A COLD NEW YEAR

STEPHEN L BRAYTON

CONTENTS

Prologue	1
Chapter 1	5
Chapter 2	10
Chapter 3	21
Chapter 4	29
Chapter 5	33
Chapter 6	42
Chapter 7	49
Chapter 8	57
Chapter 9	64
Chapter 10	73
Chapter 11	78
Chapter 12	95
Chapter 13	105
Chapter 14	119
Chapter 15	136
Chapter 16	144
Chapter 17	153
Chapter 18	159
Chapter 19	170
Chapter 20	176
Chapter 21	187
Chapter 22	195
Chapter 23	204
Chapter 24	214
Chapter 25	222
Chapter 26	229
Chapter 27	240
Chapter 28	246
Chapter 29	256
Chapter 30	264
Chapter 31	271
Chapter 32	278

Chapter 33   285
Chapter 34   290
Chapter 35   298
Chapter 36   306
Chapter 37   310
Chapter 38   318
Chapter 39   325

Acknowledgments   335
About the Author   337

PROLOGUE

Sunday

SHE FEELS a nudge on her shoulder. "Doing all right?"

She turns to the man. He waits for her answer while he pours orange juice into a mixed drink. "Yes. Fine." She wonders how he has time to talk, considering how busy he must be.

He wipes spilled alcohol from the counter. "Almost midnight."

She nods.

"Any resolutions?"

She winces in annoyance. The guy may be the father of one of her friends, but he's never been so… attentive. She doesn't understand why he would be talking to her with so many other customers. Instead of answering, she turns her focus back to the crowd. The music swells, and the undulating mass of bodies presses close. Glasses and bottles clink. The cheesy disco ball revolves over the stage, throwing a revolving confetti of lights over everything. Shouted conversations are indistinguishable and drowned by sporadic laughter. Revelers dance, laugh, and snap selfies. Couples cling to each other in lust, love, and desperation.

The end of the year is nigh. A new set of twelve months for many people means a fresh start, changes for the better, a launching point for the fulfillment of hopes and dreams. Improved health from weight loss or no-smoking programs. A solid financial future through wiser investments.

That's all she's heard over the past month, like a deep-voiced television announcer ready to offer the services of some high-priced company. To her, it's all crap. She knows the next year will bring nothing but more betrayal and heartache.

She notices the bartender still hovers near. To get him off her back, she says, "No, not really."

Alone near the end of the bar, she wonders, not for the first time, why she is here. Enjoyment of the final minutes of the year is lost to her. Her friends badgered her to come, but she saw no point to the celebration, no reason to let loose. Not with what's been happening for the past three months and, now, with what happened before Christmas. Or rather, what *didn't* happen. For her, the New Year offers nothing. No plans, no changes, no purpose, no direction. Just a gray fog.

The man leans closer. "I understand you've had some modeling pictures taken?"

So what? And how would he know?

He smiles. "I know a few people who might be able to help. You know, if you want to take the next step."

What people? Agents? She had the pictures taken as a lark, encouraged by… whatever his name was? Jack? Jamie? Pathetic, how she can't remember a guy she met at the end of October. She hadn't had any thoughts about how she might make something of them. The photographer had commented on her "natural beauty," girl-next-door, but refined. Because of time constraints, the woman had made quick style changes to her brown hair, added minimal makeup to smooth her cheeks and lips. The woman promised to feature the pictures on the studio's website.

She left happy, but with no contacts in modeling—and no idea how to make contacts—she never thought it would be something to consider as a job. And after that morning—Christmas morning—in the bathroom, she hadn't cared anymore, had forgotten about the pictures. What she wanted to happen didn't, so nothing else mattered. No wonder she'd forgotten his name—Jeremy? John? He was nothing. Hell, the negative sign in the test stick's window could have been his fault.

She sees her friend amid the crowd on the dance floor, lost in her own carousing. Arms draped around the neck of a tall, dark-haired guy, bodies contorting in rhythm to the music and each other.

The man behind the bar darts glances her way. Waiting. She could walk away. Or walk out the door, catch a ride… home, but that meant facing the betrayer who posed as her mother. Run away? Sure, that's an option, but she has the problem of not knowing what she wants or where to go.

"I just don't care anymore," she whispers.

Yet, a small part of her has taken notice of the offer made. She did have fun posing for the photographs, even if she knew they weren't going to produce any positive results.

Maybe, though, there is a chance, however small…

What the hell?

She turns to the bartender again.

As if he knew her intentions seconds before, he leans close, eyebrows raised in anticipation.

She nods. "Show me."

CHAPTER
ONE

WEDNESDAY

COLD AIR PREVENTS me from returning to the black depths of oblivion. That, and the faint clip-clop of heels on the hardwood floor in the hall. The footsteps stop, and the door to the front reception room opens.

Did Anne forget to lock up before she left me on the couch? Or did she just not care to?

My hand pauses before I can take another puff from the Lucky Strike. I wait in mild interest, anticipating it's a client, even as I hope it's anything but.

Not now. I just woke up not too long ago. My body still feels the aches from hauling myself off the couch, and my mental faculties have yet kicked into second gear.

A couple of more steps, a pause that lasts a million seconds, then the knob to my office door turns, and the door opens.

Not Anne. I should have recognized the steps as not coming from my ex-wife. Perhaps my hebetudinous physical condition and muddled mental state have swamped the acuity as I drowned my liver and brain cells over the last three days and nights. Ten bars… no, eleven, and at least four house or office parties. The alcohol intake tempered by tidbits of food and several packs of cigarettes…

The woman still stands in the doorway, looking as unsure of her situation as I am of her. A thought brushes my mind that I don't know the time. Mid-morning? Later? My office opens at eight, but my wind-up watch shows six. I stare at the face and realize the second hand has stopped. Two shakes of my wrist result in nothing.

I shrug and direct my attention back to the woman who has not yet entered the office. She wears a heavy, fur-lined coat, scarf, and gloves. So bundled in outerwear as she is, I can't tell what's underneath, but below the coat, there's a black, calf-length skirt and hard-soled winter boots. The latter have left a moist trail behind her.

Gretel makes the path through the dark woods.

"What time is it?" a voice croaks. I realize it's mine and cough to shovel away the rocks in my throat.

"Pardon me?" She shakes errant, tarnished brown bangs from her similarly colored eyes. Black smudges of liner mar her makeup, and her tired face reveals a lack of proper sleep. Hints of former beauty and attractive qualities peek through, but time has intervened, depleted, and strip-mined away the former luster. Today, her expression conveys a mix of confusion, pain, and angst.

"No pardon necessary," I reply. "I just asked the time."

She hesitates and tilts her head. A glimmer of moisture from her eyes reflects the morning light.

Do I know her? She looks familiar.

"A little after eleven," she states.

Why isn't Anne at her desk? She's never late.

My office shares the third floor with an architect and a mail-order distribution company. I'd move out if it weren't for the cheap rent. The other businesses renting space in the five-story building, ranging from a hair salon to a lawyer's firm, are moderately to highly successful, in part because of Anne's investments in them. Anne owns the building, so if her tenants are happy and stable, she is, too. She also takes part in my business, Habeck Investigations, sitting in reception and handling calls, accounting, and new clients. Unlike the others, mine is a less than mildly prosperous venture. With her successes, I haven't figured out why she stays with me.

Yes, Johnny, our relationship is complicated.

Seconds tick by and, when neither of us says anything, I wave her in, take a last drag of tobacco, stub out the butt on the desk next to the overflowing aluminum ashtray, and toss the corpse upon the pile of its brothers. I don't bother asking for her pardon. I know how I must look, how hoarse my voice sounds. "What can I do for you?"

She primly sits on the edge of the visitor's chair four feet away. "I—was told you'd be able to help me," she starts.

I help myself to another cigarette and puff once before responding. "With?"

"My daughter has disappeared. I was hoping you could find her."

I sigh and lean back in my chair. I don't need this, not today. The old year barely dead, I'm tired, hungry, and I think the blasted radiator went back to sleep. Minutes ago, I had shuffled to the thermostat on the wall by the door and squinted until my vision cleared. Anne had reset the gauge to sixty-six. I had fingered the tab back up to seventy-five and looked longingly at the dirty white radiator to my right. Stupid thing didn't respond to my silent plea. I had waited. Finally, half-heartedly, it had wheezed reluctant gasps. Unfortunately, the warmth emitted wasn't enough to fill the entire room. It barely reached my desk.

Not needing another problem this morning, I attempt to dismiss the matter in front of me. "The police—"

"I've tried the police," the woman says. "I made a report, but they don't seem interested. Too many New Year problems to sort out. At least, that's what Anne said to me. She told me to come to you."

I arch an eyebrow at my ex's name.

"Your—"

"I know who she is. You are—"

"Arlene Lansing." She gets the last interruption. "Her sister."

Yes, there's the resemblance. The high cheekbones, the soft chin. I sniff and narrow my eyes in attempted recollection. "I haven't seen you since…"

"The wedding," she supplies. "Yes, Sabastian." Her words come out with the slightest of barbs attached.

I wince, not in pain, but in resigned disgust. Another misery this morning to remind me of my in-laws', or rather, my former in-laws' resentment and antipathy toward me. The feelings are mutual, but Anne would argue that they're not justifiable on my end.

"Why did Anne send you to me?" I ask.

She reins in a retort—something sharp and biting, no doubt—and composes herself to say, instead, "She told me you are worth the effort, that when you take on a case, you stay with it, no matter what."

My heart aches a mite at the rare compliment from Anne, even if it comes indirectly from a woman I haven't seen in two decades.

Arlene inhales to say something further, pauses, and then, barely above a whisper, utters, "Please."

I sniff again and stretch my facial muscles, contorting my expression. It's one of the little idiosyncrasies Anne says irritates her. Opening a drawer, I rummage through the detritus for a writing pad and broken stub of a pencil. Also, I find the microcassette recorder I use on occasion. Next to it is an open package of cassettes. I remove one, insert it into the machine, glance at Arlene in a silent request for her permission to record the discussion—she gives a quick nod—and place the recorder on the desk in front of my writing pad.

Years ago, Anne tried to get me to switch to a recording app on a cell phone. Three seconds of my blank expression erased that notion. Cassettes I understand. *Play*, *Record*, and *Stop* buttons I understand. I avoid cell phones as much as possible, let alone any of the zillion *apps* that exist.

Record on, pencil in hand, a dying cigarette dipping in the corner of my mouth, I look droopy-eyed at the woman I recall as being a cool and disciplined professional. "So, tell me about your daughter."

WHILE ARLENE AND I TALK, I kill three more cigarettes. Anne will remind me how she doesn't like my smoking in the office. The wadded empty pack rests next to the pile of butts in the ashtray, a poor representation of a tombstone.

Since I rarely visited Anne's family while we were married and never after the divorce, I struggle to recall the family tree. It isn't especially over-blossomed, but enough so ancestors would be relieved to know a few branches continue to grow.

Anne's parents live in the northern part of the state, both retired, and visit the big bad city two or three times per year. Besides my ex-wife and Arlene, four years her sister's junior, there is Aaron, an older brother. He lives in California with his wife and five kids.

I never produced any children with Anne, but Arlene added to the world's population with two. Annabelle, nineteen, and Amos, twenty-one. I stifle a smirk at the ridiculous practice of giving progeny alliterating names passing to another generation.

Arlene's daughter still resides at home while she, in her mother's words, "decides what to do with her future." Apparently, she had decided, at least in the short term, to participate in the year-end celebration. "I last saw her riding away with a couple friends about eight o'clock that evening."

I struggle to keep from drifting back to sleep. Only fifteen minutes ago, I awoke, sprawled on a five-foot couch, eight inches too short to accommodate straightening my legs. I knew where I was even before opening my eyes. My memory is not a pesky, mischievous imp. Rather than taunt, it revealed itself, wiped away the stupor into which I so diligently and alcoholically put myself through the previous days. I knew I was in my office, and I even knew the date. January third.

However, with the woman in front of me and the story she's telling, I hope she can stave off the tears a while longer. Her lower lip trembles, but that could be the result of the chilled air. I hope it's the cold, because I don't know if I can handle tears with the way I feel this morning.

Arlene waits for either a question or permission to continue. Wishing for a drink, I shake my head in a vain attempt to wipe away the mental fog.

"Did you two discuss when she would be home?" I ask.

"We didn't set a specific time, but she said she'd be in contact if she decided to stay with her friends. I… didn't want to give her restrictions."

Of course not. Why set limitations for a girl seven months out of high school, still sleeping in the same room she's had her entire life, and who hasn't yet chosen what she wants to be when she grows up? What problems could arise?

I make a mental note to see if my assumptions are correct when I meet Annabelle's friends.

"She's a good girl," Arlene insists. "I trust her to make responsible choices."

I let my silence be the judging statement. Why push it? The woman is already worried. Five seconds pass before I prod, "So?" When she looks at me, I add, "The next day?"

"I waited until the afternoon and, when I hadn't heard anything, I called around. I don't know her friends very well, just a few names. The two she went out with said they lost Annabelle sometime during the night." She throws up her hands. "Can you believe it? They lost her and didn't think to look for her, just left her. It's like they don't care."

Without ever meeting Annabelle's friends, I make assumptions about who they are. Or rather, what they are. I've met these types before. From my school days into the workaday world of nine-to-five jobs. People who are friends because it suits their needs or because that relationship fills a void. However, when something comes along that grabs their attention, the apathy for others rises to the surface.

I ask for the names of Annabelle's friends, but Arlene provides only first names.

"When I called the police, they said they'd make a report, but they didn't sound too motivated," she says. "Technically, Annabelle's an adult, but..." Her words trail off as her jaw quivers. Not cold this time. "Roger was gone all yesterday looking for her."

She's lost me for a moment. "Roger?"

"My husband," she says, as if I should know—and I should. "He's combing the streets again today. I was so desperate, I called

Anne yesterday. She convinced me to wait another night, then come see you."

I mull over the situation for a full minute. The questions in a missing person's case are uncomfortable to ask, and most people take offense or assume something not yet proven. I start with the most obvious and save the others for later if further evidence pops up. I keep my eyes on the notebook and pretend to jot ideas. "You've checked the hospitals?"

"Yes. Nothing."

"No news reports? Television or radio mention… a woman found?"

"What?" She understands in a flash. "No!"

I might have heard something if I hadn't been fuddled for three days. I don't even know who won the college football bowl games. Well, not that I care. For me, it's pro or no.

"Will you help me?" she asks.

I fidget because I want another cigarette. A sickly-sweet odor drifts up my nostrils. It's coming from me. Yes, I concede, the party, for the moment, is over. Time to get back to the real world, lace up the shoes of employment, and step out into the noisy city, one riddled with ugliness.

I don't have much to work with on this case. A supposedly innocent girl lost at a party, forgotten by friends, and no reports from authorities she's in the hospital or dead. I'll have to tap what leads I've been given. A blown sigh escapes me. Although I've hacked through the dense foliage to see the beginning of a vague trail to follow, I'm inclined to decline the case, back on out of the trail, go home, and sleep away the rest of the day.

This isn't the first time I've had that notion. Even when I don't wake up after a bender, I often look at my life and wonder why.

Take my office. I hate it. Water spots darken the ceiling like a tea-colored Rorschach test. The hardwood floor is scuffed, scratched, and pitted. Dust bunnies reproduce in the corners. Stringy cobwebs cling to the walls like Halloween decorations.

The irony is that the office suits me. Its décor and functionality are decades obsolete… as am I. Even though I wasn't born in the big bad city of New York, Chicago, or Los Angeles, I grew up into a world I didn't understand and one that sped so far ahead, I will never catch up. Iowa's capital has been my home and my bane for forty-three years. I distress at the constant advance of technology and am confused by anything relating to a computer or a cellular phone. I buy legal pads, spiral notebooks, and pencils. The black phone on the desk is a rotary dial. Remember those days, Johnny?

People walk around with science fiction devices sticking out of their ears while they talk to the air as if they're delirious, or dance fingers on matchbook-sized objects—Androids (the name itself is technologically rebarbative) or iPhones, "I" for idiot—while driving shapeless cars.

I carry a creased notepad, a leaky ballpoint, and drive a puke green, dented, and rusty 1975 Plymouth Shitbox with cracked plastic seats and a grungy steering wheel. The passenger side mirror hangs askew, and I haven't seen the floor wells in years due to the accumulation of trash.

This is my life.

Yet, years ago, I leaned toward being a cop. An attempt to venture away from the archaic lifestyle into which I saw myself falling. Had I married Anne with that notion in mind?

By the time the police stint failed, I realized I was entrenched in the ruts I had tried to avoid. However, a weak spark of the "desire for good" still existed. If I couldn't help myself, I'd try my best to help others by figuratively hanging out the private investigations shingle. As a cop, I had to accept the assignments dispatched. As my own boss—save for Anne's guidance—I set my work hours and turn away people and cases I don't want.

Those people and cases have been many… yet, I'm still here.

Another sigh. Yes, I'll take Arlene's case. After all, it's my job.

I nod acceptance. Arlene almost melts with relief.

I need a shower, shave, more cigarettes, and, if I don't want a total stomach shutdown, I'd better give it something besides Ten High. "Give me half an hour, or rather… make it an hour," I amend as it dawns on me I do not know where my car is.

Yes, I recalled most of the revelry, all but the end of last night. I ended up on the south side of the city in an Indianola Avenue dive. Then I ran into the biggest blur in the timeline of events. In my mind's eye a stuttering film sequence flickers. I'm moving to assist another drunk who's sick, and retching sounds emanate from the restroom. Sometime later, a feeling of hands assisting me, a fuzzy image of… oh yeah, Anne. Had she driven me back to the office in my vehicle?

That's why I added the extra thirty minutes to meet Arlene at her house. "Tell me your address," I say.

"Why?" Arlene asks. "Don't you want to speak to her friends?"

"I will, and it may be as simple as asking them questions, knocking on more doors, and finding Annabelle passed out in a motel somewhere. However, nearly three days have passed with no word from anyone, giving good or bad news."

Arlene bites her lower lip. "Do you think she's been kidnapped?"

My shoulders rise and fall before she finishes the question.

"Who knows? Possibly, but if so, why? You've received no ransom calls?"

"No."

I don't suggest that if Annabelle has been kidnapped, her captor's plans may not be monetary. "Whatever the scenario, I want to take a look at her room, her possessions, get a sense of who she is. Maybe she left some evidence of her intentions for New Year's Eve."

Arlene's head cocks at a five-degree angle, expression confused.

I stare straight into her eyes. "Children… often run away."

"Oh!" The idea hadn't entered her mind before I mentioned it.

"You're her mother. Do you know if she's said or done anything to indicate dissatisfaction with home life? Has her attitude changed abruptly in recent days, months?"

Arlene studies the floor for a full minute. I guess she's trying to recall any incident worth noting, conversations held. When she speaks, her demeanor changes. She's calm, almost morose. "Sabastian, I don't want to dredge up the kind of… life you and Anne had together." Her voice drops an octave, and the tone dulls, flattens. She looks as if my question has allowed her to step off a fast-moving train, to take a rare respite on an otherwise hectic journey. "I want to say when you look at Anne, you see a character molded by her family. She's been very successful in everything she does."

Except for me.

"It's more than that. She's driven. Our parents were driven. Not to be the richest or to acquire fame or power, but to be the best wherever their interests lay. Aaron, Anne, and I never were given a chance to rest on our laurels. Vacations were what other people enjoyed. Each of us had jobs outside of school, starting in the fourth grade. Mother and Father never tried to influence the directions our lives took other than to always push to do better, move ahead, never back down, or slack off. Do you see what I'm talking about?"

"Yes." From our marriage ceremony to her entrepreneurial spirit, Anne strives to create success, which makes my heart a lead weight on the bottom of a dark swamp because she couldn't change me, couldn't mold me into what she considered successful. I was her one failure.

"Aaron married up in class and, subsequently, joined it. He and his family are financially set, even if the children fail, which none of them will, at last report. They are destined to outshine their father."

"And your children?"

"The drive continues," she replies with a sad smile. "I knew what I—what my husband and I—were doing, but couldn't stop. By the time we saw the result, it was too late."

I hike my eyebrows in question.

"Amos struggled all through school. He made passing grades, but it was a challenge. He doesn't handle pressure well. I wouldn't be surprised if he suffers a heart attack in his thirties. I feel terrible to think that way, but it's true."

"And Annabelle?"

Arlene sighs. "She gave up years ago. Her grades were middling, if passable. Roger and I couldn't understand her attitude."

"Rebel?"

"She doesn't care. Amos moved out at seventeen, ready to face the world for better or worse. Currently, he attends the Des Moines Institute of Business." She huffs a short, breathy laugh.

"We even said he could live in the dorm instead of commuting." A sigh. "Annabelle still lives at home. We can't motivate her to commit to a decision on her future. Last summer, we convinced her to apply for a job, even if only part-time. We were ecstatic when she was hired on at the mall, but of course, disappointed when she quit three months later."

"Where was she employed?"

"A place called Lupo's, in the Merle Hay Mall. It's a clothing and jewelry store for teenagers. Since she didn't own a car, we gave her rides, or she asked her friends."

"Do you know if she takes drugs? Alcohol?"

"No. Well, I suppose when she goes out with her friends. They probably drink, even though they aren't of age."

With Annabelle rejecting the family drive with vehemence and a depressing attitude, I'd be surprised if she didn't indulge. However, Arlene still hadn't answered my earlier question. "So, have you noticed any unusual change in her attitude? Anything she's not doing that she used to or vice-versa?"

Arlene considers, and her chin drops an inch. I wait while she organizes her thoughts.

She inhales, holds the breath for a moment, and then speaks, "Sometime in early October, she suddenly became even more distant than usual. She remained quiet during dinners and spent most evenings in her room."

"Did she give you a reason?"

"No, and I regret not asking. At first, I figured it was another phase, or maybe she was seriously contemplating registering for college."

"Did she indicate which way she was leaning?"

A minute, then a head shake. "No, and it wasn't too long after that she quit her job. Afterward, she occasionally went out with friends, but didn't seem interested in family. Also, she started wearing different clothes."

"How do you mean?"

"Darker colors. Black jeans, black sweaters. Not as many T-shirts, and those were plainer and darker. She stopped wearing make-up or caring for her hairstyle."

How a withdrawn attitude and darker clothes would indicate thoughts of secondary education, I don't know, but maybe that's the train track Arlene's mind is on. I have a vision of the girl's devolution and don't like what it may imply. "Sounds like depression."

She shrugs and smears a tear across her cheek. "I don't know. Roger and I thought she'd come out of it. We didn't take the time to talk to her about it."

I rub my forehead with two fingers. The morning doldrums still muddle my brain. "Arlene, I'm sorry, there's this group of youths who sound like what your daughter has become. They're not prevalent, but I see small groups of them now and then. They dress weird and…"

Arlene thinks for a second and comes up with the answer. "… You mean goth?"

On rare occasions, the news reports about this lifestyle or one of its members around town. While I understand their rejection of traditions and norms, their methods—clothes, music, and the like—baffle me. What are they trying to accomplish or represent?

"I don't think so," Arlene says. "They wear heavy make-up, and Annabelle went the other way. Almost none. Yes, she did dress dark, but I don't recall noticing any of her friends following suit. And I don't think she made different friends."

At least none about which you knew, I think. I nod and review my notes. Not much written, but the new phase of Annabelle's life over three months might be another lead I can pursue. I underline the capital letters of the Des Moines Institute of Business, wondering what a talk with Amos might net me. "Okay," I say, and close the notebook.

Arlene gives me a grim, optimistic look, stands, and departs. Mixed in with that look is a wondering about my resolve to follow through with this case.

I don't fault her. If I saw me this morning, I would have wondered, too.

CHAPTER
THREE

AFTER ARLENE LEAVES, my stomach gurgling intrudes upon the quiet office and reminds me of the scant attention I've paid it in the last half hour.

I haul myself out of the chair, shiver, and step to the window to peer through the open blinds at my slice of downtown Des Moines. I tilt my head at the correct angle, which causes a sharp pain in my temple, to see a sliver of Seventh Avenue to the west, not much, and no direct view to where it passes in front of the office building. Straight ahead, across the alley, is the horizontal opening between thick concrete levels of a parking garage. Snow covers the ground, the colors running the Ansel Adams spectrum, from pristine white where it piles to a depth of four inches on the dumpster, to a mourning dove gray near the mouth of the alley, to sludgy black on the street. Before I turn away from the window, I focused on a reflection of my face. Bloodshot eyes ache. Itchy patchy stubble has advanced like an army over my cheeks and neck. My porous nose and lips dry and chapped.

I don't see my car from this angle and wonder, again, how I arrived at the office. At my desk again, I fall into the chair, which shows its displeasure by throwing the bad ball bearing to the point that one wheel won't roll. From the bottom left drawer, I remove the amber red bottle of Ten High bourbon and upend the last half inch down my throat. It tastes like a tongue depressor, but I'm used to it. Sort of. Take that, stomach, and shut the hell up. The bottle clonks against the floor. I can't even hit the wastebasket from eight inches. I stare at the empty bottle like it is the cause of all my problems. In a way, it is.

However, I can tend to my hunger issues. I find my rumpled overcoat on the floor in the reception office, but the outside temperature, somewhere south of twenty, attacks my body, none-theless. The sun's reflection off the white snow shoots shards of pain behind my eyes and elicits a renewed grumble from my stomach. I squint at my car, parked askew in a metered slot, one wheel upon the curb. Did I drive here on my own, or did some-one, also intoxicated, deliver it? Try as I might, I am unable to fill that particular memory hole. Maybe later, on the drive home, I'll make the effort. First, food.

Downtown is not devoid of places to eat. One can find anything from a hole-in-the-wall diner where the health inspec-tors loathe to visit, to a fancy seafood joint featuring twenty-dollar appetizers. There's traditional and glitzy overpriced.

I avoid them all, especially the too-bright, too-loud, too-crowded areas on the skywalk. Instead, I frequent a quick-stop place around the corner from my office building. It sells basic items: gum, smokes, newspapers, sandwiches, and cookies… all in an area no bigger than my kitchen, give or take a few square feet.

The owner is five-foot tall and two-foot wide. She always

wears the same stained white apron over non-descriptive brown or black clothes. Something akin to a nurse's paper hat somehow remains stationary on top of short-cropped, thin, black hair. She is not overly friendly, nor overtly rude, just basic and no-nonsense. The world has passed by her shop and before her tired eyes, and she sees similar weariness in my pupils. We understand each other without any in-depth discussion.

An unnecessary bell tinkles as I enter.

Recognizing me, she reaches over to a glass-fronted cooler the same height as her, opens the rubber-sealed door, and withdraws two sandwiches: one chicken salad, the other egg salad. From a rack on the opposite wall, she plucks two packs of Luckys and adds them to the food on the counter.

I pour a cup of coffee blacker than Hades's deepest pit from a pot almost undisturbed since six o'clock that morning. The acrid odor rising from the extruded polystyrene foam cup burns my olfactory nerves like acid before I seal it in with a plastic lid. As I consider the chip selection, she says, "Ain't no pretzels today, Mr. Habeck. Sorry. The truck don't come 'til tomorrow."

I've never learned her name; but, somehow, she knows mine.

One eye narrows as I peruse the other choices. Brand name chips and novelty snacks. A bag labeled Funyons looks revolting. Another name, Snackaritos, is equally unattractive. I wonder if I ate this garbage in my younger years. Nowadays, they portend instant heartburn. However, so do many other foods in my dismal diet.

With a short, snorting sigh, I snatch a bag containing a mixture of miniature crunchy bread sticks, pretzels, toasted Chex cereal, and those too-salty, hard-as-door-stops melba toast rounds. I guess I can pick out what I don't like.

She rings up the items, and I hand her some crumpled bills. She in turn drops tarnished coinage in my hand. After bagging the food, she offers the obligatory "thank you." I'm just about to turn and leave when something causes me to hesitate. The woman fidgets, as if there might be a man crouching in the corner with a gun waiting for me to depart so he can rob the place.

I contemplate whether I should say anything. Part of me knows I'll regret it and urges me to turn around, walk back to the office, and figure out how to find Annabelle Lansing with the scant leads I have. The other voice kicks my mental shins, admonishes me to be caring. I have been a regular customer over the years, and if something has altered the routine...

"Is something wrong, ma'am?" The words are out of my mouth before I can stifle them.

She jerks her head to look at me as if, instead of speaking, I had touched an electric wire to her chin. In an instant, she looks away, then down. After a moment of costive indecision, she peers up at me. "Mr. Habeck," she says in a near whisper. "Do you... I mean, would you... have a few minutes?"

I nod.

A look of determination seeps into her expression. She bustles out from behind the counter, past me to the glass front door. In what I take to be a single oft practiced movement, she engages the lock with one hand and flips the "closed" side of a sign outward. Along the same path, she returns behind the counter. "Mr. Habeck," she starts again. "I was wondering if you might be able to help me."

I don't belong here, in this confined space, surrounded by foodstuffs—ninety percent of which I'm never going to examine, let alone eat. I'm locked in with a woman I know only by sight, but probably wouldn't recognize outside of her shop. I want to leave, take my lunch, return home, shower, and change clothes. However, what would this woman feel? Probably disappointment, but I can't say it would change the nature of our relationship, as it were. As skewed as this moment is, I guess I care what she thinks, or would think, if I walked away.

"Okay," I say.

"Mr. Habeck," the woman says. "I have a problem and I ain't sure where to turn. Maybe it's nothing, but I thought of you… you know, bein' a detective, maybe you could look into it."

"What's the problem?" Yep, I'm committed now.

"Well, it—it's my nephew. He lives with me."

I wait, give her an encouraging half-smile.

"I live in a small house. I'm not married. My husband, uh, he left some years ago, but that don't matter. Anyway, two years ago, I agreed to take in Timothy for most of the school year."

"He's the nephew?" I ask.

"Yes."

"His father?"

"His father, my brother, is involved in international investments and works in Europe most of the time. He's a widower, and it don't work to have the boy with him, so I look after him, see he gets a good education. Timothy's a real good boy. Very smart. Fifteen, but already a handsome young man."

"Yes, ma'am," I say, and my stomach churns a reminder that it's still waiting for one of the sandwiches to offset the earlier slugs of whiskey.

"It's been good to have him around. Course, I pay a neighbor to watch him after school until I get home." She pauses, back to uncertainty after her long introduction. "This year, he's been… different."

"Different how?"

"Moody, don't talk as much. His grades have dropped and… he's been stealing from me."

"Drugs?"

The woman nods. "I've heard him on his cell phone when he thinks I'm not around. I don't know why his father bought him something like that; he's too young. No sense in it."

I agree with her. Of course, I don't see the sense of the contraption in the first place.

"He's making deals with his… contact?" she says.

Close enough.

"He has a bank account for a weekly allowance, but money's gone missing from my purse from time to time. Combined with the other things…" She's too flustered to finish.

I sigh, still unsure why I'm here. "This sounds like a matter for the police."

"No!" she states with conviction. "I don't want no trouble. I want this taken care of… privately. Quietly."

She gives me a knowing look and I can almost read her thoughts. I don't like what they're asking.

"Mr. Habeck." She draws closer. "I've heard Tim speaking a name. If you could—"

My shaking head interrupts. "Ma'am, you misunderstand my job. I don't do that type of—"

Her widening eyes interrupt me. "Oh, no, Mr. Habeck," she moans, "I… didn't mean… no! What I was hoping is maybe you could, you know, investigate this person. See if there's anything you could do to… I don't want Tim involved. He's just a kid."

And you're a little more naïve than I first thought.

"The police—" I begin again, but am shut down.

"I don't want no trouble. I don't want nothin' gettin' back to his father. If you find something, you can decide what to do." She meets my eyes, and her voice lowers. "Please, Mr. Habeck. We don't know each other very well, but I think I can trust you." She pauses. "If it's money, I can—"

My raised palm puts me one up in the interruption game. "It's not the money, ma'am." I sigh again, deeper this time. I'm so tired I could crawl into the backseat of my car and sleep the rest of the day. My neck is concrete stiff and torquing it to different angles doesn't help.

What am I to do?

This is part of the do-I-care-what-others-besides-Anne-think-of-me discussion I often have with myself regarding my cases. Since I decided to stay and hear her out, I guess, in this instance, I do. However, she's handed me something with which I shouldn't have any involvement. Seriously, look at me. I conduct background checks, question witnesses for court cases. At times, I haul in easy skip traces and occasionally seek missing persons. I do not look into the dangerous life of a pusher. This is better handled by the police.

Ah, hell…

Earlier, I decided to help Arlene. Why not add another burden to my day?

When I ask, she tells me that she overheard Tim say the name Jackie Midnight.

I know of Jackie Midnight. Most privately and publicly paid investigators either have general knowledge or have had contact with him. The latter is usually in the form of harassment and short-term arrests because, as obvious as the slimeball's activities are, he's coated in Teflon, and the prosecutors' attempts to make something stick end in frustration.

Knowing the area where Midnight conducts his enterprises—a small tract of downtown and a swatch of territory east of the Des Moines River to the fairgrounds—I do not relish the idea of getting too close to him. He and his crew, understandably, do not like authority, and, more than once, competing interlopers have suffered the consequences of intrusion.

A rival gang from the Harding Street neighborhood once tried to cut in on Midnight's action. They knocked around his boys, stole cash and product, and all but stood in the middle of the street openly challenging the man.

Jackie Midnight, in his unique, eminent style, did not come out with guns blasting. His is a swift, selective, and, in all cases, secluded vengeance. One morning, the members of the Harding gang found their leader behind a taco joint, gutted like a deer. Beside him, bound and gagged, sat two lieutenants, the bones in their knees and ankles so shattered, one doctor actually threw up at the destruction inflicted.

No evidence ever connected Midnight, but everyone understood the message.

Without showing any reaction, I tell her I'll think about the matter and see what, if anything, I can do.

"Thank you," she whispers, and her hand on mine is soft.

Walking back toward my office, I realize something. I still don't know the woman's name.

CHAPTER
FOUR

ANNE

ANNE ENTERS the office of Habeck Investigations at noon. Not for the first time—or even the fifth—she chides herself at her gross tardiness. She also remembers the fault can't be laid at her feet alone.

She wrinkles her nose at the harsh odor of cigarette smoke that lingers in the air. Sabastian's car is gone from out front, and she hopes he's already on the trail of her missing niece.

Bad luck and trouble, she thinks, and hangs her coat on the rack by the door. They depict the morning thus far. A tenant in the apartment building she owns in the Sherman Hill neighborhood called two minutes after she awoke and pleaded for leniency on the rent. Next Monday at the latest, he said. Two months' rent, she told him, and knew he might scrape up one.

Three other tenants with complaints also comprised the morning's agenda. Still, she expected to be at the office by midmorning, ten at the latest. However, the resolutions to the issues took longer than necessary because she had to deal with "Monday morning attitudes" on a Wednesday. Most of the business week, she could approach tenants and clients and have a courteous and professional conversation. Why did Mondays bring forth the acidity? And how did it seep into the middle of the week?

She caught every red light on the way downtown, even after the flat. Changing out the tire in ten degrees didn't bother her, but frozen lug nuts and a low spare were problematic. In the middle of the third stubborn lug nut, her sister, Arlene, called again about Annabelle. A minute of back-and-forth exchanges, Anne's fingers numbing even through the gloves, but she finally convinced Arlene to hire Sabastian.

She did wonder whether her ex-husband would be coherent enough to take the case. During the first seventy-two hours of the new year, Sabastian had worked his way through one of his worst benders in recent memory.

He had been more out of it than other times she had been called to retrieve him, but throwing him in the backseat of his junkyard-bound Plymouth and lugging him onto the office couch was a well-practiced routine. Standing in the office now, she smirks at the memory, and recollects the previous times she collected him from a bar or a party he crashed. Yes, she could have taken him home, but for some reason, she found bringing him to the office and dumping him on the couch easier.

The heater in Sabastian's office kicks on, and she enters the room to reset the thermostat back to a reasonable temperature. At her desk, she plucks a can of air freshener from the bottom drawer and spritzes away the cigarette odor as she chalks up another loss in her continuing battle with Sabastian about smoking in the office. How many times has she told him, "It's not professional. Residue builds up and yellows the ceiling and carpet."

Her words don't register.

That had been a major obstacle when they were married. His drinking and smoking—even in the house—she could tolerate to a point. His inability—or unwillingness to even try—to comprehend and accept modern and ever-changing technology, she thought to be a sweet eccentricity. No, the major issue that led to the divorce was his ignoring her attempts to change his lifestyle—for the better—and to be more respectful of others.

Also contributing was the suspicion of his philandering with a cop. Too often, she'd heard about "drinking buddies" becoming bedmates. His vehement denials lacked full credibility, especially when he was still intoxicated.

She sits at her desk, powers up the computer, and answers a few emails. Afterward, Arlene calls to update her that Sabastian took the case and would be visiting the house soon.

"He didn't look too good," Arlene says. "I know you said… well, you've spoken about his drinking, and… well…"

"When did he say he'd be there?" Anne says.

"In an hour," Arlene answers. "Anne, I'm so worried. Annabelle's been gone… gone…"

Anne waits, allowing her sister the moment. She, too, is worried. Yes, Arlene should have acted sooner, but now is not the time to chide or scold her about how she's managed her family. Instead, she waits for an opening in the woman's short-lived break down. "Arlene, listen. Everything will be all right." Of course, she can't promise that, but her sister needs something to cling to. "Sabastian will do what he can."

"But—"

"I can imagine what he looked and sounded like when you spoke to him." Anne doesn't have to imagine, she's seen it first-hand too many times. "Remember, I told you that once he's taken a case, he'll see it through, no matter what." At least that part is true. No one will fault his tenacity.

Anne spends another five minutes reassuring her and promises to visit later, to call if she has any news. She also promises to assist Sabastian any way she can. After she ends the call, she has a twinge of momentary doubt that Sabastian has the mental and physical capacities to cope today. Often, she worries that his drinking will incapacitate him so much he'll make a mistake.

She shakes her head at their situation. Divorced, but still together. She pays his office bills, helps with his investments, and plays secretary to his detective, all the while valiantly trying to push him in the right direction.

Countless times, she's wondered why she doesn't just let him go. Yes, he drinks, but is one of those "functional alcoholics" able to do a job, even while under the influence. Heaven knows he drives that way. Is the world too busy and complicated that alcohol is the only relief, the only way to make it tolerable for him? Is her persistence to bring him into modern life, her way of "trying to save him"? She never thought she would become one of "those women" who try to rescue a drunk who won't or can't be rescued.

No, I'm not that kind of person.

Still, her stubborn pride won't let her cease.

Stubbornness… and something else she cannot allow to surface.

She sighs once, resumes a business demeanor, taps the keyboard to awaken the monitor, and gets to work.

BAREHANDED, I wipe the snow from the windshield. My excavation reveals an unexpected treasure: two parking tickets. Either I'm in front of an expired meter or my vehicle was present at rush hour. I don't bother to look at the tickets, just crumple them into a sharp-creased wad and toss them over my shoulder into the landfill of my backseat as I land behind the wheel. I toss the sack of lunch onto the passenger seat and clear the cup holder of debris for the coffee.

When I turn the key—found in a pocket of the overcoat—the metallic grinds from under the hood remind me that I have neglected to get an oil change for far too long. So long, in fact, the ink on the little reminder paper slip in the plastic tab stuck on the inside of my windshield has faded to obscurity. Belts squeal when I flip on the defroster. The wipers stutter across the glass and leave moist, angular tracks.

When I chunk the column shift into gear and step on the accelerator, the car bucks, the engine groans and coughs, and, after rubbery squeals, the bald tires find traction. I lean over and, with one hand, fumble with the glove compartment. It falls open and hangs from one bracket. Papers and trash tumble out like the myriad items in Fibber McGee's closet. I search for the backup bottle of bourbon to fill the flask. My fingers find the bottle, but it's empty. I growl in annoyance and head to the Seventh Street Bridge and then the south side of town.

A quick stop at a corner liquor store for three bottles of bourbon—one for my apartment, my office, and my coat flask—and four packs of Luckys, thinking that even though the shop owner put two packs in with my meal, I'd better stock up rather than get caught short. I leave the engine idling, but no one steals my car.

Four minutes later, after one cigarette and three attempts to negotiate the icy incline—and the coffee tipping out of the holder to spill into the floor well—I park at the top of the drive next to my half of the one-story duplex.

My neighbors are twenty-something nincompoop newlyweds —they still haven't removed the streamers from their car's back bumper and there's still a faint outline of "Just Married" in soap on the back window—who, every other week, argue to the point where doors slam and thrown objects crash into the walls. These incidents are followed two days later by loud make-up sex.

My side of the rental unit is designed with a medium-sized kitchen, opening to a cluttered living room. Beyond are a tiny bathroom, a cramped bedroom, and an extra storage room I gave up trying to make into a home office. Spiders, cockroaches, and mice find better use of my basement than I do.

I step over the pile of mail gathered inside my door and dump my overcoat on the sofa strewn with clothing, place the liquor and cigarettes on the table, and ignore the evidence I haven't vacuumed, dusted, or tidied up since the last time I had the Plymouth's oil changed. In the bathroom, I avoid the reflection in the mirror. Out of my clothes, I spend the next fifteen minutes under a lukewarm dribbling shower. Afterward, a shave with a dull blade—still without looking in the mirror. Try it one time, Johnny—it's an experience. Then I rummage through dresser drawers until I find a wrinkled pair of slacks and a shirt with the bottom button hanging by one thread.

In the kitchen, I splash hot water over clumpy instant coffee. No sugar or cream. I top it off with some of the bourbon. Since dirty dishes lay stacked in the sink, I scrounge the cupboards and come up with a large saucer to hold my sandwiches and snack.

At my kitchen table, eating, I wince at various aches and pains. Sitting at the office desk and during the interview with Arlene, I didn't register them. Maybe the residual torture of awakening on the couch and having the morning sun, colored white by the high clouds, piercing my gray irises directly to the center of my brain and the subsequent rolling off the couch to land forehead first on the hardwood floor kept the others at bay.

However, movement over the last twenty minutes or so has awakened those sustained the previous night. From a bruised knee to a scrape on my inner forearm to a swollen index finger. Focusing on each, my memory taunts me with how they came about. A drunken stumble, not grabbing onto a counter with a sharp edge, and misgrabbing one of those new, no coin, pay-by-card-at-a-kiosk parking meters.

With conscious effort, I close the door on the memories—successfully—and will away the pain—not so much. Halfway through a cigarette, I slip on my overcoat and head back outside.

Not because I am finished with breakfast or because my faculties have normalized after a few days' drinking, but because the voices through the wall evolve from loud to yelling and incomprehensible screamed words. Dickhead and his new wife next door beginning another interminable argument resound through the wall.

———

Arlene and Roger Lansing live in a stately manse on Polk Boulevard north of the freeway. With the majority of streets still choked by snowdrifts, twenty-five minutes tick away before I arrive at my destination. The main arteries are cleared first; but, in my opinion, the plow drivers throw darts at a metro map to choose their subsequent assignments.

The lot resembles its neighbors. A tall, two-story, many-windowed house colored with dark, rustic reds and browns. Snow caps a row of knee-high shrubs and patches of dormant flowerbeds. Trees look as if they've been blueprinted in their design and placement. The only corner cut is the narrow drive, barely wide enough for my car.

Arlene answers the door on the first ring. She takes my coat and drapes it on a jutting peg of a dark wood coat rack. After I stamp the snow from my shoes, she leads me down the central hall. Stairs near the front entrance ascend to the second floor, but Arlene explains that there is another flight at the back of the house near the kitchen.

I pass openings to a living room, sitting room, den, and library. Each room is spotless, the furnishings ornate, but tasteful. My cynical side thinks no one actually lives in these rooms and the real house must be elsewhere. Their depuration is so complete, I expect to see velvet-covered ropes blocking the entrances and a uniformed attendant nearby with a stiff-necked attitude that says "look, but don't touch, sit, or breathe on anything."

Framed family pictures line the hall. Collages. Single family members. Mom and Dad, son and daughter.

I pause at each to study the timeline presented.

Pictures tell so much about people. Forget the "worth a thousand words," pictures show personality, inner character, and emotions. Spirit or ennui. Even a smile can't hide the truth. Quite the opposite, a smile can enhance the contentment or turmoil within. No exception with the Lansing family photos.

Roger and Arlene's wedding ceremony. The happy couple about to slice the three-tiered cake. Roger in his suit, looking proud, if a bit diminutive. His smile and eyes don't quite believe what is happening. Arlene, in a white dress that must have been designed by Vera Wang. Fashion overkill.

The parents with baby Amos. The kid, frozen forever in tears. Roger's expression displays sunken cheeks and weary eyes.

A collage of Amos throughout his childhood. Maybe because of the blatant way Arlene spoke about him at my office, I see, even in his youth, the stress and pressure are etched upon his face.

The parents and Annabelle, the daughter's face in semi-profile.

"We tried to get her to smile," Arlene interjects.

Annabelle's collage. Bored, dispirited. Such sadness, I think, should not be so prevalent in a young girl.

Throughout the years, the daughter matured with more of mother's features: high cheekbones, lush brown hair, curve of her chin. Nowhere is there a hint of father's genes.

A recent picture of Roger and Arlene. She looks as if she's

posing for a spotlight article in a professional magazine. He has not fared well over twenty years. Black hair thinned to wiry threads streaking a shiny pate, gaunt face, sunken cheeks, dark eyes.

At the end of the hall, we enter a kitchen designed by and for a chef. A health inspector's utopia.

In contrast to the downstairs, Annabelle's bedroom at the end of the second-floor hall is characteristically teen. A poster of what I assume is a current popular boy band hangs on the wall next to one of a strange, almost abstract scene of skulls and broken hearts. One lonely stuffed bear, white fur gone gray and thin after years of cuddling, lounges on the bed. A frilly lamp sits on a white painted desk that has gracefully curved edges. A six-foot vanity mirror stands in the far corner. Black construction paper covers the silver.

"Do you know why she covered her mirror?" I ask.

Arlene shivers and hugs herself as if the idea is too terrible to contemplate.

With a thumbnail, I slice a segment of tape in the upper right corner and slowly peel back the paper. I don't want to ruin any potential clues, but want to see underneath. I must break a second piece of tape before I'm able to see the entirety of the mirror.

Cracked from a blow to the center.

What does this mean? I glance at Arlene and raise my eyebrows in a silent repeat of my question.

"I don't know," she says. "I don't know when she broke it, only noticed it when I passed by her room one day. When I asked her about it, she practically slammed the door in my face."

While Arlene hovers in the doorway, trying not to wring her hands in anxiety, I poke through Annabelle's belongings. I open dresser drawers and gently push aside articles of clothing. Nothing, until… In the middle drawer of the desk, I find three joints shoved to the back. I show them to Arlene. Again, she shakes her head. "I had no idea. I don't believe this. Why would she take drugs?"

I finger through outfits in the closet. The girl owns a fair amount of clothes, but has not been excessive in her purchases. The styles look current based on what I've seen the kids wear, but I understand women's fashion about as much as I comprehend the internet. There are only a handful of shirts and blouses I'd consider gaudy or radical. However, she pushed aside many regular outfits in favor of easy access to the darker clothing her mother mentioned in my office. She exiled her other stuffed animals to a far shadowy corner of the closet. They look forgotten, abandoned, like refugees crammed into the hold of a grounded ship.

Celebrity magazines, tabloids, old textbooks, and romances reflect her reading interests. Each cover of the latter features landscape vistas with titles in script fonts, perhaps a woman in a long western-style dress looking longingly at the horizon.

I wince at the nauseating covers of rock music vinyl records—I hear they're making a comeback, Johnny—and the unfamiliar names of the musicians. The earbuds that could be programmed to a cell phone I leave untouched. I'll have to tackle the laptop computer by her bed, but can do that later.

I sit on the bed's blue-and-pink striped sheets. The mussed-up spread, blankets, and pillows are not quite the detritus from a tornado, but they're close. When I gaze at the room in its entirety, it evidences the archetypal teenage girl and the gradual change over time to a darker persona. If Arlene hadn't told me something of the family drive for success and Annabelle's indifferent attitude regarding that drive, I might not view the room and its inhabitant as out of the ordinary. Maybe they aren't. Maybe the other family members are the ones not normal.

I slip my hand between the mattress and box springs and probe the length of both sides of the bed. I recheck the bookcases, the desk drawers, and the closet, hoping to find a journal or diary, but neither appear anywhere in the room. I ask, "Do you know if she kept a diary?"

She shakes her head. "No. I didn't know girls still kept those. Everything is all social networking on the computer."

Someone told me the latest fad was to write in online journals or to create videos with the option of allowing the entire world to read or watch the entries. I ask Arlene if I could take the laptop with me to see if Anne can find anything worthwhile.

"Sure," she agrees. "If you think it will help."

The sole item of any interest sits on Annabelle's desk. It's a simple, white plastic frame holding a photograph of three people. Annabelle and a young man flank a center girl who wears a cocky smile, as if she wants to ham it up for the camera. She has her arms around her friends' shoulders, drawing—or perhaps dragging—them into the picture. The whole scene looks like one happy lark. The background is dark with shadowy figures milling about. Perhaps the picture was taken at a nightclub or house party. I hold up the picture and raise my eyebrows in question.

"Her friends," Arlene says. "She's known them several years. They picked up Annabelle Sunday night."

"Did you remember their surnames?"

She tightens her lips and looks at the floor in shame. "I'm sorry to say I had to think a few minutes before I recalled them. They're

Annabelle's friends and… well, we didn't get to know their families. They weren't…"

"Part of our world" is what she fails to say. The rebelliousness of the daughter caused the parents to spurn anything other than surface interest in her life.

Arlene tries to redeem herself by producing first and last names for me. Kym Malin and Rusty Fisher. "They told me they were at some club on New Year's."

I slip the photo from its frame. In the middle of the bedroom, I stand and look at Arlene. "Well, I suggest following up with the police. They'll want to speak with all members of the family. I assume I can contact Amos at the college. How about your husband?"

Her expression returns to the path of worry. "I don't know where he is. Out looking for Annabelle, I guess. He didn't go to work this morning."

Yes, I think, she told me this before. "Where is he employed?"

"He works for the city. A member of the urban development board. Their current project involves redesigning the southeast Fourth Street area."

"Do you know how I can reach him?" I ask.

"I can give you his cell phone number."

I take the number and ask Arlene to call him to let him know the situation, and that I'd like to speak to him soon.

I pause, but there is nothing further for us to discuss. I offer to do what I can and mumble, "Check in with you later," as I exit the house with the laptop, a list of a couple of Annabelle's friends, and Roger's phone number, not thrilled to go back out into the wintry Wednesday, but desperate for a cigarette.

CHAPTER
SIX

BY THIS TIME of the day, I think the return trip to the office should be easy. Plows have cleared downtown streets as best they could, but left a thin layer of packed snow. Fancy, streamlined vehicles, hot rod sports cars with revving engines, and others with four-wheel drive crowd the lanes. Most drivers are adept at handling winter conditions.

Some are not, and the shortcomings of human intelligence often bewilders me.

As if auditioning for a new game at the next Winter Olympics, two bozos accelerate on the green light and send their cars into opposite, but simultaneous, skids. Each overcompensates his correction, and they end up trunk-to-trunk, noses pointing at either sidewalk like spouses mid-spat. Their audience slows except for one member, who doesn't react in time because he's too busy yakking on a phone the size of a credit card. He causes a chain reaction when he bumps the car in front of him into the car in front of him and so on, for a series of four bumper-to-bumper taps.

This show takes place outside the safety of my parked car while I hope for a gap in traffic. One lane shuts down as the owners exit their vehicles to exchange profanities. Twenty minutes elapse before the street clears and I slide into the same parking slot I left this morning. Luck is with me in that time still registers on the meter, but then luck departs as the red flag clicks into view right as I close my door. I growl and rummage through pockets in search of change with one hand, while trying to hold onto Annabelle's laptop with the other. Cold numbs my fingers, and I give up.

"Screw it," I mutter and leave the Plymouth at risk of another ticket. Can I stand the heartbreak?

As I ascend the steps to my office, my stomach grouses about the sips of Ten High, a reminder that the earlier sandwiches didn't sate the hunger. I dismiss it from my thoughts when I enter the office.

Anne sits at her desk.

Look at her, Johnny. Anne Baxter—she took back her maiden name after our divorce—current landlord and secretary. The sight of her still causes my blood pressure to rise in a good way and my heart to skip a few beats. Cliche, yes, but I can wax romantic when the occasion calls for it. She's one of those women, like Ann Margaret, who, though pretty at twenty, acquired true elegance in the succeeding two decades. Her sculpted face has allowed time to roughen the edges, which adds to, rather than detracts from, her beauty.

When I first met Anne—a long, complicated story in itself—she looked like an amalgamation of several actresses from the old black and white movies. Lauren Bacall sultriness. Katherine Hepburn attitude. A hint of Bette Davis mystique. In a short time, I saw her own unique personality, so much more endearing—and genuine—than any Hollywood starlet could possess. More than outer appearances, I experienced her inner strengths, determination, discipline, and desires. While we drifted apart as man and wife, I'm still drawn to those attributes. Since she hasn't completely left my life, and still pushes me when she feels the need to, sometimes I wonder if she harbors similar sentiments about me.

Anne's stare is bland, neutral. If I didn't know better, I'd say she is bored. I do know better. The chance of her having nothing to do is about equal to that of Elvis rising from the grave to play a show at the Val-Air Ballroom next Sunday evening.

She shifts her eyes to the papers in front of her and makes a notation before saying, "I'm glad to see you took the time to shave and change clothes."

Anne effuses business, even when there's an important case underway. I'm amazed at her control, knowing the current case involves her niece. I understand. The chafing attitude means she's coping as best she can. Being in the office, working, helps.

I'm also happy she hasn't gone off on me for more than just the smoking. Even though she's the landlord and has control over the design of the office, I think she blames me, at least a little, for the appearance. The outer office features cracked, faux wood trim, faded paint on the wall contrasting with the blooming green plant in the corner, the dusted desk, chair, and filing cabinet. A faint scent of lemon wafts in the warm air. Hanging on a nail, a basic white clock with black numbers and hands shows the time at just after two.

I lay down the laptop on her desk, flick a match to the open end of a Lucky, and reply to her earlier comment. "Only thinking of you, my pet," I mumble around the stick.

A trace of irritability registers on her lips. "Don't call me pet, Sabastian. You're not Andy Capp, and don't smoke in the office."

Even before the Iowa legislature got a bug up their collective butt about tobacco, Anne had deemed the building a non-smoker's haven. I, of course, couldn't care less about the policy and she knows it. Why else would she keep a glass ashtray on hand? I pluck said object from the corner of her desk and, with my coat still donned, flop onto the visitor's couch.

"You also trailed snow through the door," she says.

My reply is an audible expulsion of smoke directed toward the ceiling. She's not really mad, just a tad upset. The attitude is a cover for the true inner feelings. At times, I think it shows both of us can't get away from acting like eight-year-olds on the playground. I push her because I "like" her. She pushes back to say, *Knock it off, and I like you, too.* The notion she still "likes" me scares me. Just a little.

We sit in silence for a long minute. She shuffles papers with precision. I smoke and stare at her with half-lidded eyes.

One may wonder, with the sensitive and personal aspects of the current case, why Anne would be so brusque with me. I mean, she sent Arlene to my office this morning, and Annabelle is her niece.

The answer lies in that enigmatic relationship I mentioned. She cares about the case. About Annabelle. She even cares about yours truly, believes in me, or else she would have suggested another investigator. Her character, though, can't resist needling me. I don't think it's a form of power play—I know who's the better.

I care about Anne and about what she thinks of Sabastian Habeck. Unfortunately, I haven't cared enough over the years about Sabastian Habeck to change to her standards. I tried. For a while—a short while—I gave up the drinking and smoking. I hobnobbed with her socialites and attended the galas and business events.

The problems were numerous and the results less than positive. Most of the people with whom she associated were more selfish than not, wanting to be seen, hoping to take advantage of an opportunity to improve their status, power, or wealth. Anne was intelligent enough to not fall into their trap and swam the shark-infested waters with ease, scrambling the best-laid plans better than a top chef with a batch of eggs.

I couldn't tolerate even their proximity. Plenty of times, I stifled the urge (and failed on occasion) to spout my thoughts or dump a punch bowl over the head of the nearest dogberry (I *did* manage to restrain that notion, but not by much).

Add to that my frustrations with the ever-changing technology and, well…

I tried, but couldn't comfortably fit into that slot on life's game board. Anne saw that I wouldn't be forced and, while we divorced, she still hung on to the notion of easing me forward while not outright shoving me.

So, at times, she transfers her frustration to me, or tries to.

Only when she's reached her toleration limit do I acquiesce.

Today, she hasn't neared that line because she really does care about the case.

After a time, she looks at me, then the laptop. "Well?"

Hear that, Johnny? How her voice softens just a fraction?

"Well, what?"

"Sabastian, do I have to drag it out of you? What progress have you made on finding Annabelle?" She shifts her eyes to the laptop. "Hers?"

I nod. "I need to check email and these social, Tweety Facepage sites."

Her lips purse. "You mean, you want me to do that."

"Thank you," I say. "I was thinking of some type of online diary… or, what do you call those things people set up to discuss everything from politics to petunias?"

"Blogs."

"I'm off to visit the cops to see if they have anything official."

"The police," Anne interrupts.

I raise my eyes to hers. "Yes."

She holds my stare for an excruciating five seconds. I want to come back with a snarky reply, but do not wish to up the level of her unpleasantness.

Instead, I sigh. "I'll talk to Pam Hollis in Missing Persons. I'm sure if Arlene filed a report, Pam probably will cover much of the same ground I will."

Anne nods, but says nothing further. It's enough to know Pam and I will breathe the same air that rankles her. Pam and I were bar buddies back in the day. Back when the cracks in my marriage to Anne widened to gaps no amount of apologetic mortar could repair. On multiple occasions, Anne suspected and accused me of philandering. There was never any proof of an affair because there wasn't one. Pam and I developed only a platonic and potent potable relationship.

Eventually, Pam hit bottom while I skimmed along, never slipping into disaster. We both ended up divorced, but it took a case of alcohol poisoning and an extended stay in the hospital to convince her to book a permanent seat on the wagon.

"After the police, where will you start?" Anne asks.

I remember the second case of the shopkeeper's nephew I accepted and outline the basics to her.

"Do you want me to prepare a report for billing purposes?"

"No," I answer. "I don't think there's much here and I won't spend much time on it."

Besides, if there was an official record, I'd have to provide the shopkeeper's name. Which I don't know.

I showed her the picture of Annabelle with her friends. "I also need to track down these people as well as Roger. Arlene said he's been scouring the streets looking for Annabelle but couldn't be any more specific."

"I'll work on that, and let you know if I find them," she says.

As I reach the door, her voice halts my stride. "Thank you, Sabastian," she says. "I know you'll do your best."

My chest tightens with a sharp ache. Not often does her voice drop to that particular inflection, the one I could never resist and still cannot ignore. I failed as a marriage partner and, in some ways, as a decent man. She struggles ever onward with her success, while I stumble, falter, and plod through much of my existence. Our current unique relationship is, maybe, a way for both of us to hold onto a slice of... something.

"Yeah," I say to the floor, breath full of smoky huskiness, and walk out of the office.

CHAPTER
SEVEN

THE DES MOINES POLICE DEPARTMENT is housed in a greystone, block building along East Court Avenue facing the river. In the afternoon's overcast, it resembles a snow-capped, medieval castle minus the turrets and towers. Within, tile floors echo the decades in tenor tones.

At the reception desk—encased in a thick-paned bubble—I announce myself and request a chat with Pam Hollis in Missing Persons. This category of police work is encompassed in a bureaucratically-named department, but the woman behind the desk understands. She frowns at me, or maybe at my appearance. I'm sure a shower and a shave aren't enough to eliminate my rumpled, three-day-bender appearance. As long as she relays my request, I'm happy.

Ten minutes tick away before a middle-aged, matronly woman appears at the end of the hall. Pear-shaped, black hair surrendering to gray, her scowl from recognition and disapproval.

"Sabastian."

The way she says my name tells me I bring back memories she's tried to lock away in a steel vault, those of regret and remorse. Of course, that's her normal reaction whenever we've crossed paths. I assume she's grateful those times have been few and far between.

"Pam."

"I see you welcomed the new year in your usual style." She knows the signs, sees the evidence under the surface.

I have no response.

She sighs at my silence. "What are you doing here?"

Officer Friendly, she is not.

"Looking for a girl. Disappeared New Year's Eve."

"I don't recall an Amber Alert coming through."

"She's nineteen."

"Legally an adult."

"Only legally," I comment.

"Physically or mentally disabled?"

"No, but still lives at home. Not in college. Rejected the family trend to dive into the deep end of the business pool."

"Runaway?"

"Could be," I say. "The mother came to me this morning."

"After three days? Why didn't she report her sooner?"

"Initial discussions have brought to life that because the girl, er, bucked tradition, there has been a fair amount of apathy from the parents. I'm sure she's been regretful for not taking action sooner."

Pam curls her lips in disdain. "Wonderful." Another sigh. "All right. Follow me."

I don't envy Pam's job. A metro cop deals with society's dregs and even the so-called white-collar criminals get smudged with black. Yes, I'm involved with some of those people in my investigations, but Pam sees them daily.

Her office is a cheap wooden desk in a row of three other desks. On it sits a dusty and scratched monitor and a chipped mug half full of cold coffee with an oily sheen on top. Nearby stands a filing cabinet that looks as if she retrieved it after someone dropped it from a second-story balcony. The department walls are baby-puke brown with fluorescent lights someone put at the "dusk" setting.

In a lot of ways, the police headquarters is modern, with up-to-date technology. But there are still small corners, parts of departments, where there is a struggle for efficiency, a longing for the "goodies" others receive. Pam is entrenched in one of these niches.

Seated, she taps a computer key. A second later, she presses the key harder and blows a frustrated horse snuffle when the monitor doesn't respond. A third stab as if she's trying to push the key through the bottom of the plastic keyboard.

"This thing was going through an update before you arrived," she said. "It has an annoying habit of going into a coma during restart." She leans down and the position she adopts in the well of the desk indicates she's extending her arm. "Gotta do a force shutdown, wait a minute, then reboot."

I would have defenestrated the infuriating machine.

She withdraws a dog-eared legal pad from the pile of papers, folders, and reports that have taken over the right side of her desk like a squatter in your foyer who won't leave. She tosses two dry ballpoint pens toward the wastebasket. She's a better shot than I am. When she finds one that gives a faded black line, she looks at me.

"Annabelle Lansing," I say.

She writes down the name, then turns her head to call out to the room in general, "Anyone remember a report on a missing girl a few days ago? Name of Annabelle Lansing?"

Low grumbles of negatives and blank stares. I wonder to whom Arlene spoke.

Pam shrugs. "Description?"

I hand her the photo of the girl and her friends.

Pam scribbles what little she can garner from the picture. She asks for contact information for Arlene and Roger. Finished, she leans back, offers another sigh, long and tired, and rubs her eyes, which only exacerbates the redness. "If I have this correct, we have a teenager out on the biggest party night of the year, at a nightclub, probably drinking illegally, maybe drugs, and she doesn't return home that night or the next morning."

"Right."

"I'm still leaning toward runaway. Maybe found a guy to go home with and decided to stay away from confrontation at home."

"Either. Maybe something else. The mother says she's been having problems in the last three months."

"Problems?" Pam asks.

"Personality changes," I say. "More withdrawn than normal. Started wearing darker-colored clothes."

"Depression?"

"It sounds as if there was a particular incident. A catalyst to cause the change. Up until October, she was employed part-time."

"The parents have no idea what happened? Either three days or three months ago?"

"The father is out on the streets looking for her."

Pam huffs, disgusted. "Fat lot of good that will do. He'll wind up missing or dead if he pokes his nose in the wrong place."

I shrug.

She leans over the desk, arms folded on top. "Sabastian, you know I love my job," she says in a low voice. "I get to help people. But I want to be honest with you. These kinds of cases aren't so easily resolved and when there are, well, the outcomes aren't what everyone hopes for. Look what we have here. A girl gone for three days after a party. Odds are, she's shacked up with someone or decided to take the first Greyhound headed to Los Angeles." She drains half the coffee, emits a choked gag, stares at the rancid liquid, and empties the mug. "Added to this case, we have a businessman in the East Village who up and disappeared a week ago and a youth who boarded a city bus at Southridge Mall and mysteriously vanished by the time it reached the depot. Mind you, the driver said it was a strange trip where the kid was the only rider for the twenty minutes downtown. No other stops, no other pick-ups. The only time the front doors were open was for a second at the railroad tracks near the depot. Then, we have to start the new year off right with the woman who goes walkabout every three or four months."

"Mendelssohn?" I say, recalling my own experiences with the daughter of an elderly art dealer on Locust Avenue. Mental problems after an abusive relationship. Evades her ongoing succession of minders. Word goes out along a telephone chain from another private investigator. Usually, only a couple days pass, and she's always found unharmed. I discovered her once outside a bar off

Hickman Avenue, way the hell out in Clive. How she managed to walk that far from home, I'll never know. Why I was in the area myself is another imponderable.

Pam's words resonate. The root of caring for others may be buried deep, but it still forces its way to the surface. Hence my taking Arlene's case (never mind the fact the missing person is Anne's niece) and the shopkeeper's problem. I understand Pam's exhaustion, frustration, and burnout. Still…

"You seem pretty dismissive of Arlene and her daughter," I say.

Her face devolves into a glower. "You know better."

I do, but want to make certain she knows it.

She reaches under her desk again—I assume to press the power button because the skewed, squeaky, low whine of electronics precedes the monitor blinking to life. "I just told you how overwhelmed we are, and look where we're starting with this. Three days after the fact." She enters her login information. "Give me a minute."

I wait, craving a cigarette, while she pecks away at the keyboard.

Finished typing, she stares at the screen. She says, "Looks like a report was entered. A detective spoke to the mother. No further updates, so I assume he'll get around to talking with other people, the girl's friends and so on."

I figure the police and I will be covering the same ground.

"We'll do our best," she says. "You know how it is."

I do. "Thanks, Pam."

She waits a beat. "Did you enjoy New Year's Eve?"

I may have, but…

"You can't remember," she intuits.

"Pam."

She holds up a hand. "I'm not judging, Sabastian."

Yes, she is.

"Not having memories of a lot of things I did while drinking is one of the reasons I quit."

"I usually don't drink that much."

"I used that excuse many times."

"Pam."

"Don't 'Pam' me. You were there, too. How many times did we wake up and couldn't remember how we ended up in that location?" She doesn't wait for my answer. "Once too often for me. The last time I dragged myself home, Bob had already called the divorce lawyer." She nods toward my overcoat. "Still carry the flask in the inside pocket?"

Right next to the cigarettes.

"Pam, I came here about a missing girl. If you're going to lecture me—"

"Do I look like a professor or your confessor?" Again, her voice drops. "After two years, Bob still won't talk to me. Doesn't trust me. Hell, I rotate through partners around here with each one wondering if I'll skip out on a case for a nip or two. Has Anne dumped you for good, yet?"

"Some days, it feels like it."

"Quit acting as if you want her to, or one day, she will. She'll have no choice."

I stand. "Thanks for your time, Pam. If you hear anything about Annabelle, let me know."

"Sabastian." She comes around the desk, puts one hand on my arm. "Listen. Do you know that since I've been sober, I've realized how much I care for other people? You and I, we were never, you know, but if we were, I don't think I could talk to you now. I don't know a lot of things, but I do care about you. I care about these guys in the office, even if they treat me like crap sometimes. I will come to care about Annabelle, even if I sound pessimistic about finding her." She steps back, shakes her head. "Hell, I don't know what I'm saying. Just… take care of yourself."

No worries, Pam.

WHEN I LEAVE the police department, my mind returns to the second case I accepted earlier: find a way to dissuade a teenage boy from associating with one of the capital's drug lords.

I should not get involved, but instead pass along the information about Timothy to the police and let them do what they can do. I sigh, remembering what I told his aunt. I will do what little I can do.

Openly seeking Midnight will be a fruitless—and dangerous—endeavor. He's rarely static, preferring to move around and oversee his operations from the ground. Yes, he has a base, a semi-stronghold, but no one in his right mind, or without a badge, walks up to the door to ask his minions for a meeting. Suspicion runs rampant, caution prevalent. Bullets and blades strike before questions are asked.

However, I know a contact who, potentially, can provide information and might serve to accomplish my mission to curb little Timmy's tendencies.

Leon "Bull" Brummell resembles a gigantic one-year-old left to fend for himself. Skin the color of milky tea. Large, round, brown eyes similar to that of a bear cub. Intelligence way below average, but not grazing the area of disabled.

I check his usual haunts and find Leon on the front stoop of the historical museum, formerly the city library, on Second Street.

The big man sits hunkered over, his bulbaceous head lowered as if studying an interesting insect on the sidewalk. What fascinates him about the stark white snow is anyone's guess.

Leon has been in Midnight's employ for only a year, but I met him a decade ago. He's always been, and is destined to always be, a metro drifter, wandering aimlessly until someone takes him in, feeds him, sees to his needs, and uses him for however long it takes to achieve a goal before booting him back to the streets. Sometimes, these people are good Samaritans; more often, though, the parties engage in various criminal enterprises.

The guy is a sad case, generally harmless unless prodded too far. Cops don't bother him unless they need information. Sure, Leon sells drugs, but his limited resources and intelligence usually keep him below the radar. Basically, no one cares.

I park in the lot and shuffle through an uneven layer of snow, hands in my overcoat pockets, a Lucky clamped between my lips. My breath and the white smoke mix and disappear in the afternoon's knife-like breeze.

I stop six feet from Leon.

He wears a nylon windbreaker more apt to temps thirty degrees warmer. Mulch-colored, thrift store corduroys hang loose and baggy over his tree trunk thighs. The label of his plain gray, cotton sweatshirt must have at least five Xs stamped on it. Put pads and a helmet on him and National Football League teams would shove multi-million dollar contracts under his squashed nose… until they discovered Bull Brummell runs with the same side-to-side motion of a duckling, with half the speed.

After a minute, he still has not registered my presence, so I mumble around the cigarette, "Hey, Leon."

His bald head rises with lethargic energy as if he's coming out of a light sleep. When he sees me, the corners of his mouth curl up perhaps an eighth of an inch. "Hey, Mr. Habeck." His slightly nasal voice belies his size and deceives the listener into hearing a nonexistent lisp.

"What are you doing here?" I ask.

"Just hangin'. You know."

"Yeah, I know." I glance around. "Done much business on such a cold day?"

"Well," he says, his massive shoulders rising like a creature pushing up from beneath the earth. "You know."

"Yeah," I repeat, "I know."

Conversation with Bull can be trying to the inexperienced.

"You still selling for Midnight?"

"Well…"

"Yes, so knock off the innocent act."

He shrugs again.

"I'm not here to roust you." I drop the Lucky and shift one foot to crush the last remnant of life from it. "I want to ask some questions."

"Sure, Mr. Habeck," he says. "Jus' don' wan' no trouble."

"No trouble."

"Okay."

"Leon." I wait until he meets my eyes again. "Do you know a boy named Timothy?"

Damn me for not getting a surname or even the aunt's name at all. "He'd be around fifteen."

Bull starts, "No—"

I ride over his words. "He's one of Jackie's customers."

Bull moves his lips, but no words leave his mouth. Indecision and a distant sense of loyalty grind against each other to keep the big man silent.

In the intervening minute, I snap a fresh cigarette to life. "Listen, Leon, like I said, I'm not here to bust your chops. In this case, I'm not concerned with the selling of blow to businessmen and women of this fair city. I'm talking about one kid. He knows better, or he should."

"I don't know, Mr. Habeck."

"This boy is hardly old enough to shave. He's obviously been pressured by the wrong crowd because his father is absent a lot of the time, and he's sliding down a slope that ends in prison or death. Now, be straight with me, Leon. Do you know him?"

He hesitates but a few seconds. "No."

"Leon."

"I don't know him, but Jackie talks 'bout him. Calls him 'that rich Hawthorne brat'."

Hawthorne. I recognize the name. Jerome Hawthorne, Timothy's father, is a bigwig in local politics when he's local. Usually, he spends time abroad, buying up more foreign businesses than is considered sane. When he's away, everyone likes him. When he's in town, the proverbial feathers fly faster than a frightened falcon. The man can raise a dust storm—or, in this season, a snowstorm—with words alone. The movers and shakers dance a frantic jitterbug with every Hawthorne instruction.

And the woman from whom I buy cheap sandwiches and gut-busting coffee is his sister? This is the day for oddball family relatives.

"How often does he buy?" I ask.

Atlas heaves his shoulders again. "'Bout twice a week, I guess. I don't know."

I draw in smoke. Tobacco and paper turn to ash with the minutest of crackles. Cars whoosh past on Second. Slush sprays and tires crunch snow.

Leon lowers his head again to study the white.

This next part is tricky. Handled incorrectly, it might result in injury or worse. If Bull cannot keep his mouth shut or find a way to do what I want done without his boss's knowledge, I could find myself on Jackie's list of those needing to be taught a lesson.

I detest violence, especially directed at me.

"Leon." I soften and lower my voice and wait until he looks up. "He's a troubled kid. Do you really want to see him sink lower?"

"But—"

"He's on the fence right now. A slight push can determine his fate."

Sabastian Habeck, philosopher.

"Leon, you can be the one to push him in the right direction."

Sabastian Habeck, motivator.

Leon cocks his head. "How would I do that?"

Sabastian Habeck, advisor.

"Since Tim has never met you, he won't know you work for Jackie. The next time Tim makes a buy, you… hide and follow him and persuade him to not continue down his chosen road. You, Bull, are the one person who can do this." The light of comprehension flickers in his eyes, but I'm not one hundred percent certain. "Your size."

"Yeah, Mr. Habeck. I understand."

The cold sneaks up under my pant cuffs, and its tendrils snuggle against my ankles. I should leave, but allow Leon to contemplate my idea a moment more. "Will you do it, Leon? For Tim? For… me?"

He audibly inhales enough air to make me fear for my survival with the lack of oxygen in my proximity, holds the lot in his lungs for a moment. Finally, "I'll think about it. I can't promise anything. Mr. Midnight. You know. But I'll think about it."

I guess that's all I can ask. "Thanks, Leon."

He gives me an askance look. "Although… you know, I mean, you think you can help me a little?"

I know what he means. Nothing comes free, and we are talking about a violent man with Jackie. "You help me out, I'll make it worth your while."

He still eyes me sideways.

I quote him a monetary figure which he accepts. Turning to go, a new thought flickers. A long shot, but…

"Annabelle Lansing. Ever hear that name? Maybe in the last couple of days or weeks?"

"No. Is she another of Mr. Midnight's customers?"

Who knows? "She went missing New Year's Eve. Over on East Fourth."

Brummell perks up a little at the locale.

I stamp my feet to reinvigorate blood flow. "Fourth Street interests you?"

"Interests Mr. Midnight," Leon replies.

"Why?"

"The remod—renew…"

"Urban renewal project?"

"Yeah."

"Why would Jackie be interested in improving the neighborhood?" I can guess the answer, just want it confirmed.

"More customers."

Of course. Knowing Jackie's reputation, he probably works quietly behind the scenes, investing drug money in the hope of recouping later.

I thank Leon for his time and depart with a, "Get to Timothy soon, okay?"

He nods and his attention returns to the nature of the universe in the white flakes of snow.

CHAPTER
NINE

ANNE HAS DEPARTED for the day but left me a note on her desk. It tells me she received no word from the police regarding Annabelle—not surprising, since I talked to them not two hours ago—and no word from or about Roger. Concerning the laptop, Anne discovered a website Annabelle frequented, something called *www.mythoughts.com*. She explains that it's an online video journal where registered users can create and post videos and invite friends to view them. Unfortunately, she couldn't find Annabelle's password to be able to access the account. Arlene couldn't provide an answer either, because she didn't know about the online activity in the first place.

I fall into her chair and light up. A weary sigh escapes as I slouch. *Mythoughts.com.* What has humanity come to when teenagers feel they have to share their thoughts with the world? Whatever happened to the days of diaries locked with plain brass hasps and a key the size of my fingernail?

Earlier, I had planned to spend time at home on the laptop.

Anne, knowing my reluctance toward technology, stepped in to complete an initial search. With productive results. I would have delayed even powering up the infernal machine—especially after witnessing Pam Hollis's frustration—and ended up stumbling all over the internet unsure where to start. Still, as many hours of work Anne has probably saved me, I need to take these next steps myself.

I reset the thermostat, readjust the chair's height for my comfort, open the laptop lid, and find and press the power button. While the screen blinks on, I sip from my flask, finish the current Lucky, light another, and settle in for the fun. (Note the sarcasm, Johnny.)

A postscript to Anne's note shows me the procedure to login and navigate to the particular site. The monitor shows a black, charcoal gray desktop. No files, folders, or game icons. Nothing but the trash can with the blue recycle arrows in the lower right corner. A system search window at the bottom sits beside a tri-colored circle icon (an internet browser) and an open envelope icon representing access to email.

Nothing else. I wonder if the blank desktop relates to the abrupt mood change Arlene mentioned. Will the reason be included on Annabelle's account at *mythoughts.com*?

I click twice to open an internet window. Annabelle must have set her default page to the video blog site because the homepage loads in seconds. It's a mess of purples and blues and reds and images on a sliding banner showing still shots of smiling and laughing people as captured by video cameras and a menu and a search box and... more to see if I choose to scroll down the page. After my eyes refocus and my brain makes sense of the page, I figure out a person can search for individual accounts.

I slug another jolt of Ten High to deal with this emetic site and the mind-numbing distractions it offers.

I move the mouse to direct the cursor to the login choice on the menu… but don't see the cursor. What? The damn arrow was right there a second ago.

I swipe my finger across the pad… watch for the streak of motion across the screen. Slower movement in a random pattern. Nothing.

Resisting the urge to palm the laptop off the desk, I wish Anne was present to do this.

I brush my finger on the pad from upper right to lower left three times. Logic tells me the cursor should be jammed into the corner.

Yes, there it is, or the right half of it. Millimeters at a time, I guide the cursor to the login menu item, my eyes unblinking the entire time lest I lose it again in the tornado of colors. When the cursor hovers over the *login*, the word color changes to blue. A single click takes me to two data field boxes. One is titled *Email* and the other is *Password*.

Anne's note included her niece's email address. She further explained she tried several common passwords. Birthday. First name and a number. Various combinations of letters on both names and using initials. All failed. She even attempted to gain access through changing the password through an email link. However, she was stymied by a security question. *What was the name of your first pet?* I understand why Anne was stuck. The Lansings never had a dog, cat, bird, or other animal companion.

Had I seen anything that might be an answer when I searched Annabelle's room? Years ago, Anne and I discussed the habit of people writing down passwords and other such security information. She told me doing so was a security risk because anyone who discovered the access code could harm not only the account's owner but potentially others associated with the individual.

I don't understand the mechanics, but I liken it to a false rumor gone epidemic.

Knowing Anne, she would never consider creating a tangible record of her online activities. Whatever security information she has is stored in the files of her vast mental archive.

I don't know if I'd recognize a password or other computer access records if I saw one, but I didn't find any slip of paper or note from a memo pad anywhere in Annabelle's room.

I close my eyes and visualize the room. It's a place in transition, evolving from a typical teen girl's room into something darker, bleaker. The posters, the clothing, the stuffed animals banished to the closet. The photo of Annabelle with her friends. Anything there? No, Anne wrote she tried those names. What's left?

Wait!

The teddy bear on the bed. The lone remnant from her collection. The one "normal" item amid the broken mirror and the other evidence of a change in her life. Could the bear be the answer? Yes, non-living, but reminiscent of a comforting animal, a substitute for a live "pet."

I snag the phone and dial the Lansing abode. Arlene picks up and gasps when she hears my greeting. She sputters words to the effect of "have you found Annabelle?".

"No," I say when I find gaps. "I want to ask a question."

I explain the issue. Arlene reiterates that she didn't know her daughter had an online presence—as Anne had noted.

"The white stuffed bear on her bed," I say. "Does it have a name?"

It does. I thank her for the information and promise to call when I learn something.

"Anne is here," she says.

I hope she'll be a calming influence.

I replace the phone in the cradle, click to reset the password like Anne attempted. The screen brings up the security question, and I type with both index fingers:

SNOWBALL

When I click *Submit*, a red dot appears over the envelope icon at the bottom of the screen. I open the email and follow the instructions for resetting the password. For simplicity's sake, I input *Snowball* plus an exclamation point and a dollar sign since the system requires two symbols or numbers. I shake my head in exasperation at the security measures for a ridiculous video site.

When I input the new login information, the screen dissolves into an image of a tome-sized journal, *Annabelle* in the space reserved for a title. *Welcome Back* fades into view below. Seconds later, the journal's cover opens to reveal what would be a table of contents in a regular book. Here, a list of menu items displays in a single column.

Add New Entry

View Past Entries

Delete Entries

At the top, a line is reserved for the title of the video journal: *Whatever.*

"Not a very auspicious choice," I mutter.

Where to start? To save myself the oncoming headache, I'd like to jump ahead to discover if she created videos on or near the time her mother noticed changes in her attitude and mood. However, to get a better idea of the girl's life, I start at the beginning. Clicking *View Past Entries* moves the menu to the top of the screen. Replacing it is a list of years, the current year first, then going back to what I assume was the year Annabelle first registered for an account. She would have been fourteen.

A click on that year brings up the months she made videos. Another click and a calendar appears; specific dates show a frozen image of Annabelle on a movie-type screen. A single tap on the mouse pad over June sixth starts the show.

The first video shows the quality—or lack of it—that I think most entries on this site would have. Everyday people wanting a piece of any spotlight available where someone notices them.

From the angle of the camera, I deduce Annabelle sits at her desk in her room. Daylight outside the window behind her provides the illumination.

She's dressed in a loose, white T-shirt, oak-brown hair gathered on top of her head in a style that resembles an egg carton after six hours with a gerbil.

Hey, everyone! This is so cool. If I added you as a friend, you'd better reply, like yesterday. I read some of your posts and left comments. If you're watching this, Jenny, I'm sorry you broke up with Richard, but he did kiss Tammy on the last day of school. She is such a slut!

Anyway, this is supposed to be about my thoughts. Hmm, where do I start? Well, my geeky brother found a job, of course, almost the day after classes ended. He's gonna be working as a mail delivery guy at Principal Insurance downtown. Dad says it'll be good for Amos to start at the bottom.

Gawd, how boring! Of course, Dad wants me to work this summer, but I'm like, no way. No one has fun around here. We've never even been on a real vacation. Yeah, we visited the Omaha Zoo one weekend and once up to the Mall of America, but never anyplace really fun for a week or two. I'd like to go to Disney World, even the Black Hills. I mean, I have to ride with some of my friends to even go to Adventureland.

Mom and Dad are always too busy, and Amos is falling right into line. He hardly ever smiles, and he barely passed his classes this year.

Well, anyway, enough of my rants for one day. Hey, Kym, I'll call you tomorrow, okay?

Bye for now.

I lean back in the chair and sigh. Why the girl felt this jejune stuff important enough to waste time sharing is beyond me. However, I'd say she's into the rejection of the family drive, as Arlene discussed, or at least possesses a mild consternation toward it. Her voice is a maturing alto and teenager perky.

Kym. Must be the Kym Malin in the photo on Annabelle's desk that Arlene identified.

Another belt from the flask and I click to the next series of videos, where Annabelle relates the days' activities. I shake my head in exasperation. Does anyone really care about this much useless minutia? When did this type of tripe become popular?

Today, Dad gave me four applications for me to fill out. I ripped them up and flushed the pieces.

Mom wants me to try out for something called 'Mock Trial' at school. As if!

My parents are driving me crazy with all the talk of work at dinner. Work, work, Mom made a huge sale, blah, blah, Dad helped open a new business in the northern part of Des Moines. Then they look at me like, 'What did you accomplish today?' I wish they would just leave me alone!

Annabelle's first videos showed her vibrant and spunky. I can chart the cracks in the veneer. She was hoping the sessions would bring her to life, or bring life to her. As time passes, I see the frustration settling in. Her countenance as well as the room's light dims each time.

Another boring weekend with my stupid brother. Dad's off to some conference in Chicago, and Mom to a real estate convention in Nashville. I tried to get Amos to take me out for pizza and Lazer Tag, you know, develop that so-called sibling bond? He griped at me about studying for a test. It's summer, but he's still taking classes. I guess I'll see what Rusty is doing tonight. He's kind of a dork, but he's okay.

"Apparently Rusty wasn't one of her 'friends' on this site," I mutter.

I click a tab to reveal the list of friends Annabelle allows to view her entries. Girls comprise the majority of the list.

The videos show parts of her intelligence and maturity. She falls into "teen speak" as it were, but sometimes she uses words and phrases of a more mature person. I can't pinpoint the exact date, but at some point, she started using this journal as a method of relieving the pressure. Did she recognize her depression? Maybe. With her parents blind to it, perhaps she was unwilling to talk to friends, or couldn't find the right friend.

A light gray column lists various effects if one were in the editing mode. Another box on the right side—again gray—shows who's allowed to view the video. The bullet point next to *Everyone* is filled in.

Rusty. The third member of the trio in the photo. He must not have been friends with her at that time.

The months scroll by, but the pattern of Annabelle's posts rarely changes. Her words, tone, and overall demeanor, however, exhibit a deepening depression. The entries tend to be more focused and dispiriting the farther I go, and the lighting in the room darkens from open curtains to closed, to a single desk lamp turned on for illumination.

I lean back in the chair and contemplate what I've seen. Did she recognize the abjection of her attitude and personality? Arlene and Roger didn't. With no one to help, I wonder where Annabelle sought assistance. With each session, the light fades from the room and her eyes. The laptop shows more sallow skin tones and a weariness in her expression and attitude.

A few entries later, I come across material relevant to the current case. As I watch further, my mood sinks as low as Annabelle's during the time she made the video entries. Her hair is unbrushed and hides one eye and part of her face. Shadows creep in from the edges, and the conversation reflects more of a soliloquy to an audience of one. By the end, she's restricted who can view the videos to herself.

After I finish with the last video, having watched all from over the last three months, I tilt my face to the ceiling and close my eyes. Only one day into this case, and it's become a complex and convoluted mess. I don't know where to start unraveling the intricate web.

Depression weighs upon me as I think of her troubles that seemed to pullulate and worsen with each entry. Much of the investigation to come, I believe, will confirm or deny what Annabelle spoke of in the videos. Either way, I hope to glean some clue to lead me to her before she disappears into a cold New Year like my cigarette smoke fades into the ether.

CHAPTER
TEN

ANNE

ANNE LISTENS, but no sound drifts from upstairs. Arlene had fixed her a cup of hot tea minutes ago before excusing herself.

Anne stares out the window at her sister's backyard. Even the one light in the living room provides enough reflection to black out the yard, contoured snow in the ambient city light. It's a pleasant view.

Not that she's been in this room too often. Which is part of the problem…

No! She stops herself from blaming herself for the problems of Arlene and Roger. However…

She sips a droplet of still too hot tea and recalls what her sister told her earlier, what Anne suspects was an extended version of what Sabastian heard that morning.

Annabelle's rejection of the family drive and the mood change since October. The first is why Anne struggles to avoid self-blame. She didn't push her niece hard, but had noticed the "busy" life-style of the parents during the rare visits.

Anne recalls her own youth, her parents urging their kids to succeed. The intensity was strong, but Anne thought of herself as the sibling who coped better by using moderation. While she developed time-management and organizational skills, Arlene enjoyed the adrenaline rush. She stayed far enough from the burnout line, but she harbored that drive, found a like-minded partner in Roger, and raised the bar for their own children.

While Amos—from last Anne had seen of him—looked like he had no clue of the meaning of moderation, Annabelle went in the opposite direction. Not a rebel, but dismissing the go-go-go of the rest of the family.

Anne offers the empty room a sad smile. Her niece, in any other family, might be considered a normal girl. Hanging out with friends, partying, taking a part-time job when one she thought she'd like came along. Okay, the marijuana hidden in her desk drawer was wrong. Otherwise, she wanted only to *be* normal.

Anne did bring up the problem of the "fight for success in everything" years ago. Arlene listened, talked about adjusting the Lansing lifestyle, but Anne suspected she had forgotten it come the next Monday morning.

What was Anne to do? What type of intervention existed to curb traits ground into the system since kindergarten? One couldn't force the Lansings to take a vacation or the trendy "stay-cation" where one enjoyed activities around town with the family. Yes, the Lansings needed those experiences, but when everything boiled down to the base, the choice lay with Roger and Arlene.

And Annabelle suffered. Apparently, even more so in the last three months. Why? What catalyst arose to dominate her life? Did it have anything to do with why she vanished at the end of the year? Would Sabastian find the reason and be able to find her?

Sabastian.

Anne utters a short, resigned, huffy laugh. She imagines if Sabastian is back in the office, he's sitting in her chair, perhaps after moving the thermostat that she turned down before she left.

How had he fared today, she wonders. Did he figure out the laptop or dump in the waste can? Did he even understand how to navigate files and the internet? Yes, but how soon would he become frustrated?

Arlene had taken a call from Sabastian who wanted to know if the teddy bear on Annabelle's bed had a name. Anne thinks it a weird question, but after consideration, "Snowball" might be the answer to the security question. Should she call the office and ask him? She wants to but... well, Sabastian has his way. Despite the urgency of the case, even with the personal connection, he'll tell her when he's discovered anything in his own time. If he has a problem, he'll call.

Too bad he didn't have that attitude during their marriage. They might still be...

Aw, hell, she didn't want to venture down that road of memories and misery... but the one thing in which she lacks strength is erecting barriers against the rushing river of memories. Some days, they flood her mind, and she ends up saturating tissues... even after all these years.

Why she stays with him—receptionist, landlord, adviser, financial assistant—well, she's never found an answer. At least one to which she'd heartily admit.

Lingering emotions? If wanting to kick his ass every time he frustrates her is an emotion...

Yes, emotions and stubbornness on her part. A sliver of the family drive to succeed in everything taken on that niggles her.

No, he's not a complete failure. Otherwise, she would have released him, kicked him to the curb long ago. She wanted—still wants—the best from him. The effort to—well, *mold* him into her ideal isn't correct—steadily nudge him doesn't resemble Sisyphus and his rock, but it's close. She read an article discussing scientists' claims that the moon moves away from Earth at a rate of an inch and a half per year. The distance over that time is a good analogy to her progress with Sabastian.

Yes, she divorced him. One more day in the same house with him and she'd have done something harmful and regretful to both their lives.

To her surprise, he accepted and handled the process quite well. To her surprise, she discovered she couldn't oust him from her life. Despite the exasperations, despite the heartaches, despite the lonely nights when he stayed out drinking, the care and other deeper feelings continue to reside within her.

He didn't drink because he hated her. What overwhelmed him —and still does—was the ever-changing world. Technology and progress and the fast pace set by the increasingly apathetic confusing world. Alcohol offers a temporary escape. He understands it's temporary. He does have the strength and the will to cope, but doesn't want to make but a meager effort now and then. He relies on her, so she stays and helps however she can.

Yes, she pokes and prods and sees results… an inch and a half at a time.

Another sip of tea—cool enough now to enjoy—she shoves aside memories and the current status of the relationship and focuses on the present. How will this case affect him? She knows he will see it through and go wherever it takes him. Not just because there's a personal angle but because he deals with every case the same way. He has that admirable quality. He won't give up.

That's another reason she stays in his life, why she still lo—

No, don't go there, she chides herself. Think of Arlene and Roger… wherever he is. Focus on Annabelle… wherever she is.

Arlene descends the back stairs, and Anne firms up her fortitude and demeanor…

… despite the niggling emotions.

CHAPTER
ELEVEN

I CLOSE THE BROWSER, power off the laptop, and stub out the cigarette in the ashtray Anne emptied earlier. Again, I close my eyes and attempt to contemplate the mindset and motivation for mankind. That exercise in futility lasts all of ten seconds. We may share experiences, occupying the same stage as others—including people like Annabelle—but the role each individual plays, every singular effect from one circumstance to the next is unique unto each individual. Although the light bar shines on the entire stage, each player walks in a spotlight reserved for him or her. Whether the spotlight guides or blinds depends on the aforementioned circumstances.

I've come to know Annabelle better over the past hour. I don't know everything and suspect there's more than what her videos reveal. She made a choice in late December. Where she ended up at the beginning of the new year still is a mystery. I need further information from others if only to confirm the truth of the videos, but I've travelled a distance on the path to finding her. Tomorrow, I'll talk to people and see if they can't be guides along that path.

The office and I sit in yellowish-gray gloom created by street-lights. I've made a little progress here at the end of the day. At least during the morning, I was asleep, an activity I enjoy. Since I opened my eyes those many hours ago, the day hasn't made much sense. The investigation to find a troubled teen has uncovered a basket full—a video blog full—of information. I can use the information in tomorrow's interviews.

All well and good… if.

The parents are the logical starting point, but one hasn't been present. If, during the day, I had spoken to Roger Lansing at least once, even for a couple of minutes to ascertain his health, I could have eased some of his wife's fears. Anne could have phoned Roger's haunts and even some long shots.

There's a comfort sitting where she does so many hours of the day. I don't think I gain much insight into anything. Maybe I seek a remnant of her presence, a lingering aura that will sustain me for a bit longer.

Maybe I'm hungry and tired and I'm playing mental games. With my mind distracted, the cigarette burns down to a sixty-fourth of an inch away from the filter. Salt-and-pepper-colored ash arcs over the end of the desk. An involuntary twitch of my hand sends a tremor through the stick and the molecular bond holding the powder together disintegrates. Ash snows to the floor. I barely notice it upon the hardwood, but Anne's eagle eyes will. It'll be another notch of disappointment etched into the big picture of yours truly. I place the dead stick into the ashtray Anne keeps on the desk. With a sigh, I decide to cash it in for the night. What else is there to do?

I trudge to the door and rest my fingers on the light switch. Almost a routine, I tilt forward until my forehead rests upon the thin door frame. I hate this part of the day. Except for the aforementioned hours of sleep, I am hard-pressed to find a particular moment during a twenty-four-hour period where I can claim actual enjoyment. Tolerance may be the best word, but when the sun sinks below the horizon and rush hour traffic slows eight-to-fivers' voyages home, my depression increases to feed a painful barbiturate through my system, especially when Anne is not near.

Until tomorrow, where do I go? What do I do? I am not a member of any group that meets regularly. Cooking, sewing, reading, writing, politics, music, foreign language—truth be told, I'm just not interested in those topics or people who are.

I don't know the schedule of local hockey or basketball games, and think the teams are all pathetically amateurish. This time of day is lonely, and my choices number two: going home to an empty house or patronizing some dive for a few drinks.

Either decision leaves me by myself, even if the bar is full. This city is oppressive, depressing, uncaring, with too many neighborhoods where strangers are looked at with suspicion, even if they're just passing through. I feel as if I can't escape.

Sure, there are many roads out of this city, and I've tried them all. Each time I hit the outskirts, something tugs at my insides, and the leash, inexorably, is drawn back. I hate the city, yet a part of me realizes that if I did snap the fetters… well, I wouldn't know where to go.

A sad case, but I rarely venture outside the county's borders.

Winter only worsens the situation. The cold and the snow trap me in a merciless enclosure.

Ten minutes later, I follow the departing downtown herd and

leave my own set of tracks in the snow over to Southeast Fourteenth Street. Just east of the capital complex, I wind around to the drive-through of a fast-food place. Into the tiny speaker at the bottom of the too-large and too-bright menu board, I order a roast beef sandwich, no fries, no drink. I dig a wrinkled five out of my pocket to pay the tab and come back with so little change a blind beggar would squawk.

Back on Fourteenth, I fumble with the plastic box containing the sandwich. I can't find the interlocking tabs and all but crumple the damn thing to open it. Thin slices of meat fall out of the sagging bun like jumpers off the side of a leaky ship.

Three bites and the sandwich sticks in my throat. The meat had been piled in a trough, drying out long before someone shoved it between the slices of limp bread. It tastes like strips of salty cardboard. I roll down the window, chuck the remainder of the sandwich out of the car, and toss the plastic box into the passenger footwell, the latest king of the detritus pile.

So much for supper.

Ernie's Tavern is a rough, wood-sided, oversized shack tucked behind a thrift store at Army Post Road and Southwest Seventh. Gravel parking lot, one low-wattage, flickering security light over the doorway, and dirty, dull neon signs in the equally dusty window. Inside, I walk on a floor black and gummy from an unknown number of shoes and liquor spills. For a while, Ernie offered bowls of peanuts in the shell for his customers, but the discards only added another layer to the rarely cleaned floor.

Dusty yellow lights enhance the shadows, the cheap wooden chairs, and the tables. The long bar is sticky and stained with overlapping, dried condensation rings. A token mirror, the silver cracked and peeling, rests against the wall. It's only large enough to reflect an unimpressive array of liquor bottles. One unisex bathroom hides in a corner.

That's Ernie's.

It's the type of place where the orders are whiskey or three brands of beer. Anyone wanting a hoity-toity mixed drink receives a blank stare from the bartender and the other patrons.

Under different circumstances, Ernie, dressed in a white apron, might look like a central casting baker, pudgy and friendly. In the dim lighting, however, he resembles his bar: tired, droopy, and torpid. He nods acknowledgment and, like any decent bartender, remembers regulars. He clinks a Maker's Mark bottle against a double-shot glass. Ernie still offers peanuts—unshelled—and he fills a yard sale reject wooden bowl from a ten-pound, clear plastic bag. The nuts are tasteless, dry, and unsalted, but they're better than the bites of sandwich I earlier choked down. He slides an ashtray next to the peanuts. No one cares about the no-smoking laws in this place, either. He murmurs a greeting, then steps away to leave me in peace. No small talk, no listening to problems; Ernie just doesn't give a damn. He's a drink dispenser, not a shrink.

I munch a handful of peanuts with a bourbon chaser, light a Lucky, and study my fellow drinkers. Besides Ernie and me, three other people help pay the bar's expenses tonight. At the end of the counter, a short, balding man, eyes closed, mouths a silent monologue over a half-empty beer glass.

Near the restroom sits a middle-aged woman who never had any looks to lose. Her face—iron-gray under the bar lights—resembles a cookie sheet needing to be scraped clean of the burnt-on remains. Shot glasses line her table like pawns on a chess board and, every few seconds, she rearranges the line by sliding out one and replacing it with another.

In a shadowed corner, a man frets over a bottle labeled Bud Wheat. His hands fidget like they're autonomous, and his facial tics unnerve me.

I smirk at Ernie, who has followed my observations even from a distance. "Wheat beer? What next, lime or berry flavored?"

"Got those, too," he mumbles.

"Philistine."

He shrugs.

I sip bourbon, and a mental switch clicks. Another scan of the bar and my attention stops at the man with the wheat beer. His chin sags, but, when I squint, I recognize him from pictures seen earlier today. "Hey, you," I call out.

The woman looks up for a moment, then goes back to her collection of shot glasses.

I try again. "Roger Lansing?"

This time, the man raises his head. The bar's lights do nothing but worsen his already haggard condition. He's a tragic caricature of the image in the various pictures lining his home's hallway. Limp hair, pallid cheeks, eyes so full of dolor, they might have witnessed a plane crash. He wears a coat designed more for November, and it sags on his weak shoulders. His ecru dress shirt and skewed tie look like he wore them to bed the previous night. He sniffs once and wipes his nose with the back of his hand. A few moments pass while he figures out who called his name. "Huh?"

I step up to his table. Today, Roger is a sadder case than me. "What the hell are you doing here?"

"Huh?"

I sigh. "People have been looking for you all day."

"I, uh—"

"Your wife is frantic."

"Who are you?"

I pull out a chair and sit. "My name is Sabastian, and I've been looking for Annabelle. Your wife hired me this morning."

"I've been trying to find her for three days." He pauses. "Who are you?"

He's a man unused to alcohol. It's muddled his senses.

I snatch the beer bottle from his fingers before he loses his grip. "How many of these have you had?"

Shoulders travel a sluggish path up and down.

I glance over to Ernie. He raises five fingers at me. "Jeez, Ernie, don't you know when to cut a guy off and send him home?"

Ernie gives me a "You should talk" look and waves a dismissive hand.

"Roger," I bark. "Listen to me. Where have you been all day?"

"Looking for Annabelle," he whines. "Where do you think?"

"You're telling me you've been driving around all day?" I don't think Des Moines is that large, even with the ever-expanding suburbs.

He shrugs.

"It never occurred to you to call someone?"

He shrugs again.

"How long were you planning on staying here?"

He tries to focus on me through an inebriated glaze. We've been talking to each other for a few minutes, and he probably cannot remember my name. After a moment, he nods and reaches for a beer bottle. Finding it empty, he pushes it aside, almost onto the floor.

I slide the empty bottles out of his reach. "Is your car outside?"

"What?"

"Give me your keys. I'm driving you home."

"But—"

"You are no good to anyone like this. Come on."

He grumbles and fumbles in his coat pocket. A ring of keys slips from his finger and jangles to the floor.

I retrieve them before he can move, clutch his coat collar, and haul him to his feet. "He paid up?" This to Ernie, who flips his hand again.

Sabastian Habeck, chauffeur and designated driver. I march Roger outside to his car.

Lansing owns one of those bulky, battle wedges of a modern Cadillac. Nickel silver, it's one of the few cars made today still sporting a hood ornament.

A small black, electronic device attached to the key ring locks and unlocks the doors, opens the trunk, and possibly turns on the radio for all I know. There is no key attached to unlock the door the way most normal people would. In the dim parking lot lighting, I can't decipher the symbols for each operation. When I push one button, a dull *thunk* sounds, but the door won't open. I press it again and the horn beeps. Another button produces a different sound. Still, the passenger door denies me access. A second push on the same button does the trick. I deposit Roger into the passenger seat and take my place behind the wheel.

Amid pale, salmon-colored leather seats and wood paneling, the cockpit dashboard looks like it was created by an aeronautics engineer. While Roger dutifully, if clumsily, straps his seat belt over his torso, I wince at the complexity of the instrument panel. No ignition, because the starter is a quarter-sized button next to the steering wheel. Remember the push starter days, Johnny? They're back, just as a new generation. Numerous indicator lights glow in a pea-soup green. LCD gauges rise and fall with the almost silent purr of the engine.

"Hell, you need a damn diagram just to figure out where the speedometer is," I mumble.

"What?" Roger asks.

"Never mind."

The accelerator and brake pedals are no different from any other car, and the gear shift looks familiar, even if it's between the seats. I manually adjust the rearview mirror, even though I could have done it electronically. I could sit here for hours and not discover all the useless thingamabobs in this car. "The hell with it," I say, and leave Ernie's behind us.

Driving west on Army Post, I review my mental map and decide to take Fleur north, a left on Ingersoll, and another on Polk Boulevard. It's the easiest and straightest route.

Lansing couldn't walk a straight line, but he's not a slurring, stupid drunk. He needs hours of sleep. His thoughts are semi-coherent, but maybe I can talk to him. Before I do, I slip the micro recorder from my coat pocket, press the correct button, and lay it on the dashboard behind the steering wheel. Unlike with Arlene earlier, I don't bother asking for permission. I doubt he would notice, even if I did. "May I ask you a couple questions?"

He turns to look at me, blinking out of a riding-in-a-car trance. "What?"

"When I talked to your wife this morning, she commented on the fact Annabelle experienced some attitude changes in the last three months. Do you know anything?"

He exhales, exhausted, and shakes his head. "I guess I noticed a few things. Different clothes, less talkative. Course, we never did have too many Daddy-daughter conversations."

His, like his wife's, is a "you don't know what you have until it's gone" attitude.

I open my mouth to inquire more about Annabelle's life when he huffs air, a mild horse snort. "It's that stupid project," he says.

"Project?" I ask. "Is this something you're working on with Annabelle?"

"No," he whines. "Work. East Fourth Street. If it weren't for that, I'd have more time."

I'm driving at five miles below the speed limit. I want to have as much time with Roger as possible before we reach his house and to avoid sliding on slick patches of ice and snow the plows missed or skimmed over. Headlights reflected in the rearview speed toward me. The driver slows—so close to the rear bumper, I can't see his headlights—then revs his engine, lurches into the left lane, and races past. The car is one of those low-riding, foreign sports jobs with a spoiler. The tires look like the mechanic installed them at an outward angle. The driver inches up so his car is even with the Caddy, the passenger window rolls down, and he shows me his hand... well, in particular one finger, then accelerates and disappears.

The puerile actions startle me for a moment, but not as much as Roger does veering the conversation to a different lane of discussion.

Instead of easing him back, I decide to ride along and see where he ends up. "Tell me about it."

And he does. His big push in the last year and a half has been to revitalize a neighborhood south of the East Village, which is a roughly seven-by-four-block section of eclectic shops, stores, and businesses on the east side of the Des Moines River. The East

Fourth area sits below East Court Avenue, the southernmost street in the Village.

He mentions names—Fisher, Marshe—and how bureaucrats have delayed any progress. Some of it sticks—Annabelle's mention of Marshe in her videos—but I find I'm concentrating on the road ahead, especially at the colored lights flashing above the crest of a hill where Fleur descends to Bell Avenue. When I reach the crest, I smile. The hot rod from earlier has its grill embedded against the streetlight pole. A Des Moines patrol car blocks the far-right lane.

Slowing to ease by, I can't help but notice the officer and the driver standing near the wrecked car. The former fails to hide his sardonic expression. The other's head droops in embarrassment.

I tap the horn twice as I pass.

Roger doesn't acknowledge the scene. He's in his own world of frustrated and sad memories. The discussion regarding the East Fourth projects lasts a minute or two longer, then fades.

I slow at the light at Forty Second and Ingersoll. Time is running out. Polk Boulevard is just ahead. I guide the conversation back to Annabelle. "Roger, tell me about your daughter from a father's perspective. I mean, you've spent the last three days looking for her. Even though you say you haven't been real close, it's obvious you care about her."

"Of course, I care!" I expect the reaction, but he immediately backs off. "Aw, shit! Okay, I haven't been the perfect dad. I've been busy. I work hard to succeed. I wanted to pass on that work ethic to my kids. Look at Amos. He's got his head on his shoulders." He huffs again. "But my Belle—I don't know what happened. I tried. I can't seem to get close. She doesn't seem to care."

"What interests her? How does she spend her time?"

Roger starts a sentence, but something seeps through the beer daze, and he can't finish. "I don't know. She hangs out with those worthless friends of hers. Nothing but trouble."

I haven't yet talked to her friends, but sense he wants to blame Annabelle's problems on them. Maybe they are the results of those problems. Either way, he can't tell me his daughter's likes and dislikes. Ice cream, books, music, movies, nothing.

"What type of student was she?" I ask.

"I don't know. Fine. She got passing grades. Her mother and I tried to push her into doing better, but she never seemed interested." He shrugs. "She wasn't a bad kid. Did typical girl stuff, I guess. Wore the clothes they wear, listened to that crap music." His face pinches. "At least up until this fall. She… She did get a job this last summer, but somewhere in the fall… around the time I started getting some real pressure from people about the Fourth Street project, I must have missed something. The times I saw her, she seemed pretty withdrawn."

Sometime in the fall. He noticed the change, too, but didn't pursue it. By that time each was caught up in his or her own problems. Even though the love for his daughter seems strong, as evidenced by his frantic search, it's misplaced. He lost touch about the time she demonstrated her enervation for one hundred percent success. She diverted down another path, and he kept moving away.

"She has the potential to be better," he admits, but doesn't believe his own argument.

"Where do her interests lie? What does she want to do with her life?"

Another shrug.

I don't know why I continue to push; his impassivity toward his daughter's future is as apparent as her own. "Photography? Writing? Design?" I grope for something other than corporate business. "Veterinary practice?"

He sighs. "I don't know."

The same three-word answer—repetitive, automatic, useless. He gives that answer to the question about Annabelle's possible location. And he doesn't have a reason as to why she would feel the need to run away—if that's the option she took.

For the moment, I keep to myself the revelations Annabelle gave me while creating her video blog. I had hoped Roger could fill in the edges. Maybe he has, but I'm too tired to realize it.

When I pull into the Lansings' driveway and park behind Anne's car, the front door opens. Arlene's dark form radiates optimism in the foyer's light. Behind her stands her sister. I quiet the purr of the Cadillac's engine and place the key ring into Roger's hand. He looks at it as if I've given him an unexpected, belated Christmas present.

"Go be with your wife, Roger," I tell him. "Go be a comfort to each other."

His eyes glisten when they meet mine.

"I won't stop looking," I promise, overriding the part of me that wants to chuck it all, go back to Ernie's, and drink myself into oblivion.

Before he leaves the car, an idea flickers. He used his current business venture as the latest excuse not to be a dad to his daughter. There's no solid connection between the Fourth Street project and Anabelle's disappearance, but it was mentioned in the videos. I grab hold of a possibility. "Roger?"

He stops and half turns back.

"Did you ever meet with businessmen and developers here at your home?"

He nods. "A few times."

"Including Marshe?" I'll replay that part of the tape, but I recall he'd been vehement when mentioning this individual. Annabelle certainly was.

Roger blows air in a short, cynical laugh.

"So, Annabelle would know some of them?" I ask. "Even just in passing?"

"I suppose."

We exit the car and meet Arlene halfway up the sidewalk. She gives me a look of profound thanks, but, before she can verbalize it, I ask. "Could you call me a taxi?"

"I'll drive you home," Anne offers.

Because of Anne's offer, she misses the quick and pained, tight-faced expression Arlene gives her. I can't imagine the anxiety Arlene has felt throughout the evening, what with both a missing daughter and errant husband. Now that Roger is home, she still needs comfort and reassurance.

"You should stay," I say to Anne. "I'll be all right."

Anne gives me an "are you sure" look, and I return a "yeah, I'm sure" half smile. She accepts with a half nod. Arlene helps Roger when he shuffles toward the stairs to the second floor and sits on the bottom step.

"Just a minute, I'll call you that cab," Arlene says.

I meet Anne's eyes again. My hand reaches for a Lucky, but a flash of hardness stops the progress—she can't help it when it comes to me—then it's gone.

Anne glances at Roger, who sits with his head hung almost between his knees. "Where did you find him?"

"Ernie's."

"How many drinks?"

"Five."

She huffs. "He should have known better."

She also knows Roger lacks the affinity to tolerate alcohol and told me once he was allowed only a half glass of champagne at his wedding. I'm surprised he was able to talk as coherently as he did on the ride home tonight.

"What will you do now?" she asks.

She's asking if I'm going to return to the bar and finish the six pack—and more—Roger started. That had been the plan, but not now. I'm too tired. "Home. To bed."

She nods and seems satisfied with my answer. "Any more leads this afternoon?"

I think about Annabelle's video blogs. For now, I'll keep them to myself. Later, Anne will have to see them. "Some. I'll follow up in the morning."

Another nod. "Okay. Thank you for bringing him home."

Arlene returns and tells me a cab will arrive soon. It does five minutes later. She and Anne assist Roger up the stairs. I check the lock and close the front door. The outside temperature has dropped during the time I've been inside the house. Specks of snowflakes bombard my skin like a horde of icy gnats, but I choose to not further impose upon the Lansings.

In the cab back to Ernie's to collect my car, I review my conversation with Roger. I didn't learn anything revelatory about Annabelle from him, but a new wrinkle may have intruded. The fact Roger's daughter may be acquainted with his professional contacts is an interesting lead. With what she revealed, the connection could be even stronger than anyone realizes. Tomorrow, I'll revisit the subject and talk to the involved players.

I pay the driver and unlock my car. I light a Lucky and start the engine. Over an hour has passed since my last one. I hadn't lit up in Roger's Caddy. Maybe I was too caught up in trying to get substantive answers from him.

I skid and slide to a grocery store to purchase some food, then fishtail all the way home. Bald tires do not grip the road for shit. This morning, it took three attempts to make it to the top of the driveway. This time, I need four.

Inside, I throw everything into the fridge save for some processed ham rounds, a single slice of packaged cheese, and a small loaf of cheap white bread. I slap together a limp sandwich and eat in the dark in front of the dusty television. The food is bland, but better than the crap I had earlier.

As I land on the couch, the phone on the end table rings. I groan. No more issues. Can't the world leave me alone?

I set the food aside, pluck up the phone, and wearily greet the caller.

"Mr. Habeck," someone says in an excited whisper. "I just wanted to say thank you. Thank you so much."

My brain, centered on other moribund thoughts, needs a few seconds to recognize the voice. When her face pops onto my mental view screen, I forget, for a moment, why the sandwich shop woman would thank me. "Yes, uh… ma'am," I stammer.

"Tim is home tonight. He's not happy, but I don't think he's taken any drugs."

"That's good."

"Whatever you did, thank you so much." She burbles on with more praise and terminates the call.

I don't know why she's so happy. My having Leon deny Jackie's product to the boy is a temporary stopgap. There are countless avenues, literally and figuratively, where one can score. If he wants it bad enough, he'll figure out in a very short time where to go.

For a moment, I wonder how she obtained my home number.

When I thumb the remote to power on the television, the screen displays an old black-and-white movie. The scene shows a desperate-looking man—the actor's name slips from my mind just as I'm about to recall it—running down a dark, lonely, tree-lined road. He keeps looking back over his shoulder as if being chased.

I wonder if he's lost or in dire straits. In either situation, I can relate.

Through the walls, my neighbors verbally snipe at each other. Outside, a car splashes through slush.

My body is tired, and my mind is as dark as the woods in the movie. The sleep from which I awoke this morning was the body's way of coping with the alcohol. With the mental focus I've had to dredge up to handle two new cases, the running around town I've done, and the thought I'll be doing more of the same tomorrow, every part of me, from my eyes to my heels, screams for real unconscious relief.

I don't know if the man finds assuagement. Sleep sweeps over me before the credits roll.

TWELVE
THURSDAY

COLD AIR WAKES ME. My body shivers. Even before I open my eyes, I know what has happened. I don't hear the low baritone drone of the heater.

The chilled air blankets any exposed skin, slides fingers under my shirt, settles into the top of my slacks near my lower back, and cups my calves above my socks. I'm almost afraid to move because the weight of the blanket is room thick.

A gooey, cobweb-like substance coats my tongue. Bits of sandwich lodge between my teeth. Swollen gums between two teeth throb with a dull ache. A microscopic spec of gristle from the ham irritates the soft skin.

A wheezy groan escapes me when I shift forward to extricate myself from the grip of the couch. My neck hasn't moved in hours, and atrophied muscles scream in protest.

After barking my shin on the corner of the end table, I trudge to a door in the middle of the hall. I open it to stare at the dusty chunk of machinery crowded into the small space. I bang a fist against the metal casing and scrape a knuckle along the ribs of a vent. Cold delays the bite of pain. I suck on the welling blood and close the door.

In the kitchen, I dial the phone with numb fingers. Five rings before the opposite phone is picked up. Someone gives me a greeting that could double as a badger's grunt.

"Habeck," I croak. "The heater is busted again."

Another animal noise comes down the line, followed by the plastic crash of the phone.

I mumble an expletive. "And good morning to you, too."

My landlord is an androgynous individual who could double as a blob of clay. Oleaginous fluid seeps from numerous skin folds, and his eyes are permanently red-rimmed and bloodshot. He has the disposition of a bear awakened a month too early from hibernation.

However, he will attend to the heater.

At a drive-through, I smoke two cigarettes and sip twice from my flask before a chirpy window clerk hands me a greasy concoction of egg, sausage, and cheese stuck between slices of someone's pitiful idea of an English muffin. The sandwich is salty, chewy, and produces heartburn's initial gurgles before I'm finished.

More snow fell during the night, and snowplows tackle the main streets first while everyone not living on the avenues of Grand, Locust, Walnut, or University is out of luck. I spin out twice and inch along without traction most of the way across town.

Smoky clouds hover low over the metropolis. The three colors of black, white, and gray dominate the world. Faces behind frosty windshields show disgust, tight jaws, set lips, and hard eyes.

Thick-clothed zombies shuffle along sidewalks or wait forlornly at bus stops.

I hate this city.

From its schlock art exhibits littering downtown to the ever-expanding modernity to the west.

From tired store clerks to the Bohemian wannabes at the universities and colleges.

From the confusing maze of the skywalk system to the troubled city bus lines.

Meth labs in the basement of apartment houses. Drug deals completed over backyard fences. Annual floods for which no one is ever prepared. A freeway system built after developers watched chimps prepare the blueprints. Unattractive golf courses and weed-choked baseball fields.

This city will pick, nip, and gripe at you one minute and forget your existence the next. You can stay or leave and the city won't care. Today's success is tomorrow's has-been. Politicians argue with each other while trying to outdo the next guy in criminal behavior. City government annually promises beneficence but delivers zero service.

I hate this city.

I wouldn't know where else to call home.

While negotiating the streets and ever mindful of the nitwit drivers, I replay the conversation with Roger recorded the previous evening. Bits of sentences are muffled or take repeat plays to comprehend, but I get the gist of the majority of the conversation.

Out all yesterday looking for his daughter who went missing New Year's Eve. I wonder if he took any time to consider the underlying problem of Annabelle's resistance and resentment toward the family drive. Plus, there were the culminating incidents that I'll check on later.

Reviewing notes I wrote while watching Annabelle's video blog, I understand some of the truth, but does that truth connect with Roger and the Fourth Street project? Having partial knowledge gives me cause for adjusting my strategy on handling interviews today. First up, if Roger is sober enough this morning to be more coherent, I may gain more insight and have better chances to make those connections.

While I wish I was still asleep, I have an inner drive to find Annabelle, to perhaps save her from herself.

Plows haven't reached as far as Polk Boulevard, and no one has shoveled the Lansings' driveway or front walk. The Plymouth's tires skid crooked tracks when I pull in. Arlene must have garaged the Cadillac or else Roger recovered enough to venture out on another foolish foray to find his daughter.

I finish a Lucky and belt back two quick hits of bourbon before exiting the car. Snow crystals invade my shoes and melt. My socks squelch with each step. A sudden blade of wind makes short work of the scant protection of my upturned collar.

At the door, I knock twice and stab a finger three times against the bell.

Roger answers. He looks as if he attempted to run home from the bar the previous evening and arrived only two minutes ago. A blind bird built a nest with his hair. A combination of raccoon black and a deep red surround both swollen eyes. A case of lip balm couldn't cure his cracked and chapped mouth. Arlene must have persuaded him to change into night clothes or dressed him herself. The way his top and bottoms are twisted and barely hanging on his shrunken, bowed body looks as if he fought the demons of hell during the night.

"Who'r'u?" This comes out as one slurred word. I guess his alcohol tolerance is pretty low. While he may be over the intoxication, similar to me the previous night, he needs real, recuperative sleep. Because of that, he struggles with his mental faculties. He doesn't recognize yours truly, his chauffer from the bar.

Hangover. I can relate.

Before I can answer, Arlene's head pops around the door frame. Her expression lightens for a microsecond in anticipation. Seeing my non-response, she winces as if someone stepped on her foot. She scoots her husband out of the way and opens the door wider.

I stomp snow from my shoes, my calves chilled and damp.

Like the last and unwanted child chosen for the team, Roger shuffles behind me as I follow Arlene to the living room.

She sits prim but anxious on the edge of a cushioned, wooden rocking chair and folds her hands in her lap.

Roger brushes past, and I catch a waft of stale alcohol on his breath. He collapses on the sofa.

I stand in the doorway while Arlene reintroduces me to her husband.

"Mr. Lansing?" I wait until he raises his head and blinks his eyes multiple times, trying to focus. If I proceed with caution and don't rush my words, he might gather his senses long enough to provide some answers. "The previous night, when I brought you home, I tried to talk to you about Annabelle. Your wife came to me yesterday afternoon. I'm trying to find a place to start looking for your daughter."

Again, I elect to keep the videos to myself. They told me a lot more than Arlene and Roger have. However, I have a sense that they've told me more than I suspect. Both parents mentioned an apathy toward her when she didn't "fall into line", as it were, when she didn't rush out at age twelve to find a job and overload herself with slaving away at the proverbial grindstone. That apathy and… other information on those videos told me a lot. At this point, I'll backtrack to fill in and confirm a lot of that information.

She mentioned her father's work in several of her videos and, during last night's drive, Roger brought up the latest project that's kept him busy. Also, there were a couple names both brought up. If there's a chance that this project and her disappearance tie together, I have to follow the leads. Maybe Annabelle's whereabouts lay at the end.

"You also spoke about your business strategy for the East Fourth Street neighborhood," I say.

I hope round two of this topic will bring to light different aspects.

His eyes close, his chin nods, and I'm afraid he's about to slip into unconsciousness. After a moment, the lids raise, but he says nothing.

"At this point, I'm gathering as much information as possible. I don't know if there is even a tenuous connection with Annabelle's disappearance, but what more can you tell me about the project?"

I lose him on the word "tenuous." However, since Arlene chooses not to intercede with assistance, I wait. Roger sighs once, long and stuttering. While his thoughts gather, his face moves as if remembering the mechanics of speech. "Do you want the God's honest truth, Mr. Haybark?" I don't bother to correct him regarding my name. "I've been working on that lousy neighborhood for too many months." His words come on weary, airy breaths, but are laced with belligerence. "It's paperwork here, permits there. Construction estimates. Zoning regulations. People want different things, but no one commits to one single idea."

"Could you help me understand some of the problems?"

"No one can agree on anything," he whines. "Fisher and his cohorts want more entertainment venues, which will only cheapen the area. He's got that nitwit Stephan Marshe on the front lines looking for quick action."

Unbeknownst to Lansing, I notice a slight start from Arlene at the mention of Marshe. Did she quickly rein in a look of frustration for her husband's troubles? Or was that to try to cover a look of familiarity?

"I want class," he continues. "Restaurants, maybe an art gallery. These shysters just want flash and music. Quick money. No one wants to invest long-term. Success and growth result in prospects for other areas. Hell, part of the problem is the damn zoning board. There is always something to prevent everyone from getting on the same path. One day, everything is fine, the next, there's a small issue with a particular building, and some bureaucratic twit digs up a previously unknown regulation. So, they argue over that for weeks." He sinks back into the cushions and closes his eyes.

Arlene remains in her chair, but makes slight movements as if to maybe console him. Indecision sets in like old gelatin, wavering and ready to crack.

"Mr. Lansing, can you think of any relation between your Fourth Street project and your daughter's disappearance?" I ask.

He shakes his head.

"Anything? If she ran away, could the reason be, in part, because she grew tired of your frustrations?"

Roger gazes at me. With this suggestion, his reaction is incomprehension. This evolves into contemplation, and then to a hybrid of rejection and consideration that I might be onto something.

However, he and Arlene remain silent. I throw out something else.

"What about one of these disagreeing businessmen or bureaucrats wanting to cause you further problems?"

With this second plausible choice, his and Arlene's expressions freeze in a rictus of fear, as if a rattlesnake slithered into the room.

"You mean someone kidnapped her?" she asks.

"It's a possibility. At this point, I'm willing to look in all corners."

His head shakes like a dog hearing a high-pitched whistle. The concept of kidnapping can't quite register.

"Could you suggest someone I could speak with next? You mentioned a Stephan Marshe?"

Again, Arlene reacts, stiffens, and shivers a bit.

Before I can inquire, Roger, who grimaced in disgust at the name, pipes up with, "Never mind him. Try Chrish… Chris Laine." Despite the sleep, the hangover persists.

"Excuse me?" I ask.

He repeats the name. "On the zoning board."

"Is he on your side?"

He expels air in a breathy laugh. "A… reluctant friend. He means well, but it's always, 'I don't know what to tell you; I'm trying my best.'" He shrugs. "He might give you more insight into the project." Roger stands, but teeters back and forth, equilibrium not quite in full force. I can almost hear sleep calling him. "I guess

I'll get dressed and hit the streets again. She's out there somewhere."

No need to have him out there as a driving hazard. "Why don't get a few hours' sleep first," I suggest. "I'll follow up on the information you gave me and report in later."

"I think Sabastian's right, Roger," Arlene says.

"But—" Roger starts.

"Let him do his job, honey. Come on, go to bed. I'll wake you if I hear anything."

As Arlene guides him upstairs, she offers me a desperate expression, a plea to find her daughter.

Leaving the house, I recall Annabelle's own words.

March 6

Dad came home today, disgusted and grousing about "no-good incompetents." He bitched all through dinner. I don't know how many times this project in the East Village has come up, but I'm tired of it. He's never happy. I can't remember the last time he had a conversation where his work didn't come up. Hell, even if we're watching a movie, there will be a scene that sets him off.

April 17

I'm counting the days until graduation. Finally, no more stupid high school. Yeah, both Mom and Dad keep urging me to fill out applications for summer work. That and their constant talk of college drive me crazy.

No, I don't know what I want to do after graduation, but more school sounds awful. Every time I think about applying for college, think about Amos and all the shit he's had to put up with. I don't want to go down the same road.

Actually, I'm surprised my parents even have time to bug me. Mom is in the middle of closing some rich guy's three-story house in West Des

Moines. I swear, if the state ever decided to sell the governor's mansion, my mother probably would have the listing.

Dad, however, is running on a never-ending treadmill with his neighborhood renewal project. Rusty's dad is also involved because his nightclub is one of the properties affected. Zemo's is kind of cool, but it is in a crappy area.

Tonight, after dinner, Dad met with a couple of associates here at the house. They all sat on the back patio. I overheard their conversation from my room. I didn't care, but it sounded as if Dad wasn't making any more progress than he did six months ago.

Plus, one of those guys kind of creeps me out. His name is Stephan, and he sounds as if he's known Dad a long time. Maybe Mom, too. I didn't like the way he looked at me earlier. Mom tried to avoid him all evening.

Well, I'm tired. I'd better finish my math homework and go to bed.

CHAPTER
THIRTEEN

JUST WHEN I start to think I'm familiar with this city—the streets and the businesses—the gudgeon in me is revealed. Entire neighborhoods are refurbished, threads of thoroughfares rewoven. Brand new skeletons of future office complexes sprout as giant erector sets.

Don't even mention the west side of the metro. I drove over there once after all the new construction, the jazzy mall, the remora fish businesses, and the clone housing developments were completed. In no time, I became lost and confused because I couldn't find an outlet back to a main street. The maze of streets seemingly wandered endlessly with houses and lawns that had only minor differences. I was rescued only when I passed the same block three times and a neighborhood watch attendant phoned a cop.

This morning, as I return downtown, I remember too late that I should have cut south off Ingersoll and picked up Grand Avenue to Fleur Drive. Instead, I enter the widened extension of Martin

Luther King Junior Parkway and, although I end up on Fleur all the same, I don't like it as much. I pass Gray's Lake, an innocuous-looking body of water that nevertheless floods in the spring if the joggers along the trail sweat too much. I drove this way the previous night bringing Roger home. At Bell Avenue, I crane my neck to see if pieces of the souped-up speeding car remain. Nothing I can spot, but I smile at the memory.

Further south, up an incline, sits the campus of the Des Moines Institute of Business. It's not very large—all of two blocks long—but I'm in trouble because I can't tell a dormitory from a cafeteria.

No college for me, Johnny.

After parking in front of an official-looking building, I take a hit from the flask and light another Lucky. The lot has been plowed, although the sidewalks are partially snow-packed. A few students shuffle by, seemingly oblivious to the season, with light jackets, no gloves or scarves. One future leader going doolally wears shorts. I want to kick his ass and bury him in a snowdrift.

I exit the car and carefully walk to the door. Inside, I'm greeted with an echoing foyer in what proves to be the Academic Center, which includes the administrative offices. After studying a black velvet board with white plastic letters, I seek out the Registrar's Office.

The dour woman behind the chest-high counter looks at me with the knowledge I do not belong. Wariness clouds her scowling black eyes that questions whether she'll be able to reach the phone to call security before I pull out a sawed-off shotgun and start blasting. She doesn't like me on sight. I don't mind, as she's no princess herself. Thin, brassy hair surrounds a face with the shape and bland features of a hard-boiled egg. The odor emanating from her pores would repel a yak.

I understand truth will set me free, so I try it. Before I left the Lansings earlier, I informed Arlene I'd be talking to her son, Amos. She let me know he was in 315W in the Fenton Residence Hall.

All I need from the woman in front of me now are directions to Fenton Hall.

Although her suspicions are not totally allayed, she obliges me by pointing out the window at the building across the parking lot and another snowy patch of lawn. She lifts one corner of her large mouth when I offer cordial thanks, probably the closest thing to a smile she owns.

I finish another cigarette crossing the campus and damn the lawmakers restricting my smoking to the outdoors. Hell, I won't be surprised if they start banning outdoor smoking on college campuses.

The residence hall is a five-story creature with offset wings. When I enter the building containing the western half of rooms, I face the dumbest and most useless security measure ever devised. Beyond a second glass door in front of me is the front "reception" desk where visitors "check in" to announce themselves and who they want to see. However, to my right, just inside the main entrance, the stairwell door stands ajar.

The person behind the reception desk hasn't noticed my presence, his attention focused on a computer monitor angled so that he has to turn away from the front entrance to view it. Only when the inner door *tonks* shut because of failing hydraulics does he turn his head.

Before I step up to the desk, I survey what greets the students and visitors of a dormitory for a business college. Beside the desk, the wall contains at least twenty rows of four-inch square mailboxes, each labeled with a room number. To the left, a hallway houses the elevator, extends past the requisite fire door into the southern half of the western wing's set of first-floor rooms. To the right of the desk, the hall extends to the northern half of rooms. There's an open lobby with couches and cushioned chairs, a television mounted in the corner, shelves of miscellaneous books, decks of cards, and board games. Each item looks well worn, in fact beaten up, as if policy states students throw them against the wall before using them.

I approach the desk and gaze upon what I hope is not the prime example of tomorrow's leadership. Black hair, bushy eyebrows, boxy face, bored expression. Dressed in baggy jeans and a T-shirt two sizes too big imprinted with a bunch of musicians in mid-scream, as if the instruments they're holding are electrocuting them. The band's name is written in an arc above the image in a font that makes the wording indecipherable.

The guy doesn't even deign to readjust the angle of the screen or turn it off. He should have chosen one of those options because anyone who walks up to the desk can also see the screen, which displays a gallery of scantily clad or completely nude women.

He gives me a suspicious squint. My guess is he's annoyed I interrupted his prurience overload. I introduce myself as Amos's uncle (okay, technically a true statement once upon a time) and state my desire to see the lad.

"Know what room?" he asks.

"Yes," I say.

He waves his hand toward either the stairwell or the elevator. The images scroll in front of his face and he's again lost in the realm of digital pornography.

Unbelievable, I think as I trudge to the stairs, not wanting to risk the elevator. No asking for identification. No calling the student in question for acceptance of a visitor. I'm willing to bet the guy would let in a squadron of machine gun-toting mercenaries without batting an eye if the leader stated he knew the correct room of a current student. Either the college's dorm admittance policy needs revising or else the desk monitors need better vetting.

At the door of 315W, I knock and receive no answer. Paper rustles from within, so I knuckle the scarred wooden door louder.

"Just a sec," a muffled, irritated voice sounds.

The opening door reveals a harried-looking youth, casually dressed in an untucked, plaid dress shirt, blue jeans, and loafers. His oak brown hair shows no discernible part. A day's growth roughens his tired face, and his eyes—inherited from his mother—are similar in weariness and are begging for sleep. "What?" His voice sounds as if it hasn't been used all morning.

I don't need to ask, but I do, just for courtesy's sake, "Amos Lansing?"

He flicks his chin at me in acknowledgment. "You are?"

"Sabastian Habeck. I'm a private investigator. Your mother contacted me this morning—"

"Annabelle," he announces with a snort. "Yeah, Mom's been bugging me for two days. I told her I hadn't a clue where she is."

I raise my eyebrows. "Mind a couple questions?"

He sighs, swings wide the door, and flaps a hand to invite me inside. Then he plops into his chair at a desk by the window.

The dorm room isn't very big, maybe ten feet wide and half as many paces in depth. Faded blue carpet stretches across the floor. Double occupancy room, one side mirroring the other, with a closet, five-drawer dresser, single low bed, desk, and shelves.

Between the desks, a twenty-inch television is sandwiched vertically between a mini fridge and microwave. The only differences between the halves are the personal and collegiate items, clothes, textbooks, and laptops.

Amos uses his computer in conjunction with a thick book open roughly two-thirds through. He notes my curiosity. "Yeah, I know. I should be on semester break, but I chose an interim class instead. I have a paper due at the end of the week and, well, it's a bit of a challenge."

"I'm sure it is," I agree.

"Statistical Analysis of Corporate Ergonomics and its Relationship to Financial Output."

I have no idea what Amos just sputtered and, I suspect, neither does he.

He closes the tome with a solid *thunk*. "What do you want to ask?"

I start with the logical first question. "Any idea where Annabelle is?"

He snorts in mild derision, readjusts the position of both book and laptop by millimeters, looks and me, and says, "What can I tell you? I'm not my sister's keeper." He snickers at his little joke.

"Did your mother explain—"

"That Annabelle went out with her friends Sunday night and didn't come home? Yeah, she told me."

"Do you have any idea where—"

"Probably drunk or stoned in some guy's bed. I don't know."

"I understand she didn't use—"

"Yeah, Mom would say that, but what does she know? Belle didn't ever bring it home. Always went out to get high."

He's starting to annoy me. I've been interrupted four times

since he opened the door. I stay mute for a moment, just to get his attention, then change tack. "What is your major?"

He stares at me, confused for a second, his mind shifted off course. "Business administration."

I stare hard at him while lighting a cigarette. "An administrator, along with his other attributes, should be a good listener."

"Wha—"

"A good listener." I blow smoke at him. "One who waits until the person speaking finishes his questions." I pause and smile. "Understand?"

He nods, but feels obligated to point out that the dorms are no smoking zones.

Again, I stare at him while a wisp of smoke curls from the end of the Lucky toward the ceiling, the only thing moving. In my initial survey of the room, I noticed the cover of the smoke alarm off-kilter and the nine-volt battery tucked away at the back of his roommate's desk. I have no doubt a baggie of hand-rolled joints, similar to what I found in Annabelle's desk, rests somewhere on the right half of the room. Five seconds pass in silence.

"The only 'zones' I know about are time and where not to park at the airport," I say. "Now, may we continue?"

Amos slumps into his chair and grinds his knuckles into his eyes. "Yeah." He sighs. "Sorry, it's this paper."

"Yes, you mentioned. Amos, if I may be frank, you don't seem to be at all distressed about your sister's disappearance."

"Why should I be?" He laughs. "She's an adult."

"She's nineteen," I say and, before he can open his mouth, I add, "Still living at home."

He whines, "Listen, why are you asking me? I've already told you I don't know where Annabelle is. Go ask her friends."

"I will," I reply. "Apparently, they lost track of her Sunday night. When today is over, ninety-six hours will have passed with no contact. Do you have any idea where she might be? Where she might hole up?"

"No."

"Has she done this in the past? Disappear for periods of time without informing anyone?"

"No."

"She's not prone to running away?"

"Oh, she's prone to," he says. "She just doesn't have anywhere to go."

I rub my eyes. Even though I lay unconscious for who knows how many hours the previous day, last night's sleep wasn't enough of the real stuff. The January chill has brought a desire for some real, recuperative sleep. Not too strong now, but in a few hours...

I'm still standing, so I grab his roommate's desk chair, set it in the middle of the floor, and sit in a similar slouch. "Amos, I can't do my job properly without some leads and, right now, I don't have many. Yes, Annabelle's friends may point me in the right direction. On the other hand, maybe they won't."

I explain my former and current relationship with the Lansings via Anne. He mentions he vaguely remembers some references to me years ago. I'm just glad he doesn't recall the exact nature of those references.

"I don't know your family other than what your parents have told me. I'm trying to form a better picture of Annabelle. I've learned a little from your mother, but I'd appreciate anything you might add."

Amos smiles in mock cheeriness. "We're an interesting lot."

"So I gather. Why didn't Annabelle… fall into line, as it were?"

The Lansing son abruptly stands and paces. He passes me on both sides in his journey around the small room.

I wait, patient, and look out at the bright cloudiness of a late Thursday morning. My Lucky has almost died before he stops in front of me.

"Mr. Habeck, it isn't just Annabelle. It's this whole family. We're not individuals. We're an entity."

"Explain," I urge.

"Do you know what pressure is?" He abruptly sits straight-backed on the edge of his chair.

"Tell me."

"Do you know what it's like to be constantly prodded to succeed? To be the best? To be reminded of others and how well they're doing? My Uncle Aaron and his kids. My Aunt Anne. Mom. You know what she does?"

"Realtor."

"Not just any realtor," Amos says. "She's with the biggest firm in the city. She's been their top seller four years running. Residential and commercial. Let's not forget Dad and his wanting to spruce up parts of the city. Can you believe it?" He pauses to inhale to his lungs' capacity. "Now, imagine you're the offspring of all this success. Everyone looking down at you, urging you, prodding you, pushing you to be better, better, always better. 'Work harder, boy, be the best, conquer life and the world.'"

I survey the room, his laptop, the textbooks, and gesture with the last inch of the cigarette. "Looks to me as if you're moving in the right direction."

Again, his body wilts. One hand wipes his face, sweeps bangs from his forehead. "You'd think so, wouldn't you?"

"You're in college. What little I understand, business adminis-tration offers a wide field of opportunity."

Amos leans forward, folds his arms on his knees. "Sure, I'm here, and I study hard. I pass all my classes, but I'll be lucky not to start in the mail room or managing some food establishment."

"Aren't you being a little hard on yourself?"

"No," he avows. "Don't you get it? Do you know how many scholarships and grants I applied for? At least half a dozen. All rejected. I know what my grades were in high school. I barely graduated in the top forty. Hell, I even applied to be on the honor council. Why do you think I'm slaving so hard to get this paper done instead of enjoying my supposed time off between semes-ters? I do try, Mr. Habeck. I do, but the more I try, I still can't seem to get ahead."

"And Annabelle?"

He chuckles and leans back. "Ah, sweet Belle. Dear, sweet, poor little Belle. I envy her. I do, you know. Envy."

"Why?"

"Isn't it obvious, man? Because she doesn't have the pressure. She's let it go. Shoved it away. Years ago, when we were still chil-dren, she rejected the family tradition of 'succeed at any cost', the need for speed, to throw for the end zone. She's free."

I disagree and tell him so. "She still lives at home, pursues no secondary education, earns no income, and depends on her parents for food and housing. What's free about that?"

He shakes his head. "You don't understand. Yeah, she's still at home, but her not caring is what I'm talking about. She can do whatever she wants, go wherever she wants with no worries about seeking the big bonuses, the awards, or the promotions.

She's apart from the entity. An individual. She does not need to impress anyone and doesn't care what the family thinks."

I pinch the cigarette dead and lean over to toss it in a wastebasket. Reaching into a coat pocket, I withdraw the photograph of Annabelle and her friends. I take a moment to gaze at the image, the three expressions, then offer the picture to Amos. "Tell me about them."

"Do nothings. Kym's the partier, Rusty's the tag-along."

"And Annabelle? What's her role?"

"Go-along."

I shift in the hard chair, straighten my back a fraction of an inch. "Amos, I've been around a long time, seen a lot of people. Sometimes, I'm even a pretty good judge of character. Do you know what the picture tells me? Kym is the central character. I may end up agreeing with you about Rusty after I talk with him. However, you mentioned Annabelle not needing to impress. Does that include her friends? I'll bet she's a go-along to fit in."

He offers a one-shoulder shrug. "Sure. So?"

"Her rejection of the family 'drive' came at a cost."

"What do you mean?"

"I'm not saying I agree with the 'need to succeed' mindset your family has. From what I've seen, I'd prescribe a healthy dose of moderation. However, by not striving to be the best or at least marginally successful, by not having a plan for her future, she, in turn, was rejected by those who moved past her, who did have at least a direction in life. So, she latches onto what's available."

Amos's attention drifts between the picture in his hand and the floor.

"She reached a point where she started caring, if not about

success, then about acceptance," I say. "She couldn't get it from her family, who was part of the crowd that passed her by. They couldn't make her a part of them, so she turned, in your words, to 'do nothings.' I haven't spoken with her friends, yet, but I don't see them visiting your parents or hear that they're out there searching for her. So, what does that mean?" I shrug and try to pick something from Annabelle's devolving demeanor in her videos. "She may have gone too far the other direction or ran into people who didn't live up whatever expectations she had. If her friends let her down, did she say anything or did she reach her limit and turn to someone or something else? I'm not saying your parents' pushing you two to succeed is right or wrong. Probably right in the wrong way, if that makes sense. I can't police your life choices or hers, but I wonder who's better off. You or her? I wonder if her way may have gotten her into trouble."

My words looked to have hit him hard.

"Your mother says Annabelle changed during the last three months. She quit her part-time job at the mall. She switched to darker clothing and distanced herself even more from your parents when at home. Do you know what might explain this attitude?"

Annabelle told me the answer in her videos. My question is to see if Amos knows. He shakes his head and remains close-mouthed.

I stand, pluck the photo from his fingers, and turn to go. At the door, I look back. His eyes haven't moved from the floor. "Go back to your report. Don't dream about freedom from success. You may envy your sister's life, her backing away from the family's urgings to be the best, but that doesn't mean she's any happier, that she feels no pressure."

Doctor, heal thyself, I think. I couldn't handle being a regular police officer under the pressure to clear cases, to adapt to new ways I didn't understand. Anne's pushing me into something better just strengthened my resistance. Not necessarily resistance to be better, but resistance to completely accepting her way. Her way meant embracing an ever-changing world with technology and new gadgets every month.

However, just because I rejected it, was I any better doing it my way?

He doesn't respond.

"Look at me, boy." When he raises his head, I say, "You're still young enough to learn moderation. Take a break once in a while."

Good words, but they hit a brick wall. Behind his bloodshot eyes, the ingrained need to succeed thrives.

Arlene probably accurately prophesied a heart attack for her son.

He whispers his own finality, "I can't."

I know.

———

The camera picks up only the back of Annabelle's head because she has her head resting in her folded arms on the desk. The window in the background shows either early morning or dusk. After twenty seconds, her head rises and the camera has a close-up view of her face. Smudged make-up. Tired eyes.

June 1

This summer is going to royally suck. Before the spring semester even ended, Dad was shoving applications at me. He reminded me that all my friends have part-time jobs. So what? That means less time to have fun.

Amos graduated. You think he'd be happy. You think he'd celebrate, take some time for himself.

A pained expression tightens her face.

I wanted to get away. Mom and Dad aren't doing any vacation this year. I thought maybe Amos and I could do at least a day trip... somewhere. Enjoy the end of high school with him.

No. He had a job lined up and started the day after Sunday graduation. He's already applied to the Des Moines Institute of Business. Whoopee! He'll end up struggling just like he did in high school. I can just see him taking high blood pressure medication before his senior year.

Gawd! It's nothing but work, work, work with this family.

———

After watching the video blogs, talking with both Arlene and Roger twice, and now talking with Amos, I have a more complete picture of the family and how, if carefully observed throughout the years, one can see the gradual downward spiral.

I am not thinking that Annabelle's disappearance was inevitable. The worsening stream could have been stopped; the secret that caused the sudden downfall might have been kept, or if exposed, the impact lessened.

Instead, here we are. Here I am trying to find a missing piece. To do what? If I find her, can the gaping wound be salved?

CHAPTER FOURTEEN

MANY YEARS AGO, a popular novelty toy was a little plastic troll head stuck onto the end of a pencil. If you wanted to be idiotically nostalgic, you might find one lurking on a dusty shelf of a mom-and-pop store alongside other similar bygone-era gimcracks. The gimmick to provide a fun-filled thirty seconds was the troll's long hair—slightly coarse, usually colored green or purple, below shoulder length. The idea was to smooth down the hair, place the pencil between your palms, pause in anticipation, then vigorously rotate the pencil in both directions. The troll's hair fluffed out in all directions, similar to the infamous Einstein photo. Return to step one and repeat.

Well, Johnny, some people thought it was fun.

After I left Amos's dorm, I called the number Anne found for one of the friends Annabelle went out with New Year's Eve. Kym Malin. Her parents said she favored a downtown coffee shop. I consider myself fortunate to find her, but wonder how often she frequents this place.

My first view of Miss Kym Malin reminds me of the troll's head. Although the length of her mane isn't quite as extreme as the demon head's, she sports a multitude of mini spikes. Like a three-layer parfait, each strand is dyed a dark brown at the point, followed by white blonde down to the black root. Her face in the photo from Annabelle's room shows soft cheeks tapering to a smooth round chin, akin to one of those Japanese cartoons. As I study her in three dimensions, her cheeks display little depth, with fair skin on what little neck is visible above a chocolate brown turtleneck that sparkles in the light. A shiny nose stud protrudes from the side of her left nostril. Jeans-encased legs cross at the ankles under the table.

She peruses a dog-eared copy of Vice magazine. The cover shows a woman with a bushel of red hair and wearing a dress held up by willpower alone, standing at an apartment window gazing down with a sexy come-on expression. The pose naturally draws attention to her cleavage. The viewer expects titillation, but is stopped short by the bold type I can read at twenty feet:

Date Night Dos and Don'ts!

"May I help you?" The squeaky voice comes from a waif of a girl to my left.

Unconsciously, I have moved forward to find myself in front of the order counter.

I gaze at the dark, dusty color tones of the brick and plaster walls, straight out of a cheap apartment. Said plaster has been chipped away on purpose or not repaired after Father Time's erosion. The holes reveal the old brick and mortar behind. The tables (dark blonde wood with black scar streaks) go nicely with the benches—stiff, straight, and hard. Contrast those with the polished stainless steel machines and the tall and gleaming glass-fronted display case. A postage stamp stage darkened by scuff marks at the back of the room decorated with a high wooden stool and microphone.

A cold mustiness mixed with the odor of steaming coffee permeates the air. If they lowered the lighting and served something harder than fifty varieties of coffee, I could feel comfortable… as long as no one used the microphone. It all belies the fact that this downtown Fourth Street joint hasn't quite lost its bongo banging, fringe artiste ambiance.

The cashier waits with a frozen smile on her face.

What the hell, caffeine sounds good after walking two blocks from the parking slot I spent ten minutes finding. Besides, I can't recall the last time I had brewed coffee that didn't taste like the blacktop used for the city's endless road construction. I keep instant at home because it's cheaper. I should talk to Anne about getting one of those single-serving coffee makers that grind the beans or else one that uses the pods and sounds like a dentist's saliva-sucking vacuum.

"Black coffee," I say to the girl.

She wears a pastel rose top and has cut her black hair in an even arc around her head to the level of her earlobes. "Mocha latte? Caramel, pumpkin spice cappuccino?"

I stare at her because I think she just spoke in a foreign language. "Coffee," I repeat.

"What kind?"

"Black."

Is that a small smirk on her face? "What roast? Light, medium, or dark."

Why can't she understand a simple order? I point behind her at the squat round pots of coffee resting on burner plates on a machine that resembles a fifties incubator. "Those coffee pots right there. Give me a cup of what's in one of them. No sugar, no syrup, no frothing."

"What size?"

What a chirpy little girl.

"Medium."

Wrong response.

"We have Grand, Super Grand, or Mega Grand," she corrects.

"Whatever a medium is."

She pours and sets the cup before me. "Would you like a biscotti? Pastry?"

I give a suspicious look at the dry, crumbly, elongated, half-moon-shaped cookie-things inside a tall glass jar next to other sugar junkie delights. "Just the coffee, thanks."

"Okay." She fingers buttons on a chunk of a register the size of a small safe for about ten seconds, then tells me, "That'll be $3.75."

I'm stunned silent and know my ears processed her words incorrectly. "Excuse me?"

"$3.75."

My eyes move to the board hanging on the back wall, the menu and prices all hand-written in different colors of chalk. I don't recognize half the items listed; however, nothing on the menu can be bought for less than $2.50.

"Sir?"

I shake my head, saddened that a simple cup of filtered beans has become so grossly exploited. I shouldn't be surprised. Even my convenience store coffee takes extra coinage every year. "Forget it," I mumble and turn to walk away.

"Sir?"

I give her a look that negates any further protest.

My little episode gained Miss Malin's attention. She watches in curiosity as I approach her table.

"Kym Malin?" She nods. "I'm Sabastian Habeck, private investigator. Could I speak with you for a few minutes?"

She gives me a wary, close-mouthed smile, eyes a combination of wariness and a hint of mischievousness. "Hello, Sabastian Habeck, private investigator." She pauses, and peers around me back toward the counter. "Something wrong with the coffee?"

I give the clerk one last glance. She purses her lips and offers a mild smirk at my refusal to pay. "If she wants that kind of money from me, she'd better carry a baseball bat," I say to Malin. "If I want to be mugged, I'll hang around certain street corners."

Her laugh tinkles with brassy delight. Malin sips her brew, still snow-capped with whipped cream. "So, detective, you sought me out and found me. What are you going to do with me?" Her eyes narrow with the humor of her words.

"Annabelle Lansing."

She flops back in her seat and shows me a pout. "Oh, her."

I pull out a chair and sit. "I understand you and your friend, Rusty, picked up Annabelle around eight Sunday night."

"Yep."

"And you recall not seeing her again sometime before midnight."

"Yep."

"You don't know where she went?"

"Nope."

"She hasn't contacted you since that night?"

Malin shakes her head.

This conversation is like stop-and-go traffic at a pesky short light. "Do you know where she might be?"

Another head shake. The hair spikes don't move. "Nope."

She smiles, and her expression tells me she enjoys the game. I sigh. To end the single-word answers, I inquire about the coffee shop. "What type of performers does this joint rate?"

"Depends on the night." Malin takes another sip of her cauldron-concocted brew.

"Saturday night."

"Open mike." Malin shrugs. "Anything from comedians to folk singers."

I pluck another day out of the air. "Thursday."

"Twice a month they host poetry slams."

I don't ask what that means and don't want to know. It sounds… alien and, at the very least, unnatural. Besides, the word *poetry* guarantees my absence. I backtrack to the original topic because I want to avoid what other weird events this place hosts. "Where did you three visit Sunday night?"

"Zemo's on Southeast Fourth. Great music, lots of action."

I narrow my eyes. "How old are you?"

She arches her eyebrows a millimeter. "What, Mr. Detective, are you implying?"

"I'm wondering how you and Annabelle and Rusty, who, I presume, aren't of age, are—"

"Allowed in? Easy. We've been there before. The owner knows us."

"Knows you? How?"

"You haven't done your homework, have you?"

"Enlighten me." My hand reaches for a Lucky, but I defer the motion in lieu of scratching my shoulder. I'll resist lighting up since I've already caused one minor scene with the counter girl.

"Duh! He's Rusty's Dad." She pauses, but I don't respond. "Randy Fisher."

I nod. Yes, Roger mentioned Fisher the previous night. One of the businessmen interested in sprucing up East Fourth. Now I have his first name. Again, I inwardly cringe at the common usage of the same letter beginning the names of parents and children.

"Oh, Randy's cool. Lets us party, keeps us out of sight if the cops show. Even slips us a few drinks as long as we don't overdo it."

"Swell guy."

She shrugs. "Well, yeah."

I shift in my chair in a vain attempt to get comfortable. "How long have you known Annabelle?"

"Since Junior High."

"Would you say you know her pretty well?"

Another shrug. "Sure, I guess."

"Is she the type of person who disappears for no reason? Is she prone to running away?"

Malin bites her lower lip in contemplation, glances away for a second, then back. A decision made. "I suppose she could do just about anything she wanted." She laughs another brassy tinkle. "Same as me."

She's trying for nonchalance, but before she answers questions, she hesitates and pulls down a thin veil. To hide or shade… what?

I remember the impressions received from the photograph I borrowed from Annabelle's room, still in my coat pocket, and what Amos told me. "May I ask what you are doing these days?"

The corners of her mouth curl upward. "You may ask." When I don't respond to her little joke, she says, "Junior college for two years, then I plan to take online courses at Woodbury University. Fashion Design."

How one attends college via the internet, I'll never understand. What happened to classrooms and professors in front of large chalkboards?

"I wish you success," I say. "I've spoken to Annabelle's mother and brother. I don't see your personalities meshing."

Malin considers and cocks her head. "Hmm! I suppose I have to admit I'm the more impulsive one. We still get along, though."

"Tell me about Annabelle. What was she like in school? Popular? Boyfriends? Did she participate in sports?"

Malin sips more of her coffee. The whipped cream is almost gone. Thank heaven she didn't stick out her tongue to lick any off her upper lip. That would have been too much. Her innuendo-layered comments, even innocent, annoy me.

"How is any of this going to help you find her?" she asks

"I haven't been given many leads," I admit. "I'm just working my way through her contacts. I don't know what happened. Maybe if I acquire a more complete picture of who she is, I might find a reason for her disappearance."

"Ran away? Kidnapped?"

"Both choices are valid."

"Wow!" She sips. "I never thought of it that way. I figured she just got fed up with our company and hooked up."

"Hooked up?"

"Sure. Found a guy Sunday night. Spent the first part of the week with him. You think maybe something else happened?"

"I'm not thinking anything. I'm only excogitating."

"Mmmm, Detective," she chides with a sly smile. "What you said. Doesn't sound quite legal, but possibly fun."

When I stare at her, again not reacting to her flirty joke, she sighs and rolls her eyes. "Okay. Annabelle Lansing. Where to start? I guess you could say she latched onto me because we took several classes together. We sat next to each other a lot, so naturally, we became friends."

"What type of student was she?"

Her shoulders quickly rise and fall. "I don't know. Pretty smart, I guess. She didn't go out for sports or theater."

"Do you know anything about her home life?"

"I don't know too much about her family other than little snippets here and there. I mean, I never spent the night or went to dinner with them. What Annabelle told me, they are very intense, always wanting to get ahead. It seemed to her like an obsession."

"And Annabelle?"

"She couldn't stand it, didn't want any part of it."

"She rebelled," I suggest. This conversation is beginning to sound similar to the one I had with Arlene.

"Not really. She just didn't care. She'd rather hang with me or a few others rather than go home."

Malin pauses, lowers her eyes to the table.

"Something cross your mind?" I ask.

She sniffs once, a thick hiss into her studded nostril. "I was just thinking, you know, picturing Annabelle in school and even after graduation."

"What do you see?"

"She was sad a lot of the time. Hardly smiled. Her attitude was like her mom wouldn't let her come out and play, she had to stay in and work. She did, of course. Play, I mean. We partied a lot, and I guess she enjoyed it. I had fun, anyway."

"I'm sure you did."

Malin gives me a devilish smile.

"How much did she… party?"

"What do you—oh… Drugs? Well, nothing more than a toke here and there."

"Anything stronger?"

"Recently she tried some coke. Never with me, but I could tell. Just by the way she acted. Not too much, just enough to get a good buzz. Same with drinking. Nothing too hard. Some beers, a shot of Jack once in a while."

Right. Coke and Jack, but nothing too extreme. Every once in a while. And the annual year's celebration would be one of those 'once's.

"What about you? Every once in a while?"

Again, with the coyness. "Well, sure. What's a party without…?" Her turn to sigh. "Actually, I've cut back to just a beer now and then."

I let her finish the last of her drink before I ask, "Do you know if Annabelle dated much? Any steady boyfriends?"

"Not really. I mean, she's pretty." Malin states this in a tone women use to mean "but not as pretty as me." "She dated some in school. I don't think she developed a thing for anyone in particular. Again, I don't think she really cared. She went out just to…"

"Fit in?"

Malin's response is a silent, closed-lip, resigned smile.

I also mentally add, "to be accepted." As what? A friend? A normal girl?

… a human being?

I venture into known territory, again as with Amos, to see what others know. "Her mother noticed a change in Annabelle within the last few months," I say. "Her attitude, the way she dressed. This would have been around the time she quit her job."

"Yeah, I know," Malin replies. "The weird clothes. And her hair."

"Did she act any different around you and Rusty or any of her other friends?"

"It was like she couldn't focus. Kept drifting away. I… tried to help her."

My turn to raise the eyebrows. A sliver of sympathy and assistance from this person? "How?"

A flicker of the eyes up off to her left and, just as fast, that veil is back.

"Well, I… I thought she needed… I don't know, a little sprucing up, to get her back to herself."

"What did you do?"

"I… know a… photographer. I recommended her."

I recall one of Annabelle's videos. This was one of the final entries where the short-lived spark was ignited. Annabelle discussed Malin's recommendation for the photographer. She was going to mention it to the guy she'd recently met. What was his name? I'll remember it later. What I do remember is that Annabelle didn't mention the name of the photographer. I pose the question to Malin.

"The Magical Lens," she answers.

"Do you know if she followed up?"

"No. If she did, I don't think it did any good. Which is too bad." The purse of her lips and another look up to the left tell me she's thinking how much to tell me… and probably more importantly, how much to keep hidden. "The owner, Sharon Kozar, does... specialty work. She's skilled at bringing out the best qualities in people."

One of the traits of liars is the looking up to the left. If not outright falsehood, then either an enhancement of the truth or, as I suspect here, holding back on the "juicy bits."

"Why do you say the session with the photographer wasn't enough to change her attitude for the better?" I ask.

Malin shrugs, takes a sip of her drink. The wind tunnel slurp indicates she reached the bottom. "I don't know. She went, when, mid or late November? She seemed happier the couple times I saw her after. But somewhere around Christmas, maybe a day or two after, she was back in her funk. I don't think she really wanted to party at New Year's. When we picked her up at her house, we almost had to drag her to the car."

"Do you know what caused the change back in October?"

Another shrug. "Who knows? She never talked about it. I figured she was dealing with something at home, maybe. I don't know." She stops and the impish grin returns. "Although, you know they say a woman can change the way she dresses when she finds a new man. Although usually with a guy, it's brighter, newer clothes. With her, maybe she had a secret boyfriend who dumped her in October." She purses her lips and raises her eyebrows. "Maybe she found someone else New Year's Eve."

She intimates another contributing factor to the apathy toward Annabelle that night. Party girl Malin looking for high times may have even been a little jealous thinking Annabelle might have found a late-night "date." Especially, if Malin, herself, didn't.

I'll wager Annabelle's attitude toward sex was, and maybe still is, the same. Uncaring, but going along so as not to be marked weird, cold, or with worse labels.

Annabelle was used by her friends and allowed the use. However, looking at Malin, at the flirting, I wonder if some of those users were also looking for acceptance, to be acknowledged. Certainly, the girl across from me is one of those "in need." I suspect she'll prove it with the answer to my next inquiry. "Tell me about Rusty."

Her laugh hits a new high, and she throws her head back. She reminds me of a soap opera snob, but her youth lessens the efficacy of the gesture. "Rusty? He, Mr. Detective, is a puppy dog. Tell him to sit up and beg, roll over, fetch, and he'll all but slobber all over you."

Her harshness is sad, if only because she enjoys treating Rusty like her personal pet.

She looks over my shoulder. A "cat ate the canary" smile forms. "Well, say his name, and he comes running."

The third person in the photo schleps through the coffee shop door. The mongrel stands only at the midway point between five and six feet, maybe an inch less. His brown hair hasn't made friends with a comb or a barber's clippers since before Halloween. He lopes along, withdrawn into himself. A puppy, Kym said. A sad creature looking for a treat, some affection, but afraid of being swiped on the nose with a rolled newspaper.

He raises his hand in a half wave to Kym and shuffles his way to the table. When he registers my presence, he stops and stares as if I might lash out with a kick to his ribs.

I study his lackadaisical style of dress. An oversized, sludge-colored sweatshirt under a stained, nylon jacket, faded, baggy jeans, and sneakers more snot gray than white.

"Uh, hi, Kym," he mumbles, turns to me. "Hey."

Malin reacts like a wrestler who's been in the ring too long, desperate to tag her partner into the match with an overbearing opponent. She stands, makes a rushed introduction—"He wants to ask you questions about Annabelle."—actually pats him on the head, and, before Rusty can blink in comprehension, sashays out the door.

Rusty and I look at each other. I offer a half-smile, amused by his frozen expression, like an abandoned animal unsure of the nature of the stranger.

"Sit down." I try not to sound as if I'm confirming he's learned the trick.

Nevertheless, he obeys and plants himself in the vacated chair.

Again, we stare at each other. Damn, how I crave a smoke.

I indicate the counter offering the expensive food and drink. "You want anything?"

He shakes his head.

"Fine. I don't blame you." I stand. "Let's walk."

He rises in slow motion, and I wonder if he's expecting to be leashed. He plods behind me out the door.

As soon as my feet touch the snow-packed sidewalk, my hands begin the automatic motions to light up. After a few deep drags, I realize Rusty is still behind me. His head is lowered, hands and forearms stuffed in pants pockets.

"You're not a personal assistant trailing after the executive," I say. "It will be easier to converse if you walk beside me."

Plows and shovels have created a miniature mountain range along the buildings and curbs. This short corridor of a street is one of the oldest sections of downtown, with fifties and sixties lettering on faded signs, large clear glass display windows, and even awnings over many of the entrances. The wind has calmed, so we pass through our own cloudy breaths.

Smoke from my cigarette hangs in the air. We walk half a block and turn to cross the street.

Rusty isn't going to speak first, so I ask similar questions as put to his flighty friend and receive similar answers.

During Sunday's revelry, Rusty the puppy never left Kym's side or at least sight line if she danced with someone else. Annabelle disappeared around eleven, he thinks. He does remember he couldn't locate her when the old year ticked off its last seconds of life. His hesitation and glances to one side, unlike Malin's, tell me he has an attraction for Annabelle, a teenage crush. Perhaps, he wanted the traditional kiss when the world moved into the new year. When I ask him where Annabelle might have gone, he echoes Malin and assumes that she met someone.

We pass a pizza joint with a sign in almost indecipherable, Asian-style lettering.

"How long have you known Annabelle?" I ask.

He shrugs and offers a vague, short answer, typical of the rest of his sentences, "I don't know. A few years, I guess."

"What do you think of her?"

Another one-shoulder shrug. "She's okay."

I flick away the last of the Lucky in frustration. Talking to this kid is hardly worth my time. I'm not going to get a bit of useful information out of him, not without either spending too many long hours or else giving him a good hard shake to rattle his little mind. "Listen, Rusty," I say and stop mid-stride.

My abrupt halt throws him, and I can almost picture the electric connection in his head zip and zap to fathom what comes next. After he regains his balance, he glances up at me.

I stare at him for a moment. "It's pretty damn cold out here, and I don't feel like screwing around. I'm trying to get a better overall picture of Annabelle. Working down the line of contacts is my best choice." I pause to light another stick. "I suppose my next stops will be her former employer and your father's nightclub. Do you know why she quit her job?"

He shakes his head.

I sigh. "What time does your father's nightclub open?"

Rusty's head cocks to one side, as if his shoulder is too tired to achieve another shrug. "Around five."

"Tell me about your Dad. What can I expect?"

Confusion veils his face, as if I've asked him about a solution to the Middle East debacle.

I come in at a different angle, "What type of joint does he run?"

"Zemo's? It's a cool place. Dad plays the latest hits and even books some local bands. Sunday night, Spinster's Nightmare played. They're kinda insane. I wish they'd put out another album."

I don't want to know what Spinster's Nightmare might look like or what type of brain-deadening noise they produce, and could easily believe they're insane. Although, I think Rusty's connotation of the word is completely opposite of mine. His answer, though, is the longest series of words the kid's put together in a row since we started talking, and I don't interrupt for fear of his going back to monosyllables.

However, Rusty stops talking and looks grim, resigned.

"What?"

"Dad's kind of alone down there. I mean, he opened the place hoping to attract other businesses, maybe more clubs, like Court Avenue."

"What happened?"

"Nothing so far. He's working with Annabelle's dad, trying to bring in more businesses, but it's not happening real fast."

"Lack of financial investment?"

"I don't know. Dad doesn't talk about it. I mean, he's succeeding, but no one else wants to move down there."

When I don't respond, he looks up at me. "Anything else?" I ask.

"I don't see Dad that much. Kym or Annabelle, either. Community college, you know. Lots of homework."

"What's your major?"

"Haven't decided," he answers. "I'm taking the core classes right now."

"Any interests in a particular field?"

Yet another shrug.

I hope fashion design and business administration aren't on his list. The former may be in trouble if Miss Malin enters the field. I don't want to imagine the clothing she'd design. The latter may soon have an anxiety-fettered, high-blood-pressured kid who'll kill himself with stress in the first six months.

"All right," I say. "Thanks for talking with me." I shake my head and watch him walk off.

He's a sad case. No initiative. Kym uses him for a false ego boost. Annabelle probably recognized him as someone as close to a kindred spirit as she could find. Two lackluster attitudes, though, are no more productive than a couple of dope smokers, no more nurturing than a bed-hopping mother. Unless he breaks free, he'll get sucked into the black hole of an equally apathetic world. His destiny is not so much lost as nonexistent.

CHAPTER
FIFTEEN

JULY 5

What a boring holiday. All my friends were gone with their own families or working. A few are preparing for college. Dad worked at the office, and Mom discussed the next "getaway" with fellow realtors. When Dad finally came home, that Marshe guy and Rusty's dad stopped by, again trying to talk Dad into changing his view on the never-ending project. Kym spent the holiday in Council Bluffs with some guy she met on Facebook. I suppose I could have hung around with Rusty, but he gets on my nerves. He's had a crush on me for years, and sometimes it's irritating.

I spent most of the Fourth in my room. I told Mom and Dad I'd look for a part-time job. I found a few that sound halfway decent. The one at the mall seems okay.

———

Malls. Strip malls. Outlet malls.

The Des Moines metro boasts four shopping malls, countless strip malls, and an outdoor outlet mall.

They're all the same, though: large and confusing. You spend too much time in search of a parking slot, traipse over acres of concrete to reach six variations of the same shoe store or sixteen others that offer the same overpriced, supposedly fashionable women's clothing.

Merle Hay Mall is no exception. Even in inclement weather, cars pack the lots. I string together four rows before I spy a blue Dodge Dart from the early seventies back out. I brake and wait for the driver to vacate the spot, but instead, the person readjusts to straighten the car and pulls in again. A blonde woman in a trench coat and hat exits. I recognize her as a fellow private investigator whose office is west of mine on Locust Avenue. She's the one who gets called first when Mendelssohn's daughter goes missing.

A horn's beep from behind urges me to drive on. At an inter-section, I decide not to continue into the next row, but reverse course around a dividing barrier and park five paces from the street, over an eighth of a mile from the mall's entrance. I brace for the cold and, head down, trudge to the glass doors.

Inside, I'm confronted by flash and noise. Masses of people roam nonstop, and half are gazing in studied concentration at cell phone screens. Clearly, some of the area schools haven't started up for the new semester. Teenage boys gather in trade-offs of brag-gadocio. Girls giggle at whatever they're sharing on their cell-phones. Couples hang onto each other as if they're mutated human entities. Amid the roar of voices, the mall's sound system emits jazzed-up Muzak.

Annabelle made her way through this surfeit of humanity to reach her place of employment, one of these retail spaces called

Lupo's. I don't know where the store is located, but consider myself fortunate I don't have to wander the halls and wings to find it. After I study a bird's eye map of the mall, I negotiate a path through the crowds to discover the store tucked back under the center court walkway.

Only the eye of this shopping hurricane has upper and lower levels, but the expected calm doesn't exist. In the middle of the floor stands a contraption built by a sadist. A child strapped into a single seat shoots into the air. His only saving grace is a pair of bungee cords I wouldn't trust as a reliable leash for a poodle. The kid shrieks in delight as he's flung up and down while Mom smiles from below, a target for the inevitable upchuck.

I shake my head and move on.

The tiny store of Lupo's gears itself toward teen and preteen girls. Shiny, gaudy jewelry is displayed under the glass counter or draped over foot-high, plastic stands. Racks filled with a myriad of clothes cram the majority of floor space. Posters on the wall depict happy-go-lucky youngsters cavorting for the camera in clothes ranging from chic grunge to fulsome.

A thirty-something woman trying to look half her age eyes me from behind the cash register in the middle of the store. She wears a frilly, white top with a narrow, but deep, V-cut in front and jeans that look fresh off the shelf. Her hair is a mix of brown and blonde with sharp ends that hang over her face. Her features would be attractive—round cheeks, almond brown eyes, pleasant smile—except she's used her make-up to cover up instead of enhancing. Her name tag reads Janet/Manager.

"May I help you?"

I'm dubious about her ability to do so.

We both know I don't belong within half a mile of this place.

Her tone lies somewhere between offering genuine assistance for purchases, perhaps for my daughter, and wondering if I'm a pervert in a too-obvious search for my next victim.

"Sabastian Habeck," I say and follow with my profession. "Could I have about ten minutes of your time?"

"What about?"

"Annabelle Lansing. I understand she worked here last year."

"Yes." Still cautious. "Why?"

"She's been missing since New Year's and her parents are concerned. Her mother hired me yesterday. I'm following every lead possible."

Janet nods. "Well, Annabelle used to work here, but I haven't seen her since, oh, late October."

"What can you tell me about her?"

Janet hesitates. "I'm… not sure I'm able to provide that type of information. I'm bound legally and—"

"I'm not after past behavior that may affect future employment. I'm not seeking references for another company. I'm looking for the girl herself and talking to people who might provide leads to her whereabouts. At this point, I don't know if she ran away… or worse. Nothing you tell me will be shared with anyone else." I offer a half-smile. "My profession has rules, too."

I don't tell her that no law forbids her speaking about a former employee, nor do I share that I'll pass along anything worthwhile to the police, if necessary.

"I don't know what I could tell you," she says to me. "I haven't seen her for months."

Although I know the reason why Annabelle quit, I have to tap any lead to get more of a personality. "I understand. At this point, I'm putting the puzzle pieces into alignment. I'm talking to contacts she's had in the past months. Who knows who will say something that will lead me to her."

She considers for another five seconds, stands on tiptoe to look behind me, and calls to a girl in the back corner who's firing sticky red tabs from a price gun. "Gloria, could you handle the register for a few minutes?"

"Sure."

Janet motions to me. "Let's talk in my office."

Out of earshot of the help. More beneficial for me, as this gives me a temporary reprieve from the charivari of the mall.

Through a door near where Gloria had stood, Janet leads me down a hallway ten yards long. At the end is another door, which I deduce is a rear entrance where new supplies are processed. To the left, I enter a room that resembles every small business office. A metal desk covered by a holder for paperclips, rubber bands, a half dozen pens, and as many forms and reports. A mug holding coffee. Second-hand wheeled office chair with the back recliner section askew from too much use. Peeling, dull gray paint on the file cabinet with one drawer out of alignment. Boxes of miscellaneous items—returns, samples, damaged—are stacked along the far wall.

Janet sits in the desk chair and gestures to a straight-backed chair next to a set of wooden shelves. Said shelves contain more merchandise no one has paid attention to in months. I wouldn't want to disturb the layer of dust layering the products lest I want a sneezing fit.

Despite the clutter, Janet is no doubt in charge. I'll bet she knows where everything is located and, to her, all is in order. As partial proof, she rolls to the filing cabinet, pulls open the second drawer, and, from a sea of colored folders, withdraws a single manila folder, Annabelle's name inked on the tab. She opens it flat on her desk and peruses the two sheets of paper. The twitch of her lips and the slight, resigned shrug let me know she's deciding what to share.

"Annabelle started middle of last July and quit near the end of October. I had hoped she'd stay through the busy Christmas season. I had to do a rush training of someone new."

"How well did Annabelle do her job?"

Another half shrug. "Pretty well, considering."

"Considering what?"

"Well, I almost didn't hire her. In the initial interview, her attitude was… less than motivated. In fact, she told me the only reason she applied was that her parents pressured her."

"Why did you hire her?"

"Mr. Habeck, I'm a good judge of character. In most instances, I can tell if a person is right for the particular position available, even those without experience, such as Annabelle. I sense how a person will perform, how well she'll relate to the customers."

"You saw something in Annabelle?"

"I'll admit, I'm not a hundred percent accurate in my judgment. I've had my share of…"

"Duds?" I offer.

"Precisely. However, behind Annabelle's lackadaisical manner, a spark of desire waited to be fanned. Deep down she wanted to work, to get her feet wet, maybe to try something new…" Janet pauses.

I arch an eyebrow.

"You're surprised?" she asks.

"A bit. I understand the family is success and business-oriented, and Annabelle was the black sheep in the drive department."

Janet nods. "That's a possibility, but her rejection doesn't mean she didn't want to venture out at her own pace. She proved to be a very productive employee. Memorized procedures, made friends with coworkers, familiarized herself with the line of products, and usually was the first to greet customers. I also saw she possessed a keen insight for each customer. She knew what fit each person and showed the comparisons if she felt their choices were incorrect."

"For instance?"

"Say a girl liked a particular pair of earrings. Annabelle would see they were wrong for her. She derived a lot from the customer's dress and personality. She'd show the girl how another pair would look better even if the second choice was lower priced. I didn't care because she formed a bond with the person, made the sale, and, many times, the customer bought something more. More importantly, that person became a potential repeat customer and next time might bring friends along."

"So, what happened?"

Janet's frown conveyed regret. "The spark died. As I recall, one day she came in and acted listless, forgetful, tired. I had to work to get her to say more than three words at a time."

"Did she tell you the reason for the abrupt change?"

A head shake. "I tried. When nothing changed after a couple days, I met with her in private. When she wouldn't talk, I had no choice but to assert authority. She had to either perk up, leave her troubles outside, or face consequences. She lasted another week and then didn't show up for work. I called, but she barely mumbled 'I quit' and hung up. Do you know what happened?"

I do but keep it to myself and shrug. "No one I've spoken to thus far understands, either."

"Whatever caused her change must have been… I don't know, awful? Deeply personal, certainly."

"I agree. Have you heard from her since?"

"No. I emailed for her to return her name badge, since we'll reuse the holder."

I can't think of any question that might elicit more details, so I thank Janet and rise to leave. At the door, I halt when she asks, "You say she's gone missing?"

I nod.

"I hope the reason is simple, and you find her holed up some-where safe."

A shared hope, but I fear it's not as simple as Janet wants to believe.

CHAPTER
SIXTEEN

THE MALL'S population swelled during my talk with Janet. Another Mother of the Year reject has strapped her young'un into the bungee chair. This kid, appropriately, demonstrates his victim status by screaming at a pitch to pierce eardrums.

I shake my head and walk away.

Around me, people teem. Teenagers gabble like geese after breadcrumbs. Women carry shopping bags that bulge with merchandise. Husbands with resigned expressions lounge in cushioned chairs or couches.

Blacks, Asians, Latinos, Arabs. Accents from Australia, India, Africa, and Russia reach my ears.

Clothing ranges from miniskirts—in January?—to jeans. From casual to professional. From outfits that should be worn to bed to stuff surely fashioned by a blind designer on hallucinogens. Sandals with socks. Multi-colored sneakers. Three large women wear too short skirts. A pair of lean, twenty-something men walk ahead of me holding hands. Both wear matching, oversized T-shirts and pants, the latter of which droop to display three inches of the underwear beneath. Frayed cuffs brush the floor with each step, and I wait in anticipation for one or both of these mutton heads to trip. I'm disappointed when they don't.

Before I reach the short extension of the main channel that leads to the mall's entrance doors, my attention is diverted by a group of half a dozen youths gathered near the end of a wooden bench. One sits, two slouch, one squats as if picking something off the floor. The other two lean against a mammoth, ceramic planter.

All in black with two in white shirts under black vests, pasty faces, and raccoon eyes. They could be a troupe of repertoire theater actors waiting for the house lights to dim. I suspect they're part of the subculture that Arlene and I discussed as an avenue down which Annabelle might have walked.

The goth population came and went in popularity three or four decades ago, but, like the hippie-peace-man-free-love years, there are still remnants to be found if one looks long and hard enough. How many of these kids think they've discovered something new? Unlike the hippie generation, where I still see sexagenarians in flower-power shirts and peace sign imprinted headbands, most of the goth crowd tended to mature and move onto something more sensible.

Maybe this group will discover all the make-up isn't good for avoiding acne… or gaining respectable employment.

Could Annabelle have gone through this phase? Arlene said she had started to shun make-up, but the dark clothing fits. Might she have latched onto this particular group? Over a half million people in the greater metro, but how many goths could there be? If the number much exceeds these six, I might entertain discussions of euthanasia. Just kidding, Johnny, but maybe tranquilizing them, a bit a grooming, and proper clothing, then putting them in front of a mirror to show them the ridiculousness of what they were.

Not sure how to talk to such a group, I try the direct approach. It was how I spoke to Anne the first time I met her. "Excuse me, my name is Sabastian Habeck."

In fact, I think I used those same words with her.

They look at me as if I have a porcupine on my head. If I recall, Anne's expression was very similar. At least for a second or two.

"I'm a private investigator. I was wondering if any of you know Annabelle Lansing."

One of them sneers and, in an accent that makes me think I've been transported to East London, says, "Sod off, dickhead."

Others expel derisive words. The lone girl on the bench widens her eyes, but looks away a second later.

Despite the attitudes, I persevere. "She's been missing since New Year's. I was told by her mother that she might have... connected with..." With what? *Those of your ilk? Your kind?*

Neither expresses a quality of tactfulness, eh, Johnny?

At a loss for words, I'm reduced to a broad, sweeping gesture to include all six.

The Brit steps up to me, stops a yard and a half away, eyes me up and down.

One of the guys making sure the planter doesn't fall over taps the other on the shoulder. "Quotation time," he mutters.

The Brit meets my eye. "'I don't belong on this earth. I always feel out of place–like a visitor.'"

"Nice one," says the one on the bench "Shakespeare?"

"Hattie McDonald," I say.

The Brit widens his eyes in surprise. "Right. The dickhead's got a bit of brains."

"Perhaps she flew away, like a bird," the slouchers says. "To be free."

One of the planter leaners pipes up, "Quoth the raven, 'Nevermore.'"

"That's Poe," the Brit says. "Wrong connotation." He turns to me. "Sorry, mate, can't help you."

Well, Anne rejected my initial offer of drinks and dinner.

I walk away to the sound of contumelious snickers, but am surprised by the esoteric references. I expected the continuation of the original dismissal. Still, I revisit the notion of long-term care for these jokers with long-term tranquilizers.

———

I catch the door before the blustery wind smacks it back into my face. The hydraulics on the mall's entrance need a readjustment. I hunch within my overcoat, shiver, finger out a Lucky, and take three steps to the right, so I'm not a hindrance to patrons. A 'No Smoking' sign hangs above my head. I glance up at it, expel an audible breath, and light up.

I stand and smoke in contemplation of the last half hour. Janet only further confirmed something happened to Annabelle to alter her slothful life. I hadn't expected revelatory details from the manager. If Annabelle hadn't discussed the issue with her parents or friends, she wouldn't confide in a part-time employer.

While Janet was another link in the chain, I made a mistake talking to the goths. We are as different as apples and eggplants.

At the car, about ready to open the door, a footstep scrape on pavement catches my attention. Standing at the rear bumper is the young girl who was seated on the bench, the one who looked away at the mention of Annabelle's name. I had hoped she'd say something, but maybe she didn't want to speak up in front of her friends.

She's donned a bulky, leather jacket, but the chalky make-up and short, black hair give her the appearance of a ghostly waif. "Mr. Habeck?"

I'm surprised by her formality, even if she mumbles the words and can't quite meet my eyes.

"Yes."

"Um…" She puts a finger to her mouth, as if to bite a nail. "I know Annabelle."

I glance around and wonder if the others in her group are near. "Okay."

She shivers.

I've already had one conversation today al fresco. "Could we sit in the car with the heater on?"

The left corner of her mouth raises in mock wariness.

I understand the possibly implied scenario—my words may have sounded improper—and dig in my pocket for my wallet and business card, which I show her. "Private investigator, remember?" I gesture at our general surroundings. "Or we could talk out here and be cold."

I'm relieved when she doesn't give me a suspicious eye, but nods acceptance. One more scan of the parking lot in case anyone thinks I'm about to kidnap a young girl, then open my side, sit, and reach across to pull up the nub to unlock her door.

She puts one foot on the frame, eases into the seat, and her hesitation tells me she's not sure where to put her feet due to the amount of trash.

"Sorry," I say.

"That's okay. My brother's car is just as messy." She's short enough to rest her feet up against the dashboard above the glove compartment. "Your car reeks of smoke," she says, nose wrinkled.

I apologize again, and she shrugs a no-big-deal reply.

The interior warms to a comfortable temperature. As old as this hunk of junk is, the heater still does its job.

"Let's start with your name," I say

"Donna. Donna Michelle."

"How do you know Annabelle?"

"Classmate at Roosevelt High."

"Have you seen her lately?"

"Not for months. She used to work at Lupo's."

"I talked to the manager. She told me in October, Annabelle went through a change of personality. Her mother said she became more withdrawn, started wearing dark clothes."

Donna smiles. "So, you thought she went goth?"

I shrug.

"Yeah, we used to talk whenever I'd see her at work. Then she quit… when was it?"

"October."

"Right." She shifts to sit straighter. "I saw her just once after that. First part of November, maybe? She was sitting in the same area where Ian and the guys were."

"Ian. He the one who acted like I ran over his dog?"

"Yeah. He's kinda cool once you get to know him."

I doubt that statement.

"He's from England. Foreign exchange student. He graduates this year."

Iowa has to put up with the troll for almost five more months. I sigh and bring the subject back on track. "Annabelle."

"Right. Well, she was looking pretty down, and when I tried to talk to her about it, she didn't say much."

"Can you remember any of the conversation?"

Donna purses her lips in thought. Her youth and innocence show beneath the make-up. "I asked her when she was working again, and she said she'd quit, but wouldn't tell me why."

I am about to chalk up another mark in the loss column when Donna pauses, then blurts, "Moms are bitches!"

"Excuse me?"

"Annabelle was quiet for a moment... then she says that 'moms are bitches'."

"And?"

"I asked what she meant, but she stood up and told me to forget it. I thought she was going to walk away, but she sat down again." Donna goes quiet.

"Something else?" I ask.

"She turned her head away, but she might have said something like, 'I don't know who I am anymore.' I wanted to talk to her about it, but then Ian, Brian, and the guys showed up."

A regular meeting spot.

"Ian laughed. 'Find us a new recruit, Donna?' And I tell everyone Annabelle was in my class, but she tells Ian to, um..."

"Sod off?"

"Yeah," Donna says, voice low. "Then she does walk away."

"Have you seen her since?"

"No. I mean, she and I are friends, sort of, but we don't hang out too much or anything."

"Do you know any of her current friends?" Other than Kym and Rusty? Surely, Annabelle hung around more people than those two.

Donna shrugs. "Not really. As I said, friends, but, you know, you lose touch after graduation."

As lucky as I am running into three of Annabelle's former classmates, I have the notion she didn't have a close relationship with anyone. What's the hip acronym used today for best friends? It used to be BFF. Whatever letter combination or word the kids use, Annabelle didn't have one. "Thanks for talking with me, Donna."

"Sure. No problem." She reaches for the door handle.

I halt her with, "Could I ask another question?"

"Sure."

I hesitate, not wanting to sound like a Father Knows Best rerun. "You act and speak like a mature, intelligent young woman. Just as a matter of curiosity, why are you with a bunch of guys like Ian?"

She half-stifles a giggle. "If you want the truth, Mr. Habeck, I'm doing research."

"Research?"

"For my sociology class at Kaplan University. It's part of my Poli-Sci major."

"I see." Not really, but I'll fake it.

She laughs, seeing that I can't pull off faking it. "It's okay. They're cool with it. Got all the permissions to cover me with the professor."

Here I thought she had been sucked down into the muck of society. "So, you don't normally dress like this?"

"Have you ever worn a leather skirt in winter?"

"Point taken." I remember Annabelle's words. "And you don't think your mom is a bitch?"

Her laughter, unlike Kym's, is genuine. "No, she's cool. Dad, too. Mom's on the city council."

A bolt of lightning would not have shocked my heart more than her statement. Maybe my luck in this case is turning in my favor. "Does she know Roger Lansing?"

"Of course. She complains about him all the time. Hey, I have to go. I have an interim class later this afternoon, and I still have to write some notes about today's experience."

I suppose I'll be included and wonder whether her words will put me in a positive light.

She starts to leave, door half-open.

"Wait, what's your mother's name?" I ask.

"Denise."

My ex-in-laws aren't the only people who love alliteration with names. "I'd like to talk with her. Is she working today?"

"Wells Fargo. Downtown. By the courthouse." Donna says goodbye and exits the car.

I have another trail to pursue. I find a pencil and notebook to record names before I forget.

Donna Michelle. Poli-Sci. I shudder at the thought of such a convoluted and complex study that asks more questions than answers. However, I think the girl will go far.

CHAPTER
SEVENTEEN

WELLS FARGO DOESN'T DO anything on a small scale. Around the metro, edifices proclaim the vast grandeur of the company. From the mothership in West Des Moines to the reconnaissance ships of neighborhood offices. Even these cannot be considered "small" because each is a tentacle of the leviathan.

The eight-story, block-long, brick monstrosity between the streets of Cherry and Mulberry, across from the courthouse, is no exception. Not when an extra parking garage similar in size and an entire block of parking spaces are dedicated to its employees.

The lobby and reception are examples of the grandiose nature of many businesses. High ceiling, sharp corners and edges, shiny marble surfaces, bright lights. Android personnel with programmed and polished smiles and demeanor.

I would go insane if forced to work in this environment. The receptionist calls up to Denise's office, explains who I am and my request for a discussion about a missing teenage girl. Presenting the issue this way may have a better chance of success than saying I want to talk about Roger Lansing's plans. I'd have a better chance persuading her to talk about Lansing if we're face to face rather than her outright rejecting me via a receptionist.

Five minutes later, the nearby elevator bell dings, the doors hiss open. The car ejects a woman wearing a pantsuit and exuding a stature of professionalism. Straight cut and light brown, her hair matches the clothes. Her face is square, eyes dark, expression concerned, but not yet fearful. "Mr. Habeck," she says. I nod and she continues, "What's this about a missing girl? Is Donna all right?"

"She's fine," I say. "In fact, I spoke with her about twenty minutes ago."

"Why?"

"She was Annabelle Lansing's classmate. Annabelle is the person I'm searching for."

She releases a sigh of relief, and her expression hardens. "I still don't understand. How could Donna help? Why talk to her or me? I don't know Annabelle other than she's Roger's daughter."

Thank you for opening the door.

"His name and the East Fourth Street project have come up. I'm sure you must be busy, but is there someplace we could talk? Maybe you could fill in some details?"

"How will that help find Annabelle?"

"I don't know. At this point, I'm following the lines of the investigation as they present themselves."

She frowns, and her attempt to find an excuse to turn me away all but leaks out her ears. "Let's go to the break room." She sighs and leads me through a door opposite the elevator. Unlike the order in the lobby, the disarray of the tables and chairs resembles the aftermath of a small whirlwind. A full-size refrigerator stands in the corner. Sink, counter, coffee maker, vending machine.

"Coffee?"

I accept. "Thank you."

She brings two cups to a table roughly in the center of the room.

I open my flask and tip a spoonful of Ten High into mine. When she raises her eyebrows, I gesture with the flask. She glances at her watch, then slides her cup toward me.

"I won't tell," I say.

She sips the brew. "I deserve it. Ten years with this company and the first week back after the holiday is always hell."

I can empathize, if not for the same reason.

"What can I tell you?" she says after another liberal drink.

"Annabelle disappeared New Year's Eve. Yesterday morning, her mother hired me to find her."

"The police aren't involved?"

"Mrs. Lansing has made a report, but her sister recommended me as a follow-up."

"Okay."

"The picture I've put together yesterday and today has been formed from various people, but Roger Lansing and his revitalization plan have come up often enough for me to take notice. I don't know if it has a connection to Annabelle, but the nightclub where she was last seen is part of both."

"Zemo's," she says.

"Yes."

"A rat hole, if you ask me. Have you spoken with the owner?"

"Not yet."

"One of the rats."

"Is he part of a 'rat pack'?"

"Interesting term, but nowhere near as commendable as the original."

"Is Roger part of it?"

"Not… yet," she says with a noticeable pause between her words.

My turn at the eyebrow raise.

She sighs. "Let me clarify. Roger has a knack for business. He's very adept at bringing companies to Des Moines. There are three or four neighborhoods where he's played a major role in sprucing up or outright saving."

"Not East Fourth?"

She huffs in exasperation. "Sometimes, you know something won't work from the beginning. I cannot fault Roger for his intentions. His ideas are worthwhile."

"What's the problem?"

Denise's tightened lips tell me she's deciding how many details she wants to share and how tactful she wants to be.

"The… other players involved."

"The owner of Zemo's."

"He's one."

I let my silence ask the question.

"I probably shouldn't mention names," she says.

I want to throw a couple at her, but again, resist exposing I know more than I let on.

"Nothing you tell me will be shared with anyone else."

"I understand, but the situation is… delicate," she says.

I sip coffee and try to decipher what she's not saying. "Do you think by associating with these… individuals, Roger may be tainted by less than desirable reputations?"

Denise stares at me and raises her coffee cup to sip. Another late-term, pregnant pause. Denise wants to give birth to her thoughts, but in her mental labor, another implication falls into place.

"You think he already is."

She releases the held breath with the merest nod. "There is nothing tangible, no concrete evidence."

"Speculation?" Another nod. "Rumors."

"Yes," she admits.

"Of what?"

Another sip of coffee, and maybe the bourbon additive loosens her reserves. "I cannot openly make accusations."

Almost there, I think. "Understood."

"The council and city planners have been resistant for a long time. One or two have delayed progress on purpose because of the people involved. In recent weeks, maybe a few months, there has been talk of under-the-table deals."

I say the word, since she's all but spelled it out. "Bribes?"

Her lips tighten again.

"From Roger to these business owners?" I ask. She raises her chin and looks away. "Payments *to* Roger."

Her eyes snap back. "I repeat. No evidence."

"Still, there is an appearance of impropriety."

She finishes her coffee and stares at the empty cup. The air between us grows heavy, and her silence tells me she wonders if she's said too much.

"Thank you for talking with me," I say.

She nods. "I didn't say anything to help you find Annabelle."

"Maybe not directly." One part of our conversation sticks out. She mentioned the rumors started "a few months ago." Maybe in

October? At or close to the time Annabelle quit her job and became more introverted? "I don't know." I remove the flask from my overcoat. "Who can tell?"

I stand, lean over the table, and pour more bourbon into her cup.

She looks up at me.

"Just don't breathe on anyone," I say.

CHAPTER
EIGHTEEN

AT UNIVERSITY AVENUE, I pull into a gas station. Although I've filled the Plymouth countless times, I have yet to completely comprehend the computerized gas pumps. Every station has its own version, and each requires a different sequence of steps to start the flow of fuel. This station allows me to pay inside after fueling. I have a credit card, but am loathe to use it… save for emergencies. After hand-numbing minutes of studying and fingering various buttons, I finally reach the point where I insert the nozzle into the gas tank's opening and pull the trigger.

Nothing happens.

Then a voice blats from a speaker somewhere above me. Experience has taught me the cashier inside is telling me the pump is on. His voice, however, comes through like a garbled CB radio response. Why does he have to inform me the pump is functioning? The lights and numbers blink, so I know it's operating.

I wait in anticipation for a few seconds—will I get fuel or has the jerk inside turned off the pump as a stupid joke?—a soft *ka-chunk*, and the wheezy sound of gas through the hose.

After I tromp through slush blackened by tires and shoes, I step through the doors to hear a greeting said double time by one of the cashiers. At the counter, I sort through crumpled bills to pay for my fuel. The kid hands me my change with almost mechanical efficiency.

"Do you have a phone book I could borrow?" I ask.

He reaches to a shelf below him and comes up with a thick, dog-eared tome with a faded, torn cover. As soon as he plops it in front of me, I'm immediately forgotten in deference to the next customer.

I slide to one side, but glance at the twenty-something, bald man who steps up to the counter. He wears an untucked T-shirt, baggy jeans, a denim jacket that exhibits numerous, fraying holes, and has enough metal studs lining the rim of his left ear to interfere with radio signals. Tentacles of a tattoo creep up the side of his neck. He places upon the counter a plastic cup filled with a sick-looking concoction colored urine yellow and freezing before my eyes. Next to it, he puts a can the size of a thermos that contains one of those popular brands of energy drinks.

I shake my head in disbelief and open the phone book. Since Denise Michelle has put me further down the Roger Lansing line of thought, I figure I may as well keep going to find a natural terminus. The next step, then, is to check the name Roger mentioned this morning.

Since the year was born within the last four days, I hope Chris Laine isn't at whatever office he usually occupies or basking under a Caribbean sun on holiday. If the latter is true, I envy him.

I find two listings for Chris Laine. The first lives along Harding, just north of Euclid. Knowing the neighborhood, I dismiss this one for the Laine living on Sixty-ninth off Aurora.

This residential patch consists of upper-middle-class people, blocks of Neighborhood Watch signs, a few fenced-in backyards, useless rear decks—the only views are the back sides of the houses on the next street—teenagers, and Labrador-sized dogs. I pull into the driveway of Laine's split-level abode. The house is constructed of gray, roughened brick. The attached garage has two doors with a third, smaller bay for what I assume is used for storage.

His street and sidewalks have been cleared of snow.

I estimate the man who answers the door to be around forty, but time will have to battle hard to overcome his youthful looks. Smooth and evenly cut weave of tight, black curls, light, walnut-toned skin, pleasant and professional features. He's dressed in tan slacks and a matching, smooth fabric sweater with the sleeves pushed up to the elbows.

Mister Casual. I see him on the cover of a business-related magazine with an accompanying article discussing *The Working Dad at Home*.

I introduce myself and wonder if he has some time to discuss Roger Lansing and the Fourth Street plans. When he adopts a confused expression, I state, "Mr. Lansing specifically referred me to you."

Still not opening the storm door, he says in his baritone voice, "I don't understand. You're a private investigator?"

I want to ease into Annabelle's disappearance, but I'm starting to feel the chill. Another gust of frosty air finds access to my coat. "Mr. Lansing's daughter is missing."

His eyes widen. He still doesn't understand, but my words are enough for him to open the door and grant me entrance.

I follow him down a short flight of carpeted stairs and along a hallway, past a cozy sitting room, or maybe a den, and into a home office. Bookshelves line the rear wall, and family portraits hang on the others. A monitor and keyboard, a large desktop calendar, Rolodex (nice to see a holdover from the past), phone, and manila folders cover the top of an executive desk.

He offers me a chair while he eases into his ergonomic seat behind the desk.

Habit has me reaching for a cigarette, but I halt my hand halfway to my pocket. My subconscious forgot for a moment this isn't my office.

Laine is straightforward, no banter about the weather, no offer of coffee. "Could you please explain the connection between his daughter and the urban renewal project?"

"I'm not sure there is one. Yesterday, Mrs. Lansing hired me when Annabelle didn't come home on New Year's Eve. The people with whom I've spoken don't know where she is or why she's gone."

"Why would you think I would have any ideas? I don't believe I've ever met the girl."

"I don't know that you do have a direct connection. However, my conversations always steer into the topic of Roger and his business plans. Since I can't see a reason for her friends' involvement other than losing track of her, I'm looking at family matters. The major topic is Roger's affairs."

"How could the project have anything to do with his daughter?"

I must treat him as I did Denise Michelle. Ask and learn or ask and confirm what I know. "I'm working on a couple theories.

Anyway, I visited the Lansings this morning to ferret out further leads. As I said, he mentioned you."

Laine settles back in his chair and rubs fingers along his clean-shaven cheek as if evaluating skin softness.

I can tell he's still unsure of this conversation, so I gently guide him. "Could you give me a better picture of what you want to do downtown?"

"Well, *Roger*," he says, emphasizing who really leads the charge—and whose shoulders bear the responsibility—"wants to revitalize an essentially ignored area. Times change and, with it, so do interests and technology. Where once thriving businesses existed, empty buildings and lost memories now stand. Roger wants to bring life back to the neighborhood."

I hope he soon stops the rhetoric. "So, what's the problem? As I understand the situation, national monuments can be built faster than the parties involved here can agree on an idea."

"This is more complicated than anyone, especially Roger, ever imagined."

"Forgive me, Mister Laine, and I don't mean to play devil's advocate, but you have the west side growing like an uncontrollable cancer. Meanwhile, places like Fourth Street and other areas are decaying or already dead. What's so difficult in throwing up a few restaurants or shops?"

He smiles like a father to a naïve child. "Without getting too deep into the myriad regulations such as parking, safety, and accessibility, let me say there are several parties interested in this project. Other than Roger, the other investors, prospective builders, politicians, and current business owners already in the area have their own concerns. Some have shown themselves to be, um, undesirable."

"If I may throw out a name," I suggest. "Randy Fisher."

"Yes." Laine purses his lips. "I have to admit, I don't like the man. This is where I side with Roger. I would like to see a touch of, um, class brought to the area and not just competitors of Court Avenue vying for the kids or the yuppie crowd."

The term "yuppie" went out before the turn of the century, but I choose not to enter into debate. I know what he means.

He goes on, "Then you have Joe Conway, owner of Conway Construction at the end of Fourth. He's not totally against the idea of more businesses, but would like to see more service-oriented companies. Construction, equipment rental, that sort of thing. He's worried about theft and vandalism if the area becomes inundated with crowds of, um, unsupervised youths. Like Roger, he doesn't want the nightclub scene to expand."

"On the other hand, Roger mentioned a Stephan Marshe, who does want music and lights," I say.

Laine nods. "I'm familiar with Stephan as well. He rents an office in the skywalk somewhere near Seventh. Conducts some type of promotions business. He also owns The Marshe Pit, out on Army Post Road, east of Southeast Fourteenth."

Do you wonder why I hate this city, Johnny? The Marshe Pit? What a god-awful name. Knowing the man is in bed with Fisher and possibly Jackie Midnight, and understanding what they envision for Fourth Street, I can imagine what Marshe's club is like. On second thought, I don't ever want to imagine.

I've driven past the building Marshe owns. The place has been at least two versions of a country bar, a rock and roll nightclub, and an alternative music venue… whatever the hell that is. None of which lasted more than five years at most.

As Laine said, times and interests change.

"I understand there exists not a little animosity between him and Roger," I say.

"They've known each other for years, but I don't know much about their history. During board and council meetings where I've seen the two in attendance, um, I'm glad neither carried weapons. They don't get along. Stephan wants quick action, and Roger will do anything, including delaying real progress on Fourth Street, to stop him. I'd say Marshe is the major insect in the ointment. I handle some of the issues with the zoning board, the city council, and politicians, and I feel for Roger. I sympathize with his frustrations. Regarding Marshe and to some extent, Fisher? Let me say this. I've spoken with both and considered their opinions and, frankly, I disagree with them. If those two, um, obstacles didn't exist, then maybe we'd have a few new buildings along Fourth by now."

Denise Michelle has already admitted to rumors of Roger taking money for swifter action. Still, to see how far the knowledge has traveled, I ask if he's heard any scuttlebutt.

"Yes, but I'd rather not go into details," he states in a flat tone.

He answers without answering. I admire his loyalty to Roger. I can learn nothing more from Laine, so I stand, shake his hand, and thank him for his time.

Back at the car, this secondary puzzle with Roger adds more to the problem. Because of Annabelle's videos, I know about Marshe. Laine filled in more of the man's character and role in the urban renewal project. A more solid connection. The players involved with Roger's plans, even though I haven't spoken to them, sprinkle a few more plastic chips onto the proverbial card table. Is Stephan Marshe the front-line man, Randy Fisher a support troop? Who else is involved?

The important question is: do any of them have anything to do with the missing Annabelle?

———

Midafternoon. I've spoken with several people already, with more to come. One in particular… but he can wait. Since the spotlight has revealed the existence of bribes, I should talk to the supposed guilty party. If he's home and not out rushing to and fro across city streets. Hell, maybe Arlene joined in them in the search. I didn't sense that characteristic during our previous talks. Maybe strong in business, but fretting at home when it comes to family.

The Cadillac still rests where I parked it the previous night. Arlene answers the doorbell. Her face is haggard. Thin, red lightning bolts streak her eyes. Sickly smudges of a sleepless night smear down to sunken cheeks. The hope that I've returned with her daughter dies as soon as she sees I'm alone.

"I'm still looking," I say.

She nods, weary and wrung out. Which may be one reason she's not out looking. I suspect Anne may have talked her out of roaming the metro the way Lansing did. If so, I find some comfort of the faith Anne has in me.

"Could I speak with Roger again?" I ask.

Another nod. I follow her to a small sitting room at the back of the house. She offers me coffee, and I decline. A large picture window frames a white desert of the backyard. Windswept snow dunes create a miniature version of an Arctic wasteland, save for a line of sentinel evergreens against the back fence.

The room conveys a conservative ambiance and is furnished with a few cushioned chairs probably used only for family gatherings or house parties. A recliner, a small sofa, a sixties wooden desk, and some bookshelves all add simple coziness.

I shift a chair around.

"I'll get Roger," Arlene says. "He's in bed but… well…" She turns and shuffles off.

I suspect Roger's sleep was due to the alcohol. Mornings after drinking, the body begs for real and recuperative sleep. I have denied my body that sustenance too many times.

Minutes later, Roger trudges into the room followed by Arlene. He wears the same clothes from this morning, albeit more wrinkled. Bed-head has fluffed his hair and his face resembles his wife's.

He perks up a fraction at the sight of me. "Annabelle?"

"Nothing yet," I say.

"He'll find her." Arlene's reassurance is half-hearted, and Roger nods half-hearted acceptance. He slumps into a nearby, cushioned chair. He eases back and rubs his eyes like a four-year-old who's trying to stay awake long past his normal bedtime.

Before I exited the car, I should have fortified myself from my flask. What I have to say may not have anything to do with why Arlene hired me… but I go where the path takes me.

"Regarding our conversation earlier," I start. Roger's eyes travel up. "I've spoken to a few people." I grab his stare, hold it. "There are hints of backroom deals."

Arlene frowns in confusion. Roger needs it spelled out for him.

"Bribes. Specifically from Marshe to you."

A gasp from Arlene and a groan from her husband tell me I hit the bull's eye.

Arlene manages to control her anxiety. "Roger?"

He purses his lips, and sadness settles into his face like a dog about to be punished for snacking on the last T-bone steak. Unlike the dog, I don't succumb to the brown eyes.

He nods. "Yes, it's true. I took money from Stephan Marshe."

"Roger!" Arlene says, both in shoch and disbelief. "How could you—"

He raises a shaky hand. "Wait, just a second. Let me explain. He gave me five thousand dollars back in October to persuade me to drop some of my objections, you know, smooth out the process so the actual renovation could begin on some of the older buildings. But I didn't do anything with it. I put it in a briefcase and stored it all in the safe at work. I told no one."

"Did he ask you about it afterward?" I ask.

"We… argued one night. He wondered why I hadn't used my influence to sway people, or used some of the money."

"Had you done either?"

Roger shakes his head. "No. I didn't want anything to do with the money. I told him so. I told him I hadn't touched it since he gave it to me." He expels air, disgusted. "Then he made another offer."

"What?"

"He said he knew a guy who could give Amos a job, give him a taste of the business world while still in college. When Amos graduated, he might be considered for a full-time position."

"How did you respond?"

Roger's head hangs in shame. "I said I'd think about it."

I almost didn't hear his words as his voice was barely audible. "Any mention of Annabelle in this discussion?"

"No."

"No offers to help her on a career path?" Another head shake, but this time it's hesitant. "Something else?"

"I don't know," he says. "Before he left, he said something about how all of this would affect my family."

"In what way?"

"He didn't say how, just for me to think about it."

And so it circles back to Marshe. Arlene remains quiet throughout the exchange. Remembering the past?

I thank the Lansings. Roger stays in the chair while Arlene accompanies me to the door. She gives me a pointed look. I think she wants to speak. To confess to the relationship with Marshe? To explain her side? Maybe to warn me about Marshe and what he might confess?

I don't know, but wait. I can almost see the debate warring in her mind. She opens her mouth, but instead of speaking, offers a final—resigned?—nod and opens the door. Donning my coat, I return the nod and depart.

CHAPTER
NINETEEN

I STOP by my office before I venture over to Marshe's.

Anne sits at her desk, posture indicating she is in business mode, ear to the phone, and eyes on her computer monitor.

I stand in the doorway and listen to her complete a deal for a new renter on a lower floor. I am forever in admiration of this woman. Never have I met a person more intelligent, who possesses more business and social savvy. Or who's more beautiful. The years haven't harmed her. Instead, she's moved through them with grace and charm.

Too bad she had to spend some of them with me.

As Anne cradles the phone, I step forward and bury another soldier in the ashtray. She offers an encouraging smile, knowing I haven't yet found her niece. I drop onto the sofa and, noticing the wet tracks across the floor, apologize for not wiping my shoes.

She nods in acceptance. "I talked to Arlene this morning. She told me you stopped by earlier to ask more questions. Any leads?"

I shrug. "Maybe."

"She says Roger wanted to go back out."

"He's on a useless endeavor," I reply. "He should know driving around this city isn't going to accomplish a thing."

"He feels he has to try something."

"He has no focus."

"Do you?" Anne's question is not condescending but genuine and sincere.

I shrug and insert my hands into my overcoat pockets.

"Where do you think she is?" Anne asks.

I take a deep breath, let it out. "Someplace that, at first, looked different than where she was. Maybe she saw a new path, decided to wander down it for a stretch, but found she didn't want to continue and was unable to get off or return."

"Drugs?"

I shrug again. A hangnail chafes against the pocket lining. I raise my hand to inspect it. When I attempt to sever the ragged piece with my teeth, I end up tearing more skin. Blood wells, dark and mean. I press another finger over the wound and say, "I've spoken with only three of Annabelle's friends, those who accompanied her to the club that night and one other from her class in school. Arlene doesn't know the names of other friends. Do you think you could find a few more? Maybe the girl is holed up with one of them."

"I can make some calls." Anne sighs. "Who else have you talked to this morning?"

"Chris Laine."

"I know him."

"Roger suggested I also see Stephan Marshe."

A crease forms in the middle of her forehead. The only times I've seen such a serious expression were when I truly disappointed her during our marriage. She nods, and I sense Marshe memories popping up. Or maybe they ooze like feculent boils from a murky swamp.

"You know him, also?"

"Unfortunately," she answers.

"Anything you care to share?"

She considers a moment. "I think you need to discover who Stephan is for yourself."

"Or what he is?"

Anne's smile turns sad. "You won't need too much time."

"I already have opinions from two sources." And from video revelations. I avoid the subject and am grateful Anne doesn't ask. I'll keep what I've seen and heard from the missing girl herself to myself for the time being. Later, I'll share with Anne.

"The remaining pieces are thin and very transparent." I sigh and stand. The bleeding in the corner of my fingernail has stopped, but the area is swollen and numb. It matches my thoughts.

I step toward the door, but Anne's voice stops me. "Sabastian."

I stop.

"Do you think she's…" She can't finish the sentence.

I can't reply with "I don't know." Instead, I say, "You know what gets me about this case?"

She blinks and waits.

"The amount of apathy shown by everyone. Annabelle's friends on New Year's and even now, days after she's missing. Her brother cares more about some report for a class he doesn't comprehend. Even Laine. He didn't know her well, but the concern was missing when we spoke."

"Roger cares."

"Not enough to call home yesterday to let his wife know he's all right. He told me last night he hasn't been much of a father. Arlene cares now, but where was she before this? Annabelle's unhappiness didn't just manifest during the last day of the year."

Anne nods. "I've tried to talk to Arlene, but she didn't know what to do. I grew up with the family's drive for success, but I haven't let it consume me like Arlene and her family. I've learned when to push and when to step back." She looks up at me. "Even if no one else cares, you do. That's what counts."

Again, I step toward the door and, again, her voice, gentle and caressing, drifts through the air. "However this ends, Sabastian, thank you."

Without turning, I know a tear is forming in her eye. Her last two words were said with a tight throat.

I never could stand to see sadness on Anne's face, so I walk away.

Back out on the sidewalk, my plan to trek the few blocks to Marshe's office and allow the cold and the snow to help me cerebrate the Annabelle Lansing matter is momentarily delayed when I see Timothy's aunt sweeping snow from the door to her sandwich shop. I didn't take time for lunch earlier, so I wait, hands in my pockets, while she clears an imperfect, half-moon patch of sidewalk.

She falters and almost stumbles when she notices me, as if I've suddenly popped into this dimension, a boggart come to claim her spirit.

I offer a slight nod.

She smiles and, without a word, enters her store. She holds the door long enough to ascertain I'll follow. The bell tinkles with more clarity today.

The woman, by rote, selects my usual fare as I contemplate the coffee. It's as black as an adulterer's heart and probably as scalding as his wife's tongue. I pour a cup and, just like the doomed couple, must suffer the experience.

I study the shelves, hoping that the dry, salty, chunky pretzels I usually tolerate have been restocked since yesterday

"Sorry, Mr. Habeck," the woman says, sincerity in her words. "The delivery man didn't bring any today. No reason given when I asked."

Although they're salt-saturated, plastic wafers, I choose a bag of the kettle-cooked chips so popular nowadays.

Like yesterday, the woman rings up the total and bags my food. We complete the transaction in silence, but I can't ignore the soft shine in her eyes and the twitch of her fleshy lips.

I take a stab. "Timothy?"

She gives me a shaky half-smile. "He stayed home last night. None too happy, though. Paced a lot. Restless. I waited until he went to bed. I couldn't sleep, kept wondering and checking."

I nod.

"Even asleep, his arms and legs jerked. He tossed and turned all over the bed. I was so worried."

I understand. The jactitation is a sign the boy's in deep. Whatever he's buying from Jackie has its hooks securely embedded. Even one night away, his body suffers.

"I don't know, Mr. Habeck. I still think he's in trouble. He was on the phone last night. I don't know with whom, but he talked about needing something."

"He's addicted to drugs, ma'am. Persuading his supplier to not sell to him isn't enough. He'll just go up the chain of command or find another dealer. He needs to be in a rehabilitation center."

She gasps as if I had suggested she lop off the boy's fingers. I don't know if she's thought of treatment centers, but maybe she can't bear the idea of doctors, psychiatrists, and counselors picking and poking her kin.

"It sounds drastic, but may be the best course of action," I say.

Her head quivers a nod, but I don't think she's convinced. I offer to help if she wants to call.

Bag of food and coffee in hand, I leave.

One of these days, I'm going to ask for her first name.

CHAPTER
TWENTY

UNLESS LEFT with no other choice, I try to avoid the downtown skywalk system. It's too bright, too flashy. The hallways are too wide, and the people too driven. From the bankers to the beauticians to the snobbish hotel employees. The women who never make eye contact walking with determination in their power suits. Older professionals wearing dark suits and straight-lipped expressions. Young, up-and-coming hotshots in sports jackets. The commonality with the majority is their babbling away on cell phones, each call the most important in their lives.

Nothing is eternal, however, and though business thrives in the skywalk, there are certain corners, now ignored and nearly forgotten, where ghosts reside, memories fade. The long-lasting chain department store couldn't compete with suburban sprawl. The hip sports bar didn't have enough draw for people who chose to stay downtown after dark. An entire horseshoe-shaped collection of luncheon eateries gone in one fell swoop as though descended upon by the plague. Two knucklehead partners who possessed no common or business sense bought a huge section of third-floor space to open one of those stupid laser-tag operations. It lasted all of two months.

If someone held a gun to my head and commanded me to walk through the two-block area of glitz and flash known as the Hub, I'd fight him for his weapon first. So, I am thankful Stephen Marshe's office lies several hallways and numerous corners away.

I duck inside the door to the Seventh Street parking garage. In an echo chamber entry frowsty with old urine, I eat my sandwiches, the coffee cup resting on a rough concrete windowsill.

Three minutes into my fare, the elevator dings a sour note, the doors squeegee open, and a woman exits. She's covered in a long coat with a collar so furry, it looks like she has a collie wrapped around her neck. Hers is a disdainful look, as if I'm the person who created the sickly-sweet smell. One step out the door and she slips on a hidden patch of ice, but catches herself at the last second.

Finished with the sandwiches, I give up after three chips, then place the wrappings and the empty coffee cup on the top of an overflowing garbage can near the door. The foam cup, at a precarious angle, falls and lands on the floor with a hollow plunk.

The elevator has returned to the upper floors, so I push the button and wait. The skywalk lies only on the third level, but I don't consider the stairs. Good thing, because shuffles and uneven footfalls echo through the stairwell. I envision an unseen movie monster slowly advancing upon the hapless, ditzy teen who chose not to get the hell out of the scary house when she had the chance —as in, two seconds after the first of her friends were killed.

Lurching around the corner, and barely able to negotiate the descent, is who I believe could be the prime suspect for the entryway odor problem. Tall and lanky, with a wire brush beard peppered to a fine ash color. His denim jacket over unwashed T-shirt and dirtier jeans shows cigarette burns up and down both sleeves. At the bottom of the stairs, he belches once before scratching his left armpit. The reek of alcohol in the cold air could intoxicate a moose. Either he doesn't register my presence, or chooses to ignore it, as he walks a wavy course across the entry and out the door. He completes the pratfall the woman narrowly avoided.

I shake my head and take a sip of bourbon as I enter the open elevator and push the button for level three.

Marshe's office sits between a bank and the defunct laser-tag cavern. This area of the skywalk is bright and almost empty. A lone coffee vendor, demeanor dreary, rests on a stool. Perhaps he longs for the days when crowds of people lunched on the floors below and visited his stand before they returned to work. From inside the bank, a pretty, middle-aged teller stands behind the counter. Hope gleams in her eyes when she spots me, a potential new customer. The popularity of this area leaves a vacant vastness and I do not envy her job. I wonder if she tabulates the number of people who traverse this section only to get to someplace else. She frowns when she sees me approach Marshe's office door.

The man's anserine humor regarding the name of the business continues here within his office. A sign on the door reads Marshe Ado About Music. I haven't even met the guy, but judging from others' comments, I already know he is a pimple on society's face no one can pop. Maybe they're afraid of the goo he'd splatter about if they did.

The reception room gleams an eggshell white, but structural cracks in the plaster walls resemble the result of a localized earthquake. A sickly, orange-cushioned double chair even the worst dentist wouldn't have in his waiting room acts as the sole seating apparatus.

Behind a particle board, earth-toned painted desk sits a woman who personifies the image of the words "Vegas hooker." Big, brassy hair, too much make-up, and the too little fabric in her clothing expose curves so dangerous the best race car driver couldn't negotiate them. Her jaw works on a piece of gum like she's trying for an Olympic gold medal in mastication. She sports cherry red, false fingernails two inches long and filed to narrow, rounded ends. The same color smeared on her lips accentuates an already wide mouth. One leg crossed over the other bounces in time to a song from a radio the size of a large suitcase on the filing cabinet. The brash voice of the singer proudly proclaims she's trouble, or some such tripe.

The "secretary" gives me a cursory once over. "Yeah?" I've heard the same tone from harried truck stop waitresses waiting for an order.

"I'd like to speak with Stephan Marshe, if he's available," I reply.

"You a singer?"

I detect a bit of nasal in her voice. "What?"

"Singer. Or play an instrument? Looking for a gig?"

Do they still call them 'gigs', Johnny?

"No, ma'am." I clutch desperately to my cordiality. "It's another type of business matter."

Unrelated to 'gigs'.

"Okay," she says. Gum snaps between her teeth like wood pops in a fire. "Whatever." She spikes an intercom button and, five feet away and through a partially open door of an inner office, a buzzer sounds.

A man's voice comes through both the speaker and the door simultaneously, "What's shakin', sweetcakes?"

At first, I wonder if he's heard of sexual harassment, but when "sweetcakes" giggles, I decide any lawsuit would be hard-pressed to prove.

"Guy here to see you," she says.

"Take his name, number, and shtick. Tell him I'll call him."

"It ain't about that," she says.

"Huh? Hold on."

A chair spring screeches, then a loud, "Yeah, I'll get back to you. No, we'll do lunch." The office door creaks open and who I assume is Marshe sticks out his head and half his torso. One hand holds a cell phone, the screen still lit after his call. He, too, looks me up and down.

"Well, you ain't the next Elvis," he says with a buddy-buddy-just-funnin' grin.

"And you're not even close to the next Colonel Parker," I counter.

He looks mildly insulted, but chooses not to respond in kind.

"What can I do ya for?"

"Stephan Marshe?"

"The one and only."

I introduce myself. "I'd like to talk to you about Roger Lansing."

The corners of his mouth drop faster than the stock market on Black Friday. His eyes dart around the room, as if the news crew from a local television station might jump out ready to catch him in an indiscretion. "I don't understand."

"Actually, I'm looking for his daughter, Annabelle. She's been missing since New Year's Eve. My investigation keeps revealing information regarding Roger and his plans for the Fourth Street renewal project. Your name came up." His eyes widen a fraction at the mention of the daughter's name.

My next question should be direct. Does he have any knowledge of her whereabouts? Instead, I wait.

He recovers and nods an invitation for me to enter his sanctum sanctorum.

I leave the secretary looking none the wiser.

His office isn't any more attractive than the waiting room. The only improvements are a computer on the desk and framed, autographed pictures of musicians and other entertainers hanging on the walls. Headshots, bands posing on stage, or casual shots of various personalities, each with an arm draped over Marshe's shoulder like they're best pals.

He eases into his chair while I stand. He taps his cell phone, checks the screen, taps it again, then looks up at me. The meretricious attitude returns. "What can I tell you about ole Rog'?"

Before I can ask my first question, he fingers his phone again. I'm still waiting for him to offer me a chair. "I understand Roger's ideas for the neighborhood don't mesh with yours."

Marshe sighs and shakes his head. "Roger just doesn't understand how business works," he says and checks his phone again. "We could have had that neighborhood rockin' six months or a year ago."

"Except for?"

"See, the idea is to get something started. Open a few clubs or bars and expand from there. But, *nooo*, Roger keeps talking about 'class.' Family restaurants, art galleries. Are you kidding me? An art gallery? Nowadays, no one gives a damn about paintings and statues. Plus, have you seen the stuff some of these so-called 'artists' produce?"

I don't like Marshe, but on this one point, I have to agree. Chimps throwing feces against a canvas background create better pictures. What is called 'performance art' is completely beyond my ken.

Marshe does the phone routine again. "I want places where you can go to relax, have a few drinks, dance a little. A place for singles to hook up. Nightlife, you know?"

"No room for compromise?"

"It's his way or nothing," Marshe states. Once again, he looks at the phone. "Sorry, checking on a deal in the works. Guy is supposed to text me a date and a price. Business, you know."

No, it's rudeness. So, I drag over a wooden chair from against the wall, sit, reach for my pack of Luckys, and light up. Marshe glances up at my first exhalation of smoke. He wants to say something, but my expression shows passive defiance. He accepts the situation.

"I understand your arguments were rather vociferous some time back," I say.

He does a one-shoulder shrug. "Not the first time we've aired our differences in public. He doesn't know when to back down and always looks the weaker for it."

Right, and I'll bet bully Roger always starts it. Marshe makes it sound like they're twelve-year-old boys on the playground. "What are the chances this issue will be resolved?"

He smirks, and one shoulder moves up and down again. "Who knows? This has been dragging on for two years. It ain't just Roger. Other people need to be persuaded, but if Roger stepped off that soap box long enough to see the light, maybe things could get moving."

Up to this point, our questions and answers have flowed like a stream with no rapids. I wonder what he'll say to my next statement. "Maybe he was too overwhelmed by the color green."

The promoter's raised eyebrows show me he understands in an instant. He's surprised I can speak the language. He leans back in his chair and scratches the tip of his nose with the nail of his right middle finger. His tongue runs the curvature of the outside of his upper teeth and back again. Eyes drop to examine fingernails. Our stream just hit the rocks, and he's trying to find the best way of avoiding too much damage. "I… cannot confirm or deny. I will say that in business, certain… contingencies come into play."

"What about the offer to help his son?"

Marshe makes a *tsking* noise. "Where did you hear that?"

I'll keep my source—Roger—to myself. "People talk."

He scratches his nose again. "You must be a persuasive guy for people to open up, especially about matters that probably don't concern them."

I blow smoke and give him a closed-mouth smile. His eyes narrow, and his square chin bobs up and down.

"All right," he says. "I'll admit I did mention I knew someone with a bit of pull," Marshe says. "We're not best buds, but he's trustworthy, as good as his word."

I doubt the feeling is mutual. "Name?"

Another lengthy pause. Another shrug. "There's no reason not to give you his name. Stanley Porto. He's the director of Port-O-Folio, Inc. in the Three Fountains complex on Westown Parkway."

Why do people have to be gelastic with company names? I hope, with an office in such an upscale building, Porto will be more professional than Marshe. "What did Roger think of the offer?" I ask.

"Still up in the air. With Christmas so close at the time, I knew nothing would happen. Now that the holidays are over, I expect he'll come around." Another check of his phone, then he tosses it on top of his desk and leans forward, hands folded as if he's about to impart the secret of the universe. "Can't say I'm surprised by his attitude. He's always been this way."

"How long have you known him?"

"Nearly all my life. Went to school together, but we never clicked. Different interests, you know. He was always business-oriented, and I settled for music and fun."

I smoke more of my cigarette.

"Same for Arlene," he says. "He ruined her."

Marshe likes to hear his own voice. I smoke and let him talk.

"If she would have stayed with me, things might have been different."

"You and Arlene dated?" I ask.

"One or two times in school. Nothing real serious." He relaxes in his chair again. "However, there was one other time. I wouldn't call it a date. More of a one-night fling."

"When was this?"

A devilish smile precedes his cockalorum. "A few years after she married Roger."

I nod. Smoke curls from the end of the stick. There's more to come. With types like Marshe, there is always more, and they want you to ask them for it. I don't. I stay silent, smoke, and stare at him. Patience isn't a virtue by which he can abide. I wait. He has to speak.

"If I recall, this was, um, *before* Annabelle came along," he drawls, tone casual as he checks his manicure for the second time. His eyes meet mine even though his head stays still. The message they relate is, *Do you understand the implication of the stressed word?*

I do. I raise my eyebrows in another question. *Is your implication true?*

He shrugs. *Who can tell?* "I'm sure you've learned by now Annabelle isn't another drone programmed for business," he says. "Perhaps... other genes helped with the resistance."

"Does Roger know?"

"About his wife's walk on the wild side or...?"

"Either. Both."

"No, to the first. Wait." He holds up an index finger. "Let me give myself an out by saying 'not to my knowledge.' At best, it's never come up in conversation. Then or now."

"And the second?"

"I don't think the issue was ever validated."

"You didn't wonder?"

He shrugs again. "Sure."

"Why didn't you follow up?"

"Truth? Didn't care."

I knew the answer before he gave it. He didn't care then and doesn't care now. I also realize he meant to bring up the subject. If I want to see a bigger picture of Roger, why not throw a little mud onto the canvas?

Does his revelation have anything to do with Annabelle's disappearance, though? It confirms what I saw in the girl's videos. She discovered her mother's infidelity, did a little math, and guessed two plus two plus nine months equaled illegitimacy.

However, why would Marshe bring up the subject now? To

damage Roger? Does Roger's distraction over Annabelle give Marshe, Fisher, and maybe Midnight an edge?

I study Marshe as the tobacco slowly burns itself out.

Does he know where Annabelle is? Is he involved in her disappearance?

This time, he waits me out. He's grabbed a temporary hold on patience and will hide behind it, a figure veiled by connotations and could-bes. He knows I desire more information, but I doubt he'll give me straight answers. Instead, he'll sidestep, lob words from around a corner, hint, and hope I'll turn desperate.

Instead, I drop the cigarette on the carpet, crush it beneath my foot. "Thank you for your time, Mr. Marshe," I say and leave.

I don't close his office door and nod a farewell to the secretary.

Her phone rings as I'm about to step back out into the skywalk. Curiosity slows my steps.

"Marshe Ado About Music," she says in a bored tone. Four seconds later, "Yes, Mr. Prentiss, he's in. Just a second."

Prentiss. For some reason, that name sticks in my mind. Later, I'll recognize the significance.

However, my next stop is a return to the Lansings. This will be the third visit, but it's time to hammer home some facts, to confirm both what I learned from Marshe and what Annabelle told me yesterday through her video blogs.

TWENTY-ONE

LIGHT FLAKES of snow drift from a dull, gray sky. Apparently, Mother Nature hasn't been satiated and plans to continue her attempt to whiten the world.

Sluggish traffic clogs the freeway and side streets. Drivers express weariness, maybe at yet more precipitation interrupting their lives.

Annabelle's disappearance has interrupted the Lansings' lives, save for Amos's. How is Arlene handling the disruption in her daily routine? She cares for a mentally and physically exhausted husband and frets over a missing daughter when normally she would be making sales and closing deals.

When she answers the door, I greet her expectancy with a small head shake. Her look turns into a silent question.

I say, "Is Roger still here?"

"Yes. He's resting. Troubled, but resting."

"Is there a quiet place we can talk where he won't be disturbed?"

She nods. "Sure."

After hanging my coat on the same peg as the previous morning, I follow to the living room. Shadows creep across the snow, and I can't help but see them as ghosts from the past. Hovering. Seeping in through the cracks to haunt the pristine interior and all those who reside there.

Arlene takes the sofa facing the entry. "Have you heard anything about Annabelle?"

"No," I reply. "However, I've had discussions with people and, the more I listen, the more a picture develops."

She nods, not sure where I'm heading. I don't want to go there. I don't want to add more pain to the problems this family has, but I feel it's part of the problem. Snippets of Annabelle's video blog regarding this matter intrude despite my efforts to push them from my memory. *Annabelle sits in darkness, the light of the monitor the sole illumination. The rest of the bedroom lies in shadow.*

"Stephan Marshe," I state, blunt and to the point.

Similar to this morning's mention of the music maven's moniker, Arlene's face twitches. "Yes, I know him."

My turn to nod. I maintain a hard stare and my voice goes cold. "Yes, you do."

Her chin raises an eighth of an inch, and her lips press together. She doesn't break the stare and receives the silent message. "He told you," she says in a low voice.

I nod.

October 11

I sat staring out my window for hours. I didn't even go down to dinner, said my stomach hurt too much to eat. No one cared that it was my birthday, anyway.

I hate this place! I hate this house and everyone in it.

Arlene's jaw tightens. "Yes. Well."

"Tell me about it."

"I don't think that's any of your business," she says. "What possible relevance can a mistake almost twenty years ago have to Annabelle's disappearance?"

I cross one leg over another and gaze out at the falling snow. The army of flakes, though not yet serious about the attack, nevertheless has sent the first advance parties following the reconnaissance team. My eyes return to Arlene, still on the edge of the sofa. "Pieces, Arlene. With connectors that may match up."

"I don't know what you're talking—"

"I can draw a possible, if sketchy, pattern that ends with Annabelle's disappearance on December 31st. Since you haven't received a communication demanding ransom, I'm going on the assumption she chose to disappear."

"Why?"

I hold up a hand. "As I said, I'm putting together pieces. Connections. I don't yet have a solid reason why she picked that particular night. Maybe to her, the time felt right." I shift in the chair and re-cross my legs. "However, for the previous three months, she's been acting and dressing differently. Then, I have Roger's Fourth Street project with businessmen whose visions and opinions cover all sides. One of those involved is Stephan Marshe. Not half an hour ago, Mr. Marshe tells me you two had an affair, and you just confirmed it. So, can you remember the last time he dropped by for a visit?"

"July," Arlene says a heartbeat later. "He and Roger talked for about…"

My shaking head stops her. "I believe he's been here at least once since July. Say, in October?"

She purses her lips. "Yes, but Roger wasn't here."

"Who was?"

"Well, I answered the door. I took off early on a Friday afternoon for a dentist's appointment. Roger hadn't come home, yet."

"What did you and Marshe discuss?"

"I told him Roger was still at the office."

I sigh. "Arlene, stop hedging. What did Marshe say? Did he bring up the affair? Did he maybe discuss an encore after twenty years?"

Silence.

"Who else was in the house at the time?" I ask.

Her eyes widen when the answer registers and her defiance deflates. "No," she says, but her whisper belies the denial.

"What did she overhear?"

Arlene shakes her head, and her corneas shine with forming tears. "No!"

"Was Roger causing some real furor at the time? Did his stubbornness finally overwhelm Marshe? I understand there was an intense argument between them one evening."

Arlene still shakes her head, but every word stings.

"What did Marshe say that afternoon?" I ask. "Did he know Roger wouldn't be here?"

I pause before I slam it home. She's already been hurt enough over the years and these last four days, but the ghosts have settled in. She needs to see them for what they've done.

"After all these years and maybe, to drive a wedge between you and Roger, did he mention Annabelle? Did he question the timing of the affair? Did he suggest he might be Annabelle's—"

"No!" Arlene bolts upright. "No, it's not true. I told him it's not true."

Most of all, I hate that bitch who calls herself my mother. I hate her! What was wrong with her that had to go and fuck that Marshe guy? What an asshole! He was gloating. She didn't know I stood in the next room and heard every word when they talked at the front door.

I can do the math. I can subtract today from February.

Happy fucking birthday to me!

"And unbeknownst to you, Annabelle overheard the conversation."

Arlene's mouth opens, but she is unable to speak. "Look at her room and the changes she's made," I say. "It's her reaction to the information about your infidelity and the possibility of being another man's daughter. Her childhood is over, so she's hidden many of the reminders. All but one of the stuffed animals shoved to the back of the closet. She hangs a poster that depicts death, tragedy, and broken hearts. She wears darker clothes, but even then, she couldn't bear to look at herself, so she broke her mirror, then covered the shattered reflection."

My repeated verbal slaps take their toll. Arlene collapses to the floor, lost in sobs. I move to help her back to the sofa, but she pushes me away. I return to the chair, sigh once, and watch her.

It's discourteous, but I reach for the packet of Luckys. Inhaling the first rush of nicotine, I wonder how I've come to be here. Opulence surrounds me, yet it is tarnished, stained with ugly secrets. A twenty-year mistake has lingered in the shadows, hidden in the corners, waiting for the chance to expose its hircine taint.

I had tolerated high school and reluctantly taken a few courses at a community college. By the end of the first year, I knew secondary education wasn't for me, so applied to be a policeman. A small-town sheriff hired me. He also fired me, citing budgetary reasons, but I knew the truth. I couldn't handle the job and its responsibilities. The paperwork. Learning to operate the technological improvements.

I still wanted to help people, so I moved to Des Moines and looked for an office, thinking I could be a private investigator.

Which was how I met Anne. She was the most beautiful woman in the world. She still is. I don't know what she saw in me. Ah, what mistakes I made.

My lips twitch in irony from remembering my past memories. Here I am, dredging up old sins at Arlene when mine could layer the bottom of Saylorville Lake. No, I didn't cheat, but Anne's accusations added to the pile of divorce reasons.

Arlene's sniffles terminate my reverie. She climbs back onto the couch and wipes her red-rimmed eyes. "It was stupid," she says. "I was stupid."

My hand acts as an ashtray, and the Lucky is down to its last sparks of life. I don't think Arlene notices when I stand to deposit the remains in a nearby trash can.

She's still lost in herself. "Roger and I had been married only a few years," she says, her voice low, tired, almost a monotone, her gaze to the floor. "Both of us were struggling to survive. Money was tight. I was still studying for my realtor's license." She sniffs. "One night, the stress was too much, and I just left. I wanted to be alone, and believe me, the apartment Roger and I shared didn't allow for alone time. Anyway, I happened to meet Stephan at a bar. We'd dated in high school, but I knew he wasn't going to be the person I wanted to be with for the rest of my life." She sniffs again and tries for a dignified justification. "We got to talking and drinking, and one thing led to another."

I hate that line. People use it to try to excuse inappropriate actions. If something happens, then someone has allowed it to happen. "What about Annabelle?"

She smiles sadly. "Think what you like, Sabastian, but I knew what I did. I also knew I'd never be with Stephan again. The next night, I felt guilty and… well, Roger and I… and nine months later, I had Annabelle."

"Did you have tests done?"

"No," she states. "I didn't. I never told Roger, and Stephan didn't say anything either."

Marshe didn't care. He'd told me so earlier. From her tone, I suspect Arlene just didn't want to know.

"After all this time, he has the nerve to bring it up again," she says.

"And Annabelle overheard."

"I don't know. Maybe. You think she did. I just don't know."

"Three months have passed. What made her decide to leave now?"

She shakes her head. More tears gather. "I feel awful. What have I done? I just want her back so I can explain and…" Her words fade away.

At the same time, someone sniffs behind me. Roger stands in the doorway. What he's heard is anyone's guess, but I suspect it's enough. I don't know enough about him to gauge his reaction, but I ready myself for the worst. His stare is blank as an erased chalkboard, and his skin the color of the remaining white dust smearing the green surface. Seconds pass, the silence orchestral in volume. Without a word, he turns and shuffles away.

"Roger!" Arlene cries and rushes after him.

I smoke another cigarette and wait. When nothing untoward occurs, I leave. Snow covers the Lansings' roof, but somehow the once pristine color has faded, the virgin white dulled to mouse gray. The house's face no longer exhibits regalia and elegance, but weariness and shame, as if disgusted by the blackness souring its core.

———

October 12

I just want to die. I don't know anything anymore. I'm so tired.

October 17

Who am I? I don't know.

I look in the mirror for traces of Dad… or him.

All I see is nobody. I am nobody.

October 29

I want to go away. Forever. I've run away before, but only for a day or two. No one cared.

Dad and… that woman don't care. Does Dad know about Marshe?

Dad. I don't know if he really is my dad. No one does.

TWENTY-TWO

MORE BITS of confetti snow fall in lazy paths by the time I park parallel to Zemo's nightclub. This stretch of East Fourth Street, south of Court Avenue, is a wide slab of pitted pavement all but forgotten by the majority of the city. Shells of buildings line both sides. Sunken roofed structures deteriorated by time and weather. The siding resembles wet cardboard. What little metal pokes from beneath the blanket of snow is tarnished or rusted. The crumbling brick foundations look as if they've been gnawed by giant rats. Gutters hang from eaves like drunks over a toilet. Dark doorways of dusty glass portend an abyss of loneliness within. I cannot espy any signs of what businesses once occupied these husks other than faded block letters stretching across a front wall like type in a large print book.

Zemo's is the high point—as it were—of the block. From my vantage point, where Annabelle Lansing was last seen is the only operation with life, save for the construction operation, closed for the night, farther south. The nightclub has an incongruous place-ment between an old print shop—I can still read the chipped paint letters on the glass door—and an unknown, black wall with a recessed entrance. Zemo's looks all but expired itself. Hours posted on the front door in a small, sans-serif font inform poten-tial patrons the establishment opens at five in the afternoon and closes eight hours later. Sunday and Monday are the only excep-tions. On those days, logically the slowest of the week, Zemo's remains closed.

The nightclub's name, in italic cursive, covers much of the front window. Dimmed lights, the dominant color red. Absent are the neon beer signs in the window, but are prevalent inside behind the bar.

High and round or low and square tables up front and along the right wall. A twenty-foot bar to the left, stage and dance floor near the back. Two doors flank the bar on either side, maybe leading to storage rooms or an office. I deduce another door next to the stage exits at the rear of the building so band members and roadies can load and unload equipment. Restrooms are tucked up front on the left.

I extinguish my cigarette before I enter. I'll be nice and obey the new don't-smoke-anywhere-people-might-object laws. Many of the lights are doused. A couple of low-wattage spots highlight the bar and the stage. Other lights that revolve, strobe, or use colored filters remain dark. The seventies-era disco ball hangs from the ceiling over the stage like a dead moon in space.

I don't frequent nightclubs. I prefer low-key holes-in-the-wall with customers whose best description would be 'grizzled'. Where drinks are served by the bottle or out of an old, loose, wooden tap and ordering wine coolers or Cosmopolitans will get you thrown out with a broken nose. Places like Zemo's are too loud with the eardrum-destroying crap someone considers music and too crowded with hormone-infested youths getting too drunk too fast—like I should talk—and all dressed in clothes no sane fashion designer would ever in his or her worst nightmare create.

May I have a brief aside to point out that a sane fashion designer is an oxymoron? Maybe Kym will change that trend. I doubt it.

A short man of Latin American lineage pushes a wide broom, left to right and back again, on the dance floor, almost by rote. The speed at which he moves indicates he could be sleepwalking, and the dust bunnies, dirt, crumbs, and other debris should have no fear of being collected, just relocated.

The second individual, dressed in a long-sleeved, black, silk shirt tucked into black slacks, reviews inventory behind the bar. The amount of shine in his raven black hair warrants an oil derrick nearby. He glances over his shoulder.

His dark, inscrutable eyes are harder and more reptilian than canine. They communicate two messages to me. One, he wonders why someone of my ilk would enter his place and isn't anxious to find out, and two, I'm not going to like him.

He's Randall Fisher II. I had stopped back at the office to update Anne on my progress and she brought up his profile on her computer, but also I recognize the features given to his son. Elongated ears flat against his head. A sleek face shows years of studying people for an advantage. He's in his late forties and trying to pass for late twenties. He opened Zemo's seven years ago. No mention on his profile how he came up with such an idiotic name for his dance joint.

His confusion mutates into a sly smile, and he places both palms on the bar's surface. "Whatcha pleasure, stranger?"

I consider for a moment. "I'm in the mood for a Tom Collins tonight." I add just enough joviality to catch him off guard for a second.

His smile broadens, and a small chuckle escapes his lips. He turns and plucks a shot glass from a short stack, peers around with one hand halted in the act of reaching for a bottle. "You look like a Scotch man to me. No, wait, bourbon."

I tilt my head in a half nod.

"Beam?"

"Maker's Mark, if you've got it." My liver may not know the difference between that brand and Ten High, but my taste buds do.

He nods and plucks the familiar, plain-labeled, squat bottle from the second tier without clanking its neighbors. With experience behind his actions, he fills the shot glass to a dime's thickness short of the top.

After a sip, I introduce myself. "I've been hired to look into the disappearance of Annabelle Lansing."

He nods before I finish my sentence. "Yes, yes, a sad case. I'm sorry it happened here."

I raise my eyebrows.

He chuckles again. "Of course, I don't know if this is where she disappeared. I meant, I'm sorry it happened at all."

"You've been questioned?"

"Well, I spoke to an officer yesterday. I told him I remembered my son's friends coming in on New Year's Eve, but we were very busy..." He lifts his arms in a what-can-you-expect motion.

I sip another quarter ounce of bourbon. "Do you know Annabelle?"

"Only through her friends. My son and Kym. They come in every so often to dance and enjoy themselves. Usually, I'm too busy to do more than exchange greetings."

I gesture with the shot glass and, as if I didn't know, say, "You own the joint."

"Yes, sir," he replies, a tad too cheerful. His manner of speaking sounds a little forced, as if he's trying to give the impression of true friendliness, but covering for something less so.

I glance around. "You just opened for the night."

The zombie continues sweeping yard-wide swaths.

"Not many customers this early, though," I add.

Fisher folds his forearms on the bar, leans over them. "Well, to tell you the truth, the party crowd doesn't arrive 'til later. I unlock the door for businessmen wanting a quick one before heading home. Gives me a chance to check inventory, clean up, maybe make some booking calls. Later, I have a regular DJ for the music."

I finish the whiskey and toss a couple bills on the counter.

Fisher offers a refill, and I accept. "Second one's on the house," he says.

I salute him with the glass and sip. We return to Annabelle. He tells me that, after an initial greeting Sunday night, he soon lost track of the youngsters. His son didn't even say goodbye. He stayed busy up until at least an hour after closing time.

"Behind the bar all night?" I ask.

He nods. "Except when I had to go to the storeroom. You know, to restock the cooler or under the counter."

After another taste of the bourbon, I change tack. "I'm learning a lot about Roger Lansing and his plans for this neighborhood."

"Are you?"

"Sounds as if you're in the middle of some of those plans."

He nods.

"What can you tell me?" I ask.

Fisher's eyes stay on me as he considers. He cocks his head and leans against the back counter. I ease onto a stool.

He inhales a deep, audible breath. "You may have noticed this isn't the most popular area in town." He waves a hand referring to Fourth Street. "Nary a solid business here in fifty-plus years. To be honest, an eyesore."

"Why'd you open here? Nearer Grand or across the river on Court would seem more sound."

"Costs, Mr. Habeck. This area isn't much to look at. Still, I hoped to attract the younger crowd. Maybe make it a bit eclectic." He sighs. "I do all right. Reputation, mostly. I admit I've let the place go downhill a bit over the years."

"Roger Lansing?"

"Actually, I was one of the first who pushed him to consider something in the area. I've been after the city to spruce up this neighborhood almost from the time I opened. They have money for a new science center, bypasses, and housing developments. Yet, the once prosperous areas, the ones that helped this city grow, just deteriorate. I managed to spur some interest and have been working with Roger to move forward."

"A businessman looking at investments," I say.

"Sure. I plan to make some money out of this. What I recoup goes to improvements on this place."

"What's the time frame?"

"I'm hoping we can get some businesses open by middle

summer. A couple restaurants, maybe another nightclub. Give Court some competition."

"How are things progressing?"

His lips crinkle to the left side of his face. "Well, I can't say there haven't been obstacles. Some other investors' ideas are a little out of line. I just want to head off the bureaucracy before it grows out of control." A forced laugh leaks out.

This one causes me to finish the bourbon to cover my annoyance. His persiflage is too false. "Roger been around the last couple of days? Asking about Annabelle?"

Fisher's head shakes. "Nope."

I don't believe him. This would be the first place I'd try. "What's your opinion of Roger? How would you judge his character?"

Fisher ponders a moment, smiles, and gives a nonchalant shrug. "He's willing to go to great lengths to succeed… just like I do."

I study him, try to divine meaning from the words he said or, like Mrs. Michelle, the words he didn't say. "Any length too great?"

His stare hardens. "Such as?"

I shrug and use the word I used with Donna's mother. "Rumors."

He runs the end of his tongue over his lower lip. "What can *you* tell *me*?"

"Some extra… transactions? Maybe to head off more delays?"

His Cheshire Cat smile grows by micrometers, and his inhalation is long and deep. "You shouldn't listen to rumors."

"How much stock should I put in them?"

"None." He crosses his arms. "Look, I don't know everything, but what I do know is best left between the parties involved. I'm sure you understand." With that, he reaches for a clipboard to mark off more inventory totals.

I plunk the glass on the counter and slide it toward him. He glances over his shoulder and I stand. I should thank him for his time, but before I can form the words, the opening door lets in outside winter air, noise, and an even shadier-looking man than Fisher.

Black, pinstripe suit, white shirt. A gold tie pin of a silhouette of a busty woman—usually seen on truck mud flaps—decorates a thin, black tie. His hair has the just-stepped-from-the-shower shine. To round out the look, he sports reflective sunglasses. "Hey, Rand-ay," he says in a smoker's voice. "Seen any good movies lately?"

I catch a glimpse of Fisher's eyes bugging out. Black Suit must have caught the full expression because his follow-up laugh is choked off.

"Cable went out… yesterday," Fisher stammers in an attempt at recovery. "When are you stopping by to fix the satellite?"

The man falters. "Uh… call the office tomorrow. I'll have someone out in the morning."

I'll give this act some credit for the ad-lib script, but it's as lame as a two-legged horse.

The newcomer slides onto a stool, three away from mine.

This gives Fisher a reason to move. "What'll you have?"

Black Suit's confusion is short-lived, but not enough; I recognize that he's a regular, and Fisher lost points with the question.

"Scotch, neat."

"Comin' right up," Fisher says in more tiresome, B-movie

dialogue. He turns his head back to me while reaching for a bottle of Dewar's. "Anything else for you, Mr. Detective?"

Black Suit now faces me, and his expression goes blank. Although I can't see his eyes—the clodpate still hasn't removed the sunglasses—I'll bet dollars to doughnuts that they're as narrow as a paper cut. He wonders if I'm a cop.

"No," I glance at each man one more time. "I have all I need."

Fisher frowns at my innuendo. Walking out, I swear I can feel the ice-cold burn from two pairs of eyes drilling into my back.

TWENTY-THREE

WHEN I REVERSE out of the parking slot in front of Zemo's, I see her thirty yards up the sidewalk. She's on her way to work the late afternoon and early evening crowd. Tonight's business might be slim pickings, especially in this crappy January weather. The snowfall is steadier, but at least the wind has calmed. However, the mercury slipped about five notches while I spoke to Fisher.

Her name is Leticia Simmons, but, in the trade, she calls herself Patra, as in Cleopatra. Whereas the skin tone of the Egyptian queen of old was more parchment than pitch, Leticia is original African-black, and, I suspect would have a glossy ebony sheen except for the life she's lived. I don't think her customers care one way or another.

Her territory comprises most of the lengths of blocks nearer to East Walnut and East Locust, but she stays close to the nightclubs and bars. Zemo's would be part of her route. She attracts politicos from the capital complex and business types from the medium and small trades on the east side. She's a familiar enough presence, some of the locals give her a grudging acceptance. The scruffy owner of the rundown Texaco station throws her a pack of generic smokes every so often, and the cook at the diner on the corner offers her coffee and a sandwich gratis. She rents a one-room hovel in the Maury Street neighborhood south of the river.

I sidle up beside Leticia and roll down the passenger window.

She's bundled up in a thin overcoat she can adjust for optimal bodily exposure. It's not enough to keep her flesh warm. She stops and gives me a blank look.

"Buy you a coffee, 'Tish?"

"Biscuits and gravy," she counters.

I want information and she knows it. Her tone tells me I can take the deal or leave. I raise my chin in assent. Hell, it is the breakfast hour for her. The opening car door protests like it's dying, and she slides into the seat. She keeps her feet above the trash heap in the foot well. When she closes the door, something breaks off behind the panel, and the rattle reminds me of a pachinko game.

Leticia is thirty-two, aged for one in her line of work. Although some women hold their youth and smooth skin into their fifth or sixth decade, the world has not been kind to Leticia, or her alter ego Patra. A sheen of dusty gray veils her face, lips a little too swollen, eyes and cheeks too sunken. She sits like a puppy about to be dumped.

I park in front of the diner right before Locust Avenue and, when we enter the eatery, the fluorescents, one of which buzzes like an irritated insect, exacerbate the weariness in her dark eyes. Her thin fingers tremble, and it's not because of drugs. At least, not anymore.

Leticia sank into the life early, smack and crack her first

demons. However, she managed to beat them back before they delivered total destruction. Maybe the tremors are the penalty her body decided to exact, a reminder of those hellish days. Or maybe she's sick of the life.

She orders coffee and a platter of B & G. I order coffee and, after the waitress, bored with existence herself, departs, I offer Leticia a Lucky. We light up and look at each other. The smoke from our lips shrouds our faces.

"You still don't care about the no-smoking laws, Sabastian," she says.

I shrug. "Bunch of liberal asses who have nothing better to do with their time." I point to the top half of the fat fry cook in his greasy kitchen behind an opening in the wall. "Besides, Sammy cares about as much as I do." Said cook keeps a cigarette drooping from the corner of his mouth like a veteran smoker. I wonder if the health inspectors know of his violation.

Leticia sucks another lungful of Lucky.

"How you been, 'Tish?"

She shrugs, looks down at the table. "Same ole. You know."

I do.

Five years have passed since I first met Leticia. She was a contact in a case back then and has been a source of information on various characters around town. We both look upon the world as a chaotic monster ready to stomp on the little, unimportant entities. Who gets flattened next is anyone's guess. Are we pessimistic? She sells her body and gives some of her take to Jackie Midnight.

And I am who I am.

I gaze out the grease-specked diner window at the falling

snow. "You're not going to stand out in that, are you, 'Tish? Not tonight."

She shrugs again and sips her coffee. The joe is scalding, but she swallows as if it were lemonade.

I let it slide. Nothing I say will change her mind. She's heard it all before. I'm not here to try to persuade her. I just hope to glean some information. "You worked the area New Year's Eve?" Her blank stare shows me the absurdity of my question. "Near Zemo's?" I add.

"Sure."

I slide the photo of Annabelle and her two friends across the table. "Happen to see this trio?"

She glances at the picture and shakes her head.

I lay my left middle finger on top of Annabelle's face. "She hasn't been seen since Sunday night. Her two companions lost track of her at Zemo's."

Leticia meets my eyes, and I sense the slightest… something behind her black pupils. Does she know anything, or is she waiting for a story?

The waitress all but drops the plate in front of Leticia and tops off our coffees.

When she departs, I say, "Annabelle Lansing." A glimmer flashes in Leticia's eyes.

"Do you know her, 'Tish? Have you seen her?"

Her head jitters a negative, and she sips more coffee, forks up a gravy-soaked bite of food. She doesn't recognize the girl, but maybe the name?

"Roger Lansing," I say. Her eyes can't hide that I've hit the target. "He's Annabelle's father," I add.

Leticia waits.

"You know about the urban renewal project." She nods. "How?" Before she can shrug or deflect the question, I answer, "From Jackie."

Another nod. "And from him, too." She scoops gravy.

"Him? You mean Roger Lansing? How?"

She explains around mouthfuls of the congealing breakfast her proximity to Roger the times when the developer scouted the neighborhood and discussed ideas with planners and potential investors. No one noticed her or paid her any attention. Racism, as stupid a concept as it is, still exists in America, even in the heartland. Add to it she's a black hooker? Well…

What those planners should have realized was that this particular person remembers things, and, if I can tap the spigot, I might learn something worthwhile. I lower my voice, even though no one is near. "I'm looking for Annabelle. She sounds like a messed-up kid who dumped the family's pressure to succeed. Unfortunately, she doesn't seem to have her own plans. Her being at Zemo's and the nightclub's owner's connection to her father's project keep cropping up. I don't know if there is something solid here, but the more I hear about it and who's interested, the less I like about the whole affair."

Leticia continues to eat.

If I don't say something to get her talking, she'll bug out of here faster than a M.A.S.H. unit in the path of a Commie advance. "Help me out, 'Tish. You know what's going on. Fisher wants more customers down here, which means more potential profit for Jackie. It's always about the money, sure, And I've talked with Roger and you've seen him; can you tell me anything? Whether it helps find Annabelle, I won't know until something clicks."

She spoons up the last of her gravy. If she had licked the plate, it couldn't be any cleaner. Leaning back in the seat, she eyes a danish, aged at least a day, with a dollop of goop on top colored like no fruit I've ever seen. When she looks back at me, I get the hint. Everything has a price. New and modern businesses in an aging neighborhood, cheap and meaningless sex from an apathetic prostitute… and the most valuable commodity —information.

I return to the table with the pastry, and she doesn't hesitate. I'll bet she's not often treated to free food.

"You know 'bout Jackie," Leticia says. Danish crumbs dot the corners of her mouth.

"Sure. More people down here means new customers."

"Same with Randall Fisher."

"He's looking to cut in on Court Avenue business."

"Sure, but not only on the music scene."

"Talk to me, 'Tish." I gesture to the display case. "Give me something good, and I'll pop for another danish."

"Naw, just one will do me." She chuckles. "Gotta watch my figure."

"Right." I blow cigarette smoke and smile.

"Jackie and Fisher both want to expand and, with new business down here, both can profit."

The way she says the word "both" opens a mental door. "They're working together," I say. Leticia nods. "Drugs." She raises her eyebrows. "More?" Her askance look tells me she'll think me a fool if I don't understand. "Sex?"

"What you think goes on in the back of Zemo's?"

"His didn't look like that type of joint."

"Only for special customers," she says.

"And Jackie provides the fluff."

Randall Fisher II is in deeper than most people realize. No surprise he's so ardently supportive of sprucing up Fourth Street. Quick money. If Leticia spoke true, quick money would come from a specific type of service.

"So this is why he's pushing," I say. "Tell me about Roger."

"He wants stuff to happen. What I've overheard, he's frustrated everything is moving so slowly."

I nod. "From what I've heard today, balls to the walls is the norm for him."

Leticia gives me a questioning expression. She probably thinks I just made a double entendre.

"Aviator term, 'Tish. Means he's flying at top speed."

"I know." She smiles to indicate the innocent teasing. "Well, he'd be flying faster if he didn't have to deal with one particular gent'm'n."

"Fly in the ointment?"

She makes a closed-mouth sound indicating something delicious. "Good looking, too. For a white man."

"'Tish," I scold.

"I'm tellin' you, I'd give him a freebie. Tall, big eyes, looks like one of those soap stars. And muscles? Man could kick your scrawny ass."

Leticia is enjoying this a little too much. Marshe isn't as big as Leticia claims, but I admit he possesses the muscular build and attractive features over which she all but gushes. He doesn't come close to soap opera handsome, but that's just my opinion. Plus, his personality is soap op villain scum. As for "kicking my scrawny ass," well, I'll side with modesty.

"May we get back to Lansing?" I ask.

"Could kick his ass, too. He's scrawnier than you."

Her pleasant laugh under other circumstances would be enjoyable. I smirk to get her back on track.

"I'm just funnin'. Anyway, this guy and Lansing go at it all but the punching. Right out in the middle of the street. Course, ain't no one around as the sun be down."

"When was this?"

"'Bout two weeks ago."

"What were they arguing about? Could you tell?"

"Baby, anyone within three blocks could hear. Lansing wanted this guy to put more money into the area. The other guy wants to see more progress before putting out."

Hang around Leticia long enough, you catch on that she's more intelligent than people think, that she flows between the speech patterns of "street" and educated to fit her mood and her pesky, teasing attitude.

"What sort of progress?" I ask.

"Evidence of more businesses ready to open. Lansing then said something about the crappy buildings."

I connect the dots. "Some, if not all, just need to be razed. Cheaper to rebuild than renovate."

Leticia gives me the look that says I've narrowly missed connecting one dot.

I back up and see it. "Businesses could open in existing structures, and some improvements can be made. But, to beautify the area, make it attractive, it would make sense to flatten everything and start over. That's what Roger wants, but that includes the stretch where Zemo's sits."

She nods.

"Any delays like a temporary closing would have an impact

on Fisher and Midnight. The question is, how does this dissatis-
fied man connect to either of the above?"

"Don' know," 'Tish replies. "Never seen him before or since."

"So what was the result of the argument between Roger and
this other guy?"

"Last I heard, they talked 'bout money again, and the guy was
wonderin' what happened to the money he gave Roger before."

"What money?" I try to keep the inquiry casual. Roger and
others already have provided information. I'm just looking for
more details.

No luck. Leticia is shrewd enough to catch the interest, though
I tried to keep it subtle. She smiles and takes another bite of
danish, making me wait. "Like you said, all about the money."

"What do you remember, 'Tish?"

"Nothing much after that. They lowered their voices and
walked the other way."

Some cases are like walking on an icy sidewalk. Small steps are
the key, and, sometimes, you slide sideways. "One more question,
and I'll let you go."

She accepts and drinks more coffee.

"Just before I left Zemo's, a slick guy in black wearing
sunglasses walks in. Probably drives the BMW parked outside."

She waits for ten seconds. "You ain't asked a question."

I sigh. "You have an unmatched talent for vexation."

"Only for you, honey. His name is Mel Prentiss."

My ears perk up. This guy called Stephan Marshe earlier.

"What title is on his business card?" I ask.

"Movie producer."

That explains his opening line to Fisher.

I almost let it pass, but she shows me a smile that tells me, again, she's holding back. I recall Zemo's and Leticia's information on Fisher's 'sideline' business, Prentiss's employment. "I'll bet he doesn't dust off any Oscars on the shelves in his office."

"His nickname is Pool Boy."

"He acts in his pictures, too?"

She nods.

"Low budget, above average returns. Does he use local talent?"

"Baby, he'd use your granny if he thought it would sell."

Why would an adult film producer be associated with a music promoter? Both are cheap hustlers and—I can't help if the old joke enters my mind—both probably think 'harass' is two words. What other attributes—or business—do they share?

We sit in silence for a while. She fingers danish crumbs into her mouth, finishes her coffee, and declines another. We exchange sad smiles, she slides out of the booth and offers a delicate wave to Sammy, who salutes with his spatula, before she exits the diner. Her figure fades from black to gray before she disappears into the white snow.

Leticia has given me more to think about, another link to explore.

I hope Annabelle wasn't coerced, suckered into, or, worse, forced into Prentiss's world.

CHAPTER
TWENTY-FOUR

WHEN I STEP out of the diner, the weather has reduced traffic noise to something akin to someone humming into a pillow. Snow falls like God's worst case of dandruff. No wind, so the Lucky's smoke surges whiter, hangs in the air, its own cloud. The cold is silent, sneaky. It surrounds a body like a shield, but will turn on its host one nerve ending at a time until it dominates and paralyzes the senses.

The cold also shrouds and infiltrates inanimate objects. My Plymouth looks dead, or at least sullen, as if it despises my leaving it to suffer a partial white burial. Something is amiss, though. Shards of the Plymouth's left headlight litter the street. This is no hit-and-run accident. From inside the diner, I didn't hear the vandal, but he left a calling card of a sort, slipped under the windshield wiper. A recent gift since the snow hasn't buried it.

Mind your own business.

I scan the area, but the perpetrator has left the scene. Only Leticia's footprints trail away from the diner, but I see faint tracks in the street leading off in the direction of Zemo's. Snow hasn't quite filled them in. Not too difficult to deduce I must be an irritation for someone to leave a cliché movie warning.

Didn't this kind of thing go out with the seventies, Johnny?

Who might be bothered by my investigation?

Fisher?

Someone higher up the food chain?

In my overcoat, I stave off the chill, but as I land on the cracked seats, the car's interior feels like I've discovered the mother lode of ghostly cold spots or interrupted a quorum of spectral forces.

The car's endurance in its deteriorated condition is nothing if not valiant, and I negotiate the streets with relative ease. I travel toward the city's heart while everyone else navigates the arteries outward, not hurrying back to the office. I could go straight home, but I want to think, and if the neighbors are squabbling, then my effort will be a useless endeavor. The office is better. I value and cherish Anne's presence—another secretary wouldn't bring the correct atmosphere and probably wouldn't last too long in the position—but when the office is empty, I can think. Some of my cases are tricky, require deductive reasoning. Many are the nights when I sit in the chair or recline on the couch and listen to the night sounds. Intermittent traffic. Chatter and laughter from passersby. A stray cat's cries for a mate. Don't they sound like a baby crying, Johnny?

Many mornings, I find myself still on the couch, Anne's frown above me.

The point is, I can think in the empty office… or maybe I'm more content and comfortable there than elsewhere, including home.

Supper is another drive-through sandwich shop. Tonight, the

bread is fresh, but fixin's are spare. I pull into a vacant parking spot—one I suspect is empty because regulations forbid vehicles during certain hours—and eat while watching the other entities of the workday pass on the way home, to supper dates, or, because it's Thursday, out of town for an early weekend.

A patrol car slows; the cop gives me a frown Anne would be proud of and waves a finger at me to move on. I nod, and he eases down the street. I sigh, wrap up the debris of the meal, and toss it in the passenger seat. I intend to throw it into the next convenient trash receptacle, but it'll probably end up with the denizens in the floor well.

Minutes later, I slide to a stop in front of Anne's building. The front bumper taps the parking meter, and the right front tire squashes against the curb. Part of me hopes an irritated snowplow driver will call a tow, but they'll wait until after rush hour to decide when to send out the plows. I should be gone by then.

A black Jaguar XJ purrs as quietly as its feline namesake in my usual spot in front of the office building. I've parked two slots behind. The driver of the other car and I risk tickets, but I don't care and doubt he does, either. Although his car is too modern for my tastes, I can't help but admire it, if only for the fact that, similar to Roger's Caddy, it sports a hood ornament. Cars should have hood ornaments. They add class and style to a vehicle, and I miss the unique designs.

I can admire the car and equally execrate its driver. As I come abreast on the sidewalk, the passenger window slides down to reveal a shadowy interior and the silhouette of the man in the driver's seat. Like a whisper on the wind, a voice calls to me, "Join me."

I don't want to obey, but he'll just wait.

The window closes. I open the door and enter. The interior of Jackie Midnight's car is just what one would expect. Black, expensive leather seats, black, handmade dashboard, black tinted windows. Even the steering wheel is encased in a dark, rich, raven wing-colored protective cover.

The man himself is a different shade of black. He's the color of smooth, shiny ebony. The only thing missing from his eight-ball-shaped head is the white circle and numeral. His arms are long and lean, while the deep purple, silk shirt can't hide the well-developed muscles beneath. The same is true for his legs encased in imported dress slacks.

He eases the car out onto Seventh. Streetlights illuminate his cheeks, mouth, and eyes, the latter of which are focused, but not stony. We could be out for a weekend drive in the country for all his expression belies.

Except I know what he does for a living and how dangerous an individual he can be. If he ever took a drive into the Iowa farmland, it wouldn't be to admire the cattle and hogs, but to find a thick cornfield in which to dump a body.

Jackie Midnight. Drug king. Pimp. Killer.

Am I scared? Yes. Do I fear for my life? Maybe. Did he order a four-word warning on my windshield accompanied by a broken headlight? Leticia said Midnight benefits if more business comes to East Fourth. Does he see me as a threat to those benefits? Why? Because of my inquiries into Annabelle's disappearance? Could this be about Timothy? Did I err in speaking to Leon about the boy? What action did Timothy's call to someone the previous night initiate?

I sense, however, he wants to talk. At least at first.

He turns east, and soon we're crossing the river. At the crest of the bridge, he angles into a parking slot. Out the window, the snow-covered water looks gray due to the waning afternoon and the custom-installed window tint. Snow partially obscures the landscape, the train trestle, the apartment buildings just up from the shore. A lone goose plods near the bike path, as if grounded during the annual trek with his buddies to warmer climes.

Jackie inhales long and deep. "Do you like the river?" His voice is velvety smooth, like aged whiskey, pitched midway between baritone and tenor. The words flow easy, not quite high-brow cultured, not quite Southern molasses-slow, but with hints of both. "I like the river," he continues. "During the summer, I'll find a spot and watch the water. Sometimes for hours. I'm fascinated by how the surface colors move along the spectrum as the sun rises or dusk settles. How the city lights twinkle on the surface in the middle of the night."

He goes silent for a full minute. We stare at the frozen river.

Soon, he reverses out of the slot, and we're back into the east-bound lane.

"It never really changes, though," he says. "Sure, it flows downstream to meet the Mississippi, but here in our little corner of the world, it doesn't change. The seasons come and go, but it's always there. The amount of water may drop or overflow to dangerous levels, but it's always there. Men may put obstacles in the way in an attempt to control it, but the river will always find its own way. Because it possesses determination and time, there is nothing capable of stopping the river."

While he speaks, Jackie tracks a random route up and down various east-side streets. Every so often, we pass individuals either walking the sidewalk or huddled in doorways. All eyes linger on the car and a few arms raise in a half salute.

Jackie's surveillance of his kingdom lets the serfs know he's near.

Night settles over the city, but true dark never comes. Street and security lights and the white, white snow act as forever beacons, creating and separating shadows. Dark patches in the urban jungle portend menace, nightmares, inevitable despair. People often lose themselves in those holes. There are certain individuals, however, who thrive in the darkness, and many work for the man beside me. He is the black shadow passing, the only true darkness on the streets tonight.

In time, Jackie zeros in on home base, behind Analu's, a Laotian restaurant that serves as one end of a strip mall at the intersection of University and East Fourteenth. The complex is shaped like clock hands set at a quarter after six, with a Walgreens ironically serving as the small hand.

The food at Analu's is spicy and overpriced; while dinners are served up front, drugs, weapons, and hookers can be purchased in the back. Jackie made a deal with the middle-aged owners of the restaurant. A simple, non-negotiable, and easy-to-understand arrangement: the couple keeps their mouths shut and doesn't cause trouble or they don't breathe any longer.

Jackie drives to the rear of the building while he murmurs into a cell phone just loud enough for me to hear. I read between the lines of his blasé patter and decipher code words informing the minions behind the barred door that he's not coming in under duress. His company does not bode a threat. At least, I hope those are his instructions, rather than ordering his boys to deliver two jabs to my kidney with a sharp object as soon as I step out of the Jaguar.

Out of the car, we approach a steel door. It opens as if

computer controlled. Inside, a guy who could be Leon's darker sibling gives me a cold stare and indicates I should turn around. His pat down finds my packet of Lucky Strikes, matches, and whiskey flask.

He doesn't find a weapon, much to my relief, but only because I don't carry one. Some of my brother detectives of decades past swore by the guns, but I'm loath to use one. Normally, my job sees no need for firepower, and I'd be sorely tempted to shoot the first person who caused me grief or frustration, or plant the butt of the gun against his temple.

Jackie leads me down a dimly lit hallway to a spacious office I didn't think could fit behind the restaurant. It's furnished with a desk, a few chairs, and a small bathroom at the far end. I don't see a computer, filing cabinets, or anything one might expect in the sanctum of Iowa's version of Tony Montana.

A small area in one corner is curtained off. Jackie strolls over and whips back the curtain. A young, thin, half-naked white woman lies curled up on what looks like an elegant day bed. He smacks her backside, which elicits a girlish whimper. "Get your ass up, Sugar Lips, and hit the streets."

Jackie reverts to a seventies movie pimp. All he needs is a sparkly, purple vest.

The girl whines, but unfolds and stretches like a lazy cat. Ignoring me, oblivious of her bare skin, she approaches one of Jackie's lieutenants and accepts a small baggie of powder before shuffling out the door. I hope she takes time to dress before venturing outside.

"Damn bitches don't know when to go to work," Jackie says, still in central casting mode. "Raymond, you need to wake her ass up earlier next time."

"Okay, boss," agrees Raymond in a voice so deep it resembles the first rumble of an earthquake.

The scene is surreal enough that I'm a bit light-headed. Maybe I'm still hungry.

Jackie swishes the curtain closed, turns to me, and the regal calm returns. The smooth professional is back. In the room's half-light, Jackie resembles a wraith when he crosses the floor to his desk. From his black, leather executive chair, he gestures to the plain, wooden chair in front of him.

I still stand just inside the office. With no sudden movements to cause a reaction from the sentinels, I walk to the chair and sit.

Jackie leans back and eyes me with speculation. No one says anything or moves, hardly dares breathe. The silence is vast, but filled with anticipation. A silence powerful enough to engulf a planet. The smallest twitch, the slightest nod, even eyes shifting a quarter inch to one side, might precipitate a firestorm, but right now, I could be alone in a room filled with statues.

A trickle of sweat forms and flows from my hairline down my neck behind my left ear. My eyes never leave Jackie. His stare locks me in place. I can only assume that what he wants to tell me —and he's said so much thus far that I'm only beginning to form a picture of its meaning—relates to Leon and Timothy. If so, I may be in more trouble than I first thought.

CHAPTER
TWENTY-FIVE

"I HAVE a lot of the river's qualities in me." Jackie speaks as if ten minutes haven't passed. My mind has to catch up. "Ever moving forward to something larger. I'm affected by various people and events, but I don't really change."

I want a smoke, but I don't dare. I don't even want to risk asking permission.

"People try to divert my course, but like the river, eventually, I find routes around the obstacles." He leans forward and rests his forearms on the desk. "Sabastian, do you understand what I'm saying?"

I nod once. Jackie nods once before his eyes rise to the ceiling. Long seconds pass, and I don't like the silence.

"Sometimes, when a particularly large obstacle attempts to block the river, the consequences can be devastating. The sudden release of water can be, well, violent is the best word, wouldn't you say? The explosion of a bursting dam."

He likes the analogy and, though I'm ahead of him, I'll let him explain. As if I have a choice.

"Other impediments don't require as much pressure to defeat." His stare pierces, bores into me. "For example… minor damage to personal property as a warning."

My car's headlights.

His voice drops two notches in volume. "I react in a similar fashion to problems. Sometimes, not often, mind you, but on occasion, I'm confronted by a problem so large and threatening, I have no other option, and my response is… potent, shall we say. Even… brutal. The threat, however, does get eliminated." He eases back into the chair.

I recall the articles about the Harding Street gang.

"More often, though, the pressure needed to wash away the obstruction is low to medium, depending on the, uh, shall we say, stubbornness of the particular problem." He leans forward, places his elbows on the desktop, and puts his hands together as preparing to pray. Instead, one index finger points at me. "At present, I have a two-fold problem." He shows me his palms. "I don't think it's difficult to solve. In fact, I've already taken care of the first part." He sighs long and deep and is just about to speak again when a knock sounds on the door.

I shift my head to see one of the sentinels check the visitor through a sliding window. Satisfied, he allows entry to a boy in his mid-teens. Even in the half-light, I distinguish youthful features stressed and anxious, hands twitchy, tousled hair the color of wet sand. He's dressed in faded blue jeans fraying at the cuffs, a sweatshirt at least two sizes too large, sneakers well past their expiration date, and a nylon windbreaker.

Timothy Hawthorne.

I've never seen him, but I harbor no doubt as to the boy's identity.

He looks toward Jackie, who raises his chin in both acknowl-edgment and permission. From his jacket pocket, Timothy removes a wad of bills and hands it to Raymond. For the payment, he receives two packets similar to what was given to the hooker. He nods at Jackie, gives me an incurious look, then departs.

I turn back to Jackie.

As if following a script, he says, "The river always wins, Sabas-tian, and so do I."

My heart sinks like a lead weight to the bottom of the pond and lands with an aching thud. As if Jackie's picking me up in front of my office wasn't confirmation enough, Timothy's presence confirms Jackie knew I'd tried to interfere with his operations.

Minutes later, Jackie and I walk back outside. Forgoing the car, but trailed by one of the bodyguards, we walk south behind the Walgreens, across University via a convenient gap in heavy evening traffic. Headlights and streetlights glare off the snow and illuminate the rest of the world, but we walk in shadow. The snow falls heavier, faster, not quite a complete whiteout, but enough to obscure vision beyond fifty yards. I'm hunched like a turtle in my overcoat, but Jackie walks as if he's taking a summer stroll through the park, unmindful of the January conditions. We walk side by side. I'm not sure why he wants to take this little jaunt, but whatever his purpose or goal, I'm bound to follow.

"Sabastian," he says. "There are a lot of forces in this town, and people must choose which side they're going to back. In my busi-ness, as in others, loyalty is valued. I'm sure you understand."

We walk behind another building, past service entry doors to a dentist's office, a video store, and an attorney. Soon, we're across Fremont, angled towards East Fourteenth.

"People who work for me, Sabastian, they know the score. I'm very meticulous in my organization. I don't necessarily micro-manage everyone, but I am aware of every facet. Who goes where, how much is taken in on a daily basis. No angle escapes my atten-tion. At the moment, I'm in the middle of certain matters of busi-ness expansion, and I don't have time for distractions."

Does he mean the Fourth Street project? 'Tish claimed Midnight had a large piece of the pie.

Just before the main drag, we cut south again behind a dry-cleaners.

"However, when something goes wrong in my business, when an individual's loyalty wanes, even for an instant, I know. I'm so in tune with my people, I'm almost psychic."

We cross a dirt path, ruts filled with snow, leading to the first line of houses set back from the street. Next to the cleaners stands a red, wooden building, formerly a barbecue joint. A thirty-yard long, seven-foot-high fence right out of Tom Sawyer blocks the view of neighboring houses.

Jackie halts when we take a step past a dumpster perpendic-ular to the building. "When there is an employee problem—" He says, indicating a large form on the ground half-buried by snow, "I rectify it."

My breath catches when I recognize the bulk of Leon Brum-mell. I don't know if he's only unconscious, but I fear the worst.

Jackie moves close to me and speaks almost as one confidante to another, "Sabastian, this is my city, and you are but a small and insignificant particle. I do not wish for you to come to my atten-tion in the future."

I'm frozen in place by both Leon's prone form and Jackie's ice-cold words. My mind rushes to issue commands to my appendages, to order movement, to mount a defense no matter how inconsequential.

Too late.

Lightning flashes as something crashes against my temple. My legs disappear, and I collapse. Part of me hopes I suffer no further injury by landing on snow-packed asphalt. I fade to black before I hit the ground.

———

Cold air forces instinctual shivers even before I'm fully awake. For a second, I don't move. After assessing the situation, I realize I *can't* move. Joints and muscles are locked, and I have no feeling in my fingers.

I open my eyes to find a blanket of snow over me.

With a deep breath, guttural groans, popping joints, and stifled gasps, I haul myself to hands and knees. My demeanor is like a grouchy Kodiak after an interrupted hibernation, only to discover its cave mysteriously missing.

My first attempt to stand disintegrates all thoughts as my head detaches from my torso and floats free, spinning like an out-of-control planetoid. One with a tender lump on its surface. With frozen fingers, I explore my temple, use the other hand to support myself against the nearby wall.

I may suffer from a concussion.

Scrambled thoughts roll to the forefront, dissolve to let others intrude.

Jackie Midnight.

Did I lose any blood?

Anne.

I'm so cold.

Leon!

I shake sensibility back into my head and try to focus on my immediate surroundings.

A larger bear, also snow-covered, lies a few feet away. I blow hot air onto my fingers. Nerve ends tingle with fresh, coursing blood. I kneel beside the big man and feel for a pulse. His skin is cold and dry, and I'm not sure if the thready beat I register is his or mine. I push him and call his name, but it's a failed effort. So is searching his pockets for a cellphone.

My watch says 10:10. The sky is overcast, clouds low. Veils of fog like will o' the wisps haunt corners and niches. I stand and half-shuffle, half-stagger back across University to a twenty-four hour laundromat. Unlike most places in the metro, this one has an attendant, a bored Asian man behind the counter who's expression changes to a wide-eyed, frozen stare when I stumble across the threshold.

On a ragged breath, I try to speak, but need a second before the synapses between brain and vocal cords connect. "Phone. Need… an ambulance." Exhausted by the effort, I collapse onto a nearby chair.

An unknown amount of time passes. Medical attendants and the police arrive. Four people are needed to load Leon onto a gurney for transport to the hospital.

An EMT wants me to follow, but I prefer to sit a while in a warm place and rest. I do allow him to inspect my head injury, and his frown indicates he'd much rather see me lying prone and hooked up to beeping machines while doctors schedule myriad tests. His frown deepens when I take a pull from my flask, followed by lighting a wrinkled and bent Lucky.

The laundromat attendant chatters a protest, but no one listens.

Sighing, the EMT steps back. "Well, you don't seem to be in immediate danger. If at any time you feel faint, light-headed, experience dizziness, speech problems, or loss of muscle control, you need to get to a hospital immediately."

I stare at him, silent, smoking. His words do not make sense. If I lose muscle control, how am I to get to the hospital? I decide not to ask him to clarify the paradoxical statement.

"Actually, you're very lucky," he continues, "Your friend, too. The combination of the building, the windbreak wall, the coats you two were wearing, plus the snow, served to insulate you from the worst of the night's weather. You easily could have frozen to death or suffered frostbite."

The only lucky I'm feeling is the one between my lips. An officer replaces the EMT as my next persecutor. I relate my story three times, and each time he tries to elicit more details.

We both know Jackie is to blame and are equally certain that, although he'll be questioned, he'll have an airtight alibi.

I catch a cab to the office to find, finally, my car gone, towed, most likely by a grumpy city employee, so another grumpy city employee could plow the street.

The jehu takes me home and, he drives away before I reach my apartment door. Inside, of course, the busted heater has left the apartment as cold as the interior of the refrigerator.

I glance at my watch again. Just after midnight into the new day and I already hate it.

TWENTY-SIX

FRIDAY

WITH THE TIME spent tolerating the ministrations of the EMT and the police interviews, the trip back to my apartment, the recuperative sleep that did nothing to reset my senses or relieve most of the aches, the sluggish movements showering, shaving, dressing, and, finally, waiting for another cab, I'm well into the eleventh hour of the morning when I reach the office.

Despite my cleaner appearance, Anne, with her enigmatic intuitiveness, knows something is amiss the second I walk in the door. Maybe she sees the residual pain in my eyes, the set of my jaw, or the slowness of my walk.

After I explain last night's encounter with Jackie, she says, "Sabastian, you should be home in bed. Do you think you can think clearly enough today?"

I nod, sit on the couch, and ask her to make some calls to retrieve my car. First, she examines my head wound and offers two aspirin. She smacks my hand when I try to wash them down with Ten High and gives me bottled water from her desk. "Why don't you go home and sleep?"

I shake my head. "I'll be all right."

"Sabastian, this is serious. You've angered the wrong people. You should give this to the police."

I shake my head and sigh. "The police know Midnight attacked me, but the man is insulated six ways to Sunday. Part of the reason for last night was that I interceded on behalf of an acquaintance to keep her nephew from buying dope. It didn't work, and now a man is in the hospital. This also has to do with the East Fourth project. Fisher, Marshe, and probably Prentiss have ties to Midnight. Maybe others are involved. In searching for one missing girl, I scratched the surface of a bigger operation."

"You need to go to the police," Anne insists.

I give a slow head shake. "I have nothing to connect to Annabelle's disappearance. According to Leticia, Fisher runs a sort of brothel in the back of his club, the girls supplied by Midnight. If she knows, then the cops are aware of it. Maybe Midnight has friends in certain departments or offers payments for turned heads. I just don't have any proof of how everyone ties together or how it all relates to Annabelle. Links from one party to another, but the chain doesn't lock anyone in place."

"What are you going to do?"

I stand. "I don't know. Last night, I wanted time to think, but that didn't work out so well."

"You need sleep," Anne says.

"I'll grab some food and talk to more people."

She sits at the desk, phone in hand, and, in a minute, she locates my car at the lot of Crow Tow, the go-to company for the city. She pays the bill with a debit card, then calls a cab to take me out to the place just off Maury.

Before I leave, I hesitate. Anne deserves to know about the videos. "When I get back, I'll, uh, show you what I've discovered."

Her lips tighten a fraction and the chin drops and rises once. The attitude wonders why I haven't revealed anything I've learned earlier, why I'm waiting until later, but has grudging acceptance of my reasons.

"Okay." She keeps my stare for an extra second before returning her attention to the paperwork on the desk.

I watch her for an extra second myself, then turn to catch my ride to my car.

Plows have cleared the main streets. Slush and compacted snow still make for slippery travel, but my taxi driver negotiates the challenge well. He does try to take me on an alternate course in an attempt to pad the fare—but I catch him before he commits to the wrong turn and put him back on the more direct path.

No tip for him.

The woman at the towing company is all business. Efficient. Non-judgmental—she's seen all types walk through the door, from the belligerent to the shamed. All of them guilty of parking where—or in my case *when*—it's not allowed.

She produces the paperwork for me to sign, hands me the receipt that I'll give to Anne, and tells me where the truck driver parked my car.

I use my coat sleeve to clear the windows and settle behind the wheel. If the cold hadn't settled in, I might have tilted over and fallen asleep. Instead, I urge the protesting motor to life and ease back out onto Maury. A quick stop at the convenience store on the corner for coffee, two too-sweet doughnuts, and two packages of Lucky Strikes, and I'm off to see if I can dredge up more information on the Lansings, both Roger and Annabelle.

———

Stephan Marshe told me the previous day that, in addition to the cash bribe to Roger Lansing, he talked with the owner of an investment firm to offer Roger's son, Amos, a job. The warning of the note and smashed headlight told me I was on the right track, even with the multiple players. The more connections I can make, the closer, I hope, I come to finding Annabelle.

The office of Port-O-Folio is on the fourth floor of a T-shaped building in the Three Fountains business park. From Forty-Second Street to the interstate and between Westown Parkway and University in West Des Moines, business thrives in red brick monuments with spacious parking lots.

Before I call for an elevator, I take time to warm up on the ground floor. Silence surrounds me except for a subtle hum in the air. It doesn't overwhelm me, but I sense the potency underneath. Electric without the sizzle.

The tote board in front of me shows that Porto leases one of five offices on the fourth floor. The others are occupied by two firms of attorneys, an accountant, and an architect.

Look, Johnny, more As.

When the elevator deposits me on the correct floor, I walk the stem of the T to the last office. *Port-O-Folio* is imprinted over the solid wooden door. Two foot-wide, glass windows flank the door.

Each shows a portion of a front counter in a darkened office. A laminated sign in one window displays the office hours and the fact the investment firm closes at noon on Fridays. I've missed him by ten minutes.

The hallway is quiet. The acoustics eliminate sounds from other companies. I smoke a Lucky while deciding my next move. I can't be miffed that I didn't get to see Stanley Porto. Luck has favored me in all my walk-in interviews over the last two days in that I've met with the intended parties with only short delays (if not getting instant access), but the closed office of *Port-O-Folio* breaks the pattern.

A minute later, my mouth moves to a resigned pout. If I can't make the connection personally, I'll be forced to conduct… internet research. I may not find direct connections, but maybe a hint of insight on the man.

I wet the butt of the cigarette under a restroom sink's faucet and dispose of it properly. At the elevator, I wait since the car has returned to the first floor. Numerals above the doors light as the car passes each floor and the *ding* indicates it has reached its destination. I move aside to allow the occupants to exit.

My heart jolts at the sight of the man who steps from the elevator.

Randy Fisher.

He does a double-take with a stutter step. His eyes slit, and his face freezes into a mask of bewilderment and curiosity. He wants to know why I'm here. I wonder who he's here to see. Surely not the architect, unless he's planning on another addition to the back of his nightclub. The attorney? The accountant? Maybe.

I step onto the elevator, but push the button to hold the door open. Fisher says nothing, doesn't stop walking, but takes glances over his shoulder. When I don't see him veer to any of the doors along the shaft of the 'T', I deduce his visit to Porto's. I select the first floor as he notices the hours-open sign.

No need to conduct another conversation with Fisher. I know where to find him if I seek further information. His presence is curious. What's his connection to Porto? Does it mean anything?

———

I'm a smidgen closer to the West Des Moines Library than to the one in Urbandale. Valley Drive—I remember when it was Thirty-Fifth Street—south over the freeway, a long straight stretch through residential blocks. The West Des Moines Police Department meets me at the first arc of the soft 'S' curve and the library rests at the second arc. From then on, the name changes to Mills Civic Parkway, which is the limit of my desire for further travel. The street becomes a main artery for an explosion of 'progress' that widens the street to three or four lanes with a confusion of turn lanes, interminably long traffic lights, and clogged streams of traffic flowing past scores of businesses, strip malls, and abominable-sized apartment buildings.

The library itself combines grandiose and utilitarian. Long, brick building with ground-to-roof windows on the west side. I find an empty slot that doesn't make me walk too far to the library's entrance, bundle the coat collar close, and stomp snow from my shoes before I enter the library proper.

The interior resembles every other library. Rows of shelves of books. Sitting areas with squat, low-backed, cushioned couches and chairs. Partitioned tables for individual study. Meeting rooms for book clubs and presentations. High ceiling. Depending on the section, the lighting ranges from florescent to chandelier-type. Every color starts at brown and strays from dark mahogany to light ash.

Libraries are supposed to be quiet places, but each has noise. Low, murmured conversations (except, ironically, from the librarian at the reception desk laughing with a middle-aged woman about the New Year's Eve recipe she tried). Soft taps on a keyboard. The copier *clanks* out paper. Magazine pages *slap-turn*. The creak of door hinges. The squeal of wheels on a metal, rolling book cart.

The recipe talk stops when I approach the main desk. The librarian tries for a friendly smile, but the wariness in her eyes denies it. My exhaustion from last night's assault and this morning's ordeal must still show in my face and stance. The other woman studies the three books she either checked out before I entered or has yet to return.

"May I help you?" the librarian asks.

"I'd like to use one of your computers," I say. Then to stave off suspicions of my purpose, I add, "I'm researching local businesses."

That last bit satisfies her. She wraps up the conversation with the woman, then leads me to a far wall and eight computers, each its own partitioned niche.

"Scan your library card to log on." She points at a box next to the monitor with a sensor window. "Copies are ten cents per page."

"I apologize ma'am," I say. "I don't live in West Des Moines, so I don't have a card to this library."

Or to any library, for that matter, but she doesn't need to know that.

Her eyes say, *Of course, you don't.* Her smile and words say, "No problem. You can use a one-time guest logon."

She clicks the mouse, showing me, and doing it for me. She even double-clicks the internet browser to bring up the search engine.

I thank her and sit. She pauses a moment, as if waiting to see what I'll input into the search bar, then walks away.

Port-O-Folio brings up a list with Stanley's company listed first. The algorithms then veer off into other directions, just in case I was inquiring about the definition of the word *portfolio*, design ideas for my house by Port.O.Folio Decorators, or Port Orford, Oregon.

Clicking on Porto's company switches me to the site's home-page, with the name at the top, a navigational menu, and a stock image of two executives looking over… well, a portfolio I assume will make one or both of them financially sound, maybe wealthy.

"Investment" and other money words and half phrases fade in and out, all surrounded by shades of forest green and more browns the library should consider adopting.

The *About* menu item goes to a page showing a respectable image of Stanley Porto and who I guess is his receptionist behind the front counter. Stanley does not look like the second half of the famous comedy duo of Laurel and Hardy, but could pass for Oliver Hardy's brother. He doesn't sport the mini mustache, but has straight, black hair, double chin, pudgy midriff under a basic, white shirt and black tie. He's not quite ready to celebrate his sixth decade of life, but well on his way.

Other pages highlight the services of the company and boast of

Port-O-Folio's inclusion in several magazines via a scrolling banner. One of the magazines is entitled *Finance*. The cover shows a drawing of a hand holding a businessman's carrying case, one for documents or a laptop. The case is engorged, I presume, with money, since several renditions of hundred-dollar bills stick out from the top and side pockets. The attention-grabbing headline reads: *Are You Ready For Retirement?*

I click back to the search list. Among the irrelevant sites, the company name shows up in a bold font in local newspaper articles. I scan through these, reading just to get the gist. Sponsoring a foundation event and one of the top twenty metro investment firms. A longer article regarding the East Fourth Street project grabs my attention and I take time to read in more detail. *Port-O-Folio*'s name came up through Randy Fisher, who mentioned the investment firm's interest in the neighborhood. The reporter chose to include only one quote from Stanley: "I'll be interested to see what happens down there."

To me, that doesn't sound like a ringing endorsement. I picture Porto in his office, feeling obligated to speak after the reporter mentioned one of his clients and choosing the blandest positive statement available.

A search of Stanley Porto brings up an even more diverse listing. When I narrow the parameter by adding a comma and *Des Moines* after his name, the results aren't minimized, but the first six center on the man. Winning a local fundraising award. The speaker at a businessmen's meeting last year. One of those who spoke at a city council meeting regarding… well, what do you know, urban renewal in neglected or forgotten parts of the city.

The man has more presence than I first thought. How direct, though?

Porto's son shares a sliver of the spotlight. One article mentions that Reginald "Reggie" Porto and his country band The Buckaroos signed with a record company, the name I recognize as mid-size, but one I wouldn't have thought would be in Stephan Marshe's sphere of influence. However, who knows how far the man's slime can ooze into respectable enterprise? Perhaps Marshe was telling the truth in doing Porto a favor by jump-starting the son's career in return for Porto helping Roger's son Amos. Is he still trying to reap the benefits? I don't know Porto, but I'll bet he has a good attorney he can tap if Marshe tries to make too many inroads.

I dig into my coat pocket and find the micro recorder. One of Annabelle's videos talked about Amos working a summer job in the mailroom at the Principal Building. Yesterday morning, Roger didn't talk about the offer Marshe made regarding another job for Amos, but I remember the previous night he did.

I turn down the volume and hold the speaker close to my ear. A minute passes before I find the correct segment.

"That damn Marshe. Trying to bribe me. First with money, then with promises of a job for Amos. Said he has an in with a guy. Stanley P—Porto. Runs that place Por—f'lio. (Slurred words as Roger tries to regain control of his tongue. When he does, the tone turns whiny.) *What kind of job? Come on, it ain't like he was gonna start in middle management. Another mail room job like he had at Prin—Principal."*

Amos didn't say anything about a job when I spoke to him. Of course, I didn't ask him, but he was so stressed and worried about his grades and the upcoming paper that any, uh, *porto* in the storm (sorry about the pun, Johnny), would have been a relief.

The idea that Marshe and Fisher use Porto's doesn't sit well. I can assume Marshe uses him for investements as does Fisher. Is the relationship between Porto and Marshe such that the latter can ask the former for a favor, even if that favor is for extra leverage against Roger Lansing? Does Fisher put some of his ill-gotten gains into Porto's firm?

Does Porto know anything of the others' real motives and business?

CHAPTER
TWENTY-SEVEN

FROM AN UPSCALE OFFICE to a place one step removed from a condemned notice on the front door. A bar so rundown even I won't patronize it takes up the left half of a black-painted, angled building on a dogleg of Southwest Ninth south of the Raccoon River. The other half contains Prentiss Productions with a facade no more impressive than the tavern's: gouged, wooden walls, chipped black paint, dirt-encrusted windows, missing roof tiles, eroded foundation.

The latter is present in most of the neighborhood residences. Two and three-story houses and apartments defy the downhill slope, but the years have taken their toll on appearance.

Parking for the black building is in the rear off Davis Avenue. Time and nature have made the lot not much more than rubble. I negotiate around chunks of concrete and asphalt strewn hither and yon like a giant's unfinished jigsaw puzzle.

Beyond the front door are a scuffed wooden floor, faded and water-stained wallpaper, three metal folding chairs, a battered filing cabinet, and a secondhand desk, behind which sits a woman with dyed black hair and too much makeup. Former 'talent', I deduce from surgically enhanced features seeking to escape the thin fabric sweater. A long, thin cigarette smolders in a plastic ashtray to her left.

I make certain to touch nothing and step up to the desk. "Is Mr. Prentiss in the office?"

She gives me a blank stare and sucks in a lungful of nicotine. "Yeah."

I wait a beat for her to catch the obvious next request, then, "If he's free, may I speak with him?"

Another smoke. "Have an appointment?"

"I'm not here for an audition, only to talk."

"What about?"

"Business."

She blows smoke, picks up the phone, presses a button. "Man here to see you. Says he's here to talk 'business'."

"All right," a voice says over the speaker." Give me a moment."

Her duty done, she ignores me, opens the middle desk drawer, and removes an emery board to scrape across the ends of her nails.

Minutes pass in silence except for the short-lived sandpaper *scritches* of the emery board. She ignores the cigarette, and it continues to waste away through wispy smoke streams. Sated by a Lucky before I entered, I'm still drawn to the stick in the holder. Fascinating how something as insignificant as curling smoke in the air captures the attention.

Minutes later, with no sign of her boss, the woman replaces the emery board in the drawer, picks up the cigarette, stands, and sashays out of the room in a bad imitation of a forties movie gangster's moll.

I'm not sure what the message is. That my impatience grows enough I'll leave? Frustrated, I make a decision. If caught, I can make excuses later.

Seconds later, I enter an empty room that I estimate takes up the majority of the space of Prentiss Productions. The back part is filled with monitors, video players, and computers. A video camera screwed into a tripod points at a blank wall in front of which sits a stereotypical 'casting couch'. A high ceiling displays an array of stage lights. Another door beyond an L-shaped counter contains a wide-screen monitor. I approach the short side of the counter and rest my forearm on top.

The minute action must have triggered the computer's mouse sensor because a soft but high-pitched whine indicates the hard drive coming back to life.

The screen is angled so if I lean forward six inches, I can read the display. It's a spreadsheet, of sorts, with a column of initials on the left, a column of dates in the middle, and a third column of what I assume are movie titles on the right. Some of the dates are from last month, but most are from later this month, February, and into March. A quick check confirms that many of the initials match what is written on the folders next to the monitor.

Almost at the midway point on the screen, I read:

A.L. 1/7? FIRST TIMERS-VOL. 4

I don't know what the question mark by the date signifies, but I imagine, of all the people who have had sex in front of Prentiss' cameras, not many have the initials A.L. By coincidence, those same initials are on a folder near the middle of the stack.

I lean away and concentrate on the indistinct murmurs from the front room. Prentiss on the phone?

A look back at the screen. The document window has been reduced just enough to reveal another window behind, the tab listing the name of the website—The Magical Lens.

A door behind me opens, and I scoot back around the counter. I'm saved from being caught snooping by the person pausing to call something back over his shoulder. "Yes, I'll get to it later."

The same slick man from Zemo's the previous night enters, carrying a short stack of manila folders. Today, he wears an open-collar, white shirt under a black vest. No sunglasses, but his hair shines a black gloss.

He doesn't offer a handshake. "Haven't we met?"

"Not formally," I say. "Sabastian Habeck, private investigator." I pause. "Fisher didn't fill you in?"

"Right." He remembers.

The questions are: how much information did Fisher give him… and how much does he have on his own?

"Have a seat," he says and gestures to the couch. "Let's talk."

I glance at the couch and don't want to imagine what activities it has experienced in its lifetime. Prentiss laughs at my discomfort and points to a high stool next to the camera. I slide it over, and soon we're facing each other across the work counter. He places the folders near the screen, gives me an askance look, and clicks the mouse. The folders disappear, leaving the blank desktop with an array of icons.

"The stage is yours," he says.

I decide to treat Prentiss as if he already knows the situation and see how far I can go. "I have yet to discover the reason for Annabelle's disappearance, if the choice was hers. I'm checking all angles, and since you and Fisher are friends, I thought you might have some ideas."

He blinks a couple times, shows a toothy smile. "Annabelle. I'm sorry. I don't know any Annabelle. There is an Anna Belle who went pro several years ago."

"Forgive me," I say. "I thought you and Fisher had discussed this last night."

He draws out his answer, "Nooo, sorry. I stopped in for a drink. We talked sports."

The lies pour like water from a leaky hose.

"How much are you involved in the negotiations with Roger Lansing and East Fourth Street?" I ask.

A head shake. "Almost nothing except for what Randy shares. Apparently, it's been a dicey issue of late."

"You have no interest?"

He shrugs. "For what reason? I have my office here and a combination studio and post-production facility in a warehouse a mile north on Murphy Street. There is nothing about East Fourth to attract me."

My turn to shrug. "From what I understand, more business on Fourth means more potential customers for Fisher... in a number of ways."

Prentiss gives me another shark-like smile. "I don't know what you mean. Just because I patronize Zemo's for a drink or two now and again doesn't mean Randy and I talk shop. Yes, he's mentioned Roger and some of the plans, but that's about it." He straightens his shoulders. "My office here isn't the Capitol Center, but consider the nature of the business. It's all legal, and so are the ages of the actresses. However, I understand the perception of the general public of what I do. I admit that my production company is not high class, but we fill a niche."

He makes sleaze, but why bring down this conversation even further with the truth? We both know the score.

A.L. is supposed to star in what sounds like a compilation video on January 7. Maybe.

If A.L. is who I think she is, I hope I find her first.

There are a lot of players in this case. The tenuous stings touch, but the solid ties have yet to be found.

CHAPTER
TWENTY-EIGHT

SIXTH AVENUE, from University north to where it sneaks behind the Bridgestone Tire plant, passes through a beefsteak of old town Des Moines. Marbled into the meat are layers of Latinos, Blacks, and middle-class Whites. Residential intersperses with businesses across the industry spectrum. A detail shop, bakery, Italian restaurant, a nightclub, and pet store.

The building housing The Magical Lens sits next to a tire shop and across Oak Park Avenue from a funeral home. One story, but deep like Prentiss's office. Weathered, rusty red wood. Hand-crafted sign under the eaves. Before I reached the entrance to the photographer's lot, I veer into the tire place. A ten-foot-high wall blocks my view of the other building. More importantly, it blocks the view of my car from the person who walks outside as I drive up.

Randy Fisher.

I recognize him in an instant and, though his presence doesn't leave me chapfallen, I wonder why the pesky nightclub owner keeps popping up. First at Porto's investment office, now here. The first I can understand, but I cannot see him scheduling a session for himself or his boy Rusty.

I swerve into the tire place because I don't want to add to Fisher's suspicions. He's already on my radar in my case. I'm sure he was involved in my car's vandalism last night, directly or otherwise.

The wall of the lot ends at the entrance. I turn in my seat and wait until Fisher's car passes before I put mine in reverse. Too late. An employee approaches. Jeans, stained, long-sleeved work shirt, oily work boots, drawn and dark-skinned face. The patch sewn to his shirt reads Felipe. I roll down my window.

"How can I help you, amigo?" he asks.

My car has needed new tires for months. I should have changed them out last fall before the cold weather set in.

I'm about to give him an excuse. *Sorry, my mistake. Just turning around.* Or *Answering a phone call…*

Okay, that one won't work since I don't own a cell phone. I remember Anne's pursed lips when I gave her a lame excuse when she commented on the tires. *Uh, I don't have the time.*

I look at Felipe. In turn, he gazes at the condition of my tires, smiles, and raises his eyebrows.

What the heck.

Minutes later, I agree to a set of refurbished tires for a reasonable cost. Felipe has the size in stock, throws balancing in for a discounted price, and says he can get started soon, the entire switchover done in forty-five minutes.

That gives me enough time to walk next door.

Instead of a bell announcing my entrance, a grating buzzer sounds. The lobby doubles as a galley of framed photos. Single-person shots of teenagers. Couples—spouses, siblings, nerdy guy with prom date. Family photos against backdrops both artificial and natural.

I step up to an empty reception counter next to a closed door. No movement or sound from down the hall or elsewhere save for the hum of centralized heating. A silver bell on the counter provides another way to gain attention, but if no one heard the buzzer, I doubt anyone would respond to a metallic ding.

The desktop below extends past the edge of the counter. I don't have to lean over to see someone left in the middle of settling accounts, both payable and receivable. Open bill statements for utilities, internet provider, and a bill for materials from Roderick Lighting. A booklet of business-sized checks with the green dot matrix background.

Three checks nearby. Two payable to Lori Kozar. One signed by Mel Prentiss, the other by Randy Fisher. The third check is a payment to Kym Malin. Empty envelopes addressed to both Prentiss and Malin.

What do I make of all this? Before I'm able to contemplate further, a door down the hall opens and two sets of footsteps sound on the hardwood floor. Two women enter the reception cubicle. This morning, the shorter chose a mauve sweater over black dress slacks. Black clouds of curls give her a grown-up Shirley Temple look.

The other stands tall and lithe and lean and smooth from skin to bronze hair that drapes six inches below her shoulder. Midnight blue slacks and jacket, white shirt buttoned to the top. The epitome of the professional woman.

Before she can speak, the shorter woman says, "Oh, look, Ms. Kozar. Mr. Fisher dropped off his check."

Kozar fails to keep the vertical forehead crease from forming, nor does she keep her lips from thinning. The expression lasts a second before resuming normal calm.

"Yes, Leena," Kozar says with clipped words. "Why don't you take everything to my office and I'll finish them later?"

Leena's demeanor falls faster than an anvil dropped from the roof. Her body withdraws into itself, meek, as if she spilled coffee over a bunch of final prints. "Yes, Ms. Kozar."

Without another word, she gathers up the checks, checkbook, and statements, and scurries from the room.

"I apologize," Kozar says, the graceful Siamese who just batted away the nettlesome mouse. "How can I help you?"

I pause before answering to consider Kozar's reaction to a seemingly innocent remark by her assistant. Okay, the girl shouldn't spout out names of… what would I call Randy Fisher? Client? Customer? Perhaps… associate? In what aspect? Whatever applied, names shouldn't be bandied about in front of strangers. However, Kozar was more… annoyed…? miffed…? on edge…? than normal. A polite request for the girl to repair to the back would have been more professional. Admonish her later.

Knowing what I do and what I've seen raises my interests and suspicions. Will my name raise hers?

I bite the bullet and introduce myself. "Are you familiar with the name Annabelle Lansing?"

The emerald in her eyes turns moldy, but this time, she holds strong save for a slight tightening of her cheeks.

"Yes," she says. "I'd have to check, but she was in here a month ago. If I recall, the session was an early Christmas present from her… boyfriend, I guess." She pauses, then as if at that moment another recollection hits her, "Oh, yes. She said she was referred by a friend."

"Kym Malin?"

Kozar's brows rise a millimeter. *Have I added a degree of heat?*

"Yes. Malin... well, she's not officially on the payroll, but she refers many clients to us."

Enough to leave the amount I saw on the check? Those numbers will keep Malin in frothy refreshments for the foreseeable future.

"I'm talking to people Annabelle met in the last two or three months," I say. "Trying to find what she'd been doing and where she might have gone after the first of the year."

"I don't understand," Kozar says.

"Her mother's worried. Annabelle hasn't been seen since New Year's Eve."

"I see. Well, I, uh, don't know how I can help. She hasn't been back since, I think, early December. Like I said, she came in with her boyfriend for some pictures."

"What was your impression of her?" I ask. "Attitude. Mindset. General demeanor."

She offered a patronizing smile, as if I'd asked to see her tax returns. "Mr. Habeck, I'm sorry. I see a lot of customers every week. Most, like Annabelle, are one-time meetings. During our time together, I'm trying to get the best possible pictures. I'm not here for a psychological analysis. I'm a photographer."

"Yes, ma'am. I understand."

"Sure, if a particular person becomes... difficult, I might remember." She shrugs. "As for Annabelle, dark hair, pretty. I can show you a gallery of prints from the shoot, but I can't recall much more."

The facts of Randy Fisher's visit, his check, and the payments from Prentiss and to Malin reeks of much more. Kozar's not telling me all the facts. If I ask about her connection to Fisher, she might say *customer*, or perhaps *family album photos*. I still don't have enough information to push.

Instead, I thank Ms. Kozar for her time. Before I try and leave, Leena pokes her head into the room. "Ms. Kozar, may I take my lunch? We worked through my normal time setting things up for—"

"Yes, yes," Kozar says. "I'll finish up."

Leena disappears. Kozar offers a strained but gracious smile and I leave.

Outside, I fire up a Lucky as I walk back to the tire shop. Halfway across the parking lot, someone behind me whispers my name in a loud hiss. I stop and swivel my head. Leena, partially hidden behind the far corner, waves at me. I start toward her, but she holds up a hand, peers over her shoulder, then quick-steps to me.

"Let's go next door," she whispers.

She donned a bulky winter coat before exiting The Magical Lens. Sky blue with puffy sleeves and a hood that has enough fur lining to see her through an Antarctic expedition.

She glances over her shoulder again before we reach the perimeter wall of the tire shop. I lead her to the spot where I'd parked earlier to hide from Fisher. Despite the coat, Leena shivers. Like a contagious yawn, I shiver, too, aware the temperature this afternoon hasn't changed. The cold front acts like a battalion of soldiers beating down the castle door as it drives into my overcoat's weakening defenses.

"I need to talk to you," Leena says.

I doubt she wants to invite me to lunch. "Yes?"

"Ms. Kozar. She—" Another shiver "—lied to you."

I glance to my right. The closed doors to the two bays keep anyone from overhearing. Traffic slushes past on Sixth.

I smoke. "How so?"

"About Annabelle Lansing."

The short answers could take a while to reach a substantive end. I won't bogart her into talking in case I scare her off, but my headaches and the cold exasperate my exhaustion.

"Why don't you tell me what you know and we can both get to warmer places?" I say.

Her brunneous eyes widen, and her head nods as fast as she shivers. "Annabelle didn't come only one time."

"She returned. Alone? With this boyfriend?"

"No… wait. Let me start from the beginning."

"Please do."

"I've been working here only since September," Leena says. "I'm trying to be a professional photographer. Ms. Kozar needed a receptionist. Well, she calls me an assistant, but I don't do a lot of assisting. I mean, she shows me how the cameras work and gives me tips on setting up shots right but—"

"Annabelle?" I interrupt.

"Oh, sure. Sorry. Anyway, for a while, I've had suspicions Ms. Kozar does more than senior pictures and photos of newborns in wicker baskets."

My lips twitch as a memory of a picture comes to mind. Baby

me in one of those straw or twig-lined beds or containers. Instead of looking cute partially wrapped in a blanket, I thought I looked like the next honoree for a Viking funeral, the torch bearer just off camera. When did I dispose of that picture… or did I?

"What else do you think she does?" I ask.

"I'm not completely sure, but I can guess." She bundles the coat tighter to her body, as if that guess adds more frigidity to the scene. "Did you see the checks on the desk?"

"Yes," I say.

"And the names?"

"Kym Malin. Prentiss Productions. Randy Fisher. You said his name."

"Right. Ms. Kozar was waiting for his payment."

"Do you know what the check is for?"

She makes a quick head shake.

"He stopped in minutes before I arrived," I say.

"Right. I heard the buzzer, but neither of us could get to it."

"Okay."

"Damn," she huffs. "I keep getting this out of order."

By this time, I'm down to the end of the cigarette. I toss it aside where it hisses to death in a layer of snow. "Take it easy, and just tell me."

"After the shoot with Annabelle, the first one, I overheard Ms. Kozar on the phone in her office. I don't think she realizes how thin the walls are. I can hear practically every word from my desk."

Decades-old building. Even renovated, unless walls were built, eavesdropping wouldn't be difficult.

"She asked for Kym Malin," Leena says. "Then she talked

about Annabelle's photo session. She wanted to confirm with Malin that Annabelle would make a good candidate."

"Candidate?" I ask. "For what?"

Leena glances around. Still no one in sight. "Dirty magazines," she says very low. "Maybe, you know, *adult* movies."

I wait. Leena, now bolstered, doesn't hesitate.

"Annabelle was in on Tuesday. I saw her for a second out the front window. They brought her in through the back door."

"They?"

"I didn't see the driver," Leena says. "Before Ms. Kozar went to the back, she asked me to tell any caller or visitor she'd be busy for an hour. And she told me not to bother her." A pause. "I didn't check, but I think she locked the studio door."

She wants to tell me more, but I have to play doubter. "Back for a follow-up session."

"Maybe." Leena hedges, hesitates. Cautious.

I soften my voice. "What is it, Leena?"

"She took… nude photos. Ms. Kozar left early that afternoon. I got curious, so I… I took the SD card from the camera and inserted it into the machine she uses to sort out images. It connects to the computer. About thirty or so photos of Annabelle… naked. Not p—pornographic, but, you know, like for a centerfold."

"You don't think Annabelle commissioned them," I say.

A head shake. "I don't know, but I didn't like it. Not just because she was nude. I didn't know Ms. Kozar did that kind of work. Annabelle… well—" Leena takes a breath and lets it all out. "I don't think she was a willing participant. She looked tired, groggy, as if…"

In an instant, her resolve falters and ceases. I understand.

Connections. Kym to Annabelle to Kozar to Prentiss. And

Fisher? Where did his link hook up? If, as Leena suspects is true, that Anabelle did not consent to the nude photos, and if what Leticia said happens at Zemo's…

Connections, yes, but still emerging from the fog. Logical explanations could solve everything.

But where was Annabelle?

I thank Leena, scoot her off to lunch, and retrieve my car after a ten-minute wait.

I'll make one more stop, but first, it's time to talk to Anne. She deserves to know what I've discovered since Wednesday.

TWENTY-NINE

THE ELEVATOR LIFTS me to my floor. When it stops, I wait an extra second for the car to settle with a minor juddering, as if a giant thumb presses it into place. The doors slide to the side and I step out. Halfway down the hall, two men with oxen frames walk toward my office. Shoulders broad enough to support yokes, the men can't walk side by side without brushing the walls.

They don't knock, but open the office door and enter. I trail along behind, stopping five feet from the open entry.

A silence follows in which I imagine Anne, sitting behind her desk, sizing up the two bridge stanchions.

"May I help you?" Anne asks.

Hear that, Johnny? They haven't said a word, but I bet they aren't here fronting for the Girl Scouts on the annual cookie sales. Yet, Anne's tone remains cool, professional. I imagine her welcoming smile… as her right hand slips under the desk.

"Your boss in?" one of the guys says.

"May I ask the nature of your business?" Anne asks.

A pause, then the same guy says, "Yeah. We want to make sure he understood some… information he was given last night."

"It's come to our attention that he may not have," the second guy says.

They're trying to play the high-minded language game with Anne. She'll win.

"If you'll leave your names and a number he can call, I'll be certain to ask him to contact you," she says.

Another pause. Are they deciding what to do next?

"If he don't understand from last night, maybe he will if we give her the same message," the second guy says.

"Yeah," his partner agrees. "Might be fun."

Aw, hell, why did they do that? I know Anne can handle herself, and I know I'm not feeling one hundred percent after my little episode last night, but I don't want a mess to clean up. I step into view, just outside the door. "You'd better rethink your plan."

Startled, they jerk toward me. One shifts so he's not hidden behind his buddy.

"You Habeck?" The first guy takes a step toward me.

I smile and hold up a palm. "Unless you're walking out of the office intending to leave the building, I don't think you should move."

Two sets of dark eyes narrow. "Why not?" asks the first guy.

I raise my chin a millimeter. "Notice the lady's hand under the desk?"

Two sets of dark eyes dart to Anne.

"She's not throwing away a tissue," I say.

Two sets of dark eyes return to me.

"If you have a message to deliver, then *say* it." I smile. "Anything else, and I'll have to replace her desk."

Two sets of pudgy lips frown. They want to do more than talk, but the threat keeps them from acting. It also removes any verbal threat they want to make. Instead, they try to deliver the message telepathically by staring at me for ten seconds. I back away and, as if rehearsed, they step into the hall and walk toward the elevator without a backward glance.

I wait until the car descends before I enter the office and close the door. Only then does Anne remove her hand. She swallows, regains whatever minor composure she lost with a long, drawn-out breath. "I don't know what you've uncovered in this case, Sabastian, but whatever it is has stirred up worry in someone."

We understand some people don't have the best intentions when they walk in the door, whether they are here for the investigation side or a business venture for Anne. Some of her tenants have turned out to be, if not hostile, then more than irked at some of her decisions. So far, nothing untoward has occurred, but if verbal push comes to physical shove, Anne is prepared with a Smith and Wesson .38 tucked under the middle drawer, positioned for an easy draw or to fire through the back of the desk.

I recall the parties I've spoken to over the last two days. "Someone thinks my questions came too close to revealing something meant to stay hidden."

"Annabelle?"

"I don't know," I say. "We should talk."

Her expression goes blank. She doesn't like the phrase any more than I do. It portends an unpleasant scene with knowledge one person isn't going to enjoy.

I notice one object missing. "Do you have Annabelle's laptop?"

She opens the top drawer of the desk, withdraws the

computer, and places it on the desk. "Thought I'd keep it out of sight during business hours."

I admire her insight. Not sure whether the two most recent visitors would have recognized it or understood its significance, but why take chances?

I remove my coat, hang it on the nearby coat rack, and sit on the couch, the laptop on the small table in front of me. Anne joins me. Her closeness creates a warm tingle on my skin. In deference, I resist the urge to light a Lucky.

As I summarize the interviews, hitting the salient points, the room darkens as the clouded sun moves toward the horizon. Neither of us bothers to turn on any lights.

I omit nothing, even bringing in Timothy and his nameless, shopkeeper aunt.

Anne frowns but doesn't look away when I tell her about Pam Hollis. I'm not five minutes into my report but her softening attitude cools.

"I never cheated on you with her," I say.

Anne nods. "Go on."

Leon. Roger. "He described some of what he wants to happen on East Fourth," I say.

"That damn project," Anne says in a low voice.

"I believe someone used the stalled negotiations as an opportunity."

Amos. "Kid'll be on blood pressure medicine before he graduates," I say.

Kym. "Showed her true colors when she recommended Kozar's studio."

Randy. "Definitely won't win the city's entrepreneur of the year award."

Annabelle's former employer at Lupo's. "I think the girl had a head for business, even if she didn't realize it."

Donna. Her mother. Chris Laine. "Bribes?" Anne asks.

Stephan Marshe and the confirmation of the affair with Arlene. "Oh, no," Anne breathes.

Porto. "No direct evidence of wrongdoing," I say. "I do find it coincidental that two players in this case use him."

Prentiss and Kozar. "What can you say? I don't know if Annabelle fell behind his lens, but she definitely was behind hers."

At this point, I power up the laptop and navigate to Annabelle's online video journal. I scroll to the entries I viewed.

The more she watches, the more Anne's stalwartness sinks, falters, weakens. By the time she reaches November of the previous year, she's pressed herself against me, as if the couch shrank little by little over the days and months of Annabelle's blogs.

The background lighting dims throughout the entries. By the time we reach the middle of November, she's raised the window blinds. Grayish-yellow light, as if from a sunrise, brightens the room. It's not a complete refreshment, but the promise, or maybe hope, of one.

November 15, 20-

I met someone at a Halloween party. I didn't want to go, but Kym dragged me to it, saying a lot of cute guys would be there. I didn't care.

I sat by myself most of the evening. I didn't wear a costume, but no one noticed. They all thought I'd come as some goth girl.

Then this guy sat down next to me and offered me a beer. He wore faded blue jeans and a leather jacket and had way too much oil in his hair.

He introduced himself as James Dean and looked at me as if I should know him. When I didn't say anything, he said, "Actually, I'm Jason Weber."

He told me he attended Drake University and worked part-time for his dad, who ran a semi-truck dealership.

Anyway, we talked for about an hour before leaving together. I don't think Kym even noticed or cared. Later, I told her I'd taken a cab home.

Jason and I drove around for a while drinking beers and smoking joints. We ended up in Walnut State Park and made out. I... think he understands me. I haven't told him about my stupid family, but maybe I will. He's a nice guy.

"Oh, no," Anne says.

December 6

Jason and I have gone out a few times, and each time he tells me I'm pretty. He also said he had a surprise for me. I kept asking what it was, but he wouldn't tell me.

Well, today he wanted to take me to a photographer for some pictures I might show to modeling agencies, that it was an early Christmas present. I called Kym and she mentioned one particular place.

I was so nervous, but the photographer was really nice and helped me pick out the right clothes and jewelry and even gave me advice on make-up and hair.

It was so cool and Jason was so sweet. I've been thinking about what I want to do for a long time. If Jason and I... well, more later. Christmas is this month, and I want to be sure he receives the best present.

The smile brightens her entire face and lifts her attitude to a high point not seen in months.

December 25

Today is going to be a great Christmas. I've never really enjoyed past years, at least as far back as I can remember. They've always been boring dates my parents felt obligated to celebrate. We either hosted or visited family members when Mom and Dad would rather have been at their offices slaving away.

The house is decorated, the tree is lit, but these people are false. I see through them. They're nothing, and they've created nothing. Amos and I, the obligatory children, are nothing. We were meant to be programmable entities, not humans with lives.

Amos can't handle it. He'll fail, and then what will happen? Amos is a nothing. I have become a nothing. The man I call Dad doesn't see me and doesn't care. My mother is a fake, a fraud. I am nothing to her because she can't acknowledge who I might be.

Enough about my stupid family. I'm a little sad because I called Jason a week ago and he wanted to take a break from our relationship. "Call me after the first of the year." Please! He didn't even want to spend New Year's Eve together. I mean, I thought he was my boyfriend.

He'll change his mind, though, when I give him the good news. Everything will change. I will be someone. Forget the stupid presents wrapped in pretty paper and bows, Jason and I will be given a gift no one can take away. Only a couple of minutes in the bathroom, and I'll be back with the good news. I may even share this with my friends. What a great way for everyone to find out.

Anne clicks the mouse, but no new window appears. "This is the last entry," she says. "Poor girl. I wish I had known. I… could have done something, talked with her."

I stay silent. The result of the test must have devastated Annabelle so much she didn't have the strength or the willpower to create further video entries.

"She wanted to feel something," Anne whispers. "She wanted someone to love and who would love her back unconditionally." She suddenly grasps my arm. "Oh, Sabastian, you don't think…"

I shake my head. "I don't know." My voice is flat. "There's more."

She swallows and turns glistening eyes to mine. Her strained expression says she doesn't want more, and the ache that gouges my heart gives me pause. However…

Kozar. Leena.

Anne's face, always so professional, so resolved, unyielding, and beautiful, crumbles to despair. Droplets form at the corners of her eyes. "You have to find her, Sabastian. You have to…" Her voice catches.

I nod once and she collapses into me, head against my chest.

The year's newness has disappeared as the cruelty and heartlessness beneath gains dominance. Outside, a heavy veil slowly slips over the sun. The light fades for an early dusk.

I don't know the direction I will take, but feel it to be a Hobson's choice. It's an uncertain future, one as cold and as bleak as the myriad shadows that create soulless and blurred patterns on the office furniture, walls, and upon two disparate creatures. We sit, Anne and I, alone together, to endure our own burdens with only brief touches and words of comfort.

I gently rest my hand on Anne's shoulder and feel the vibration of her body as she silently sobs.

I wish I could have stayed drunk and missed it all.

CHAPTER
THIRTY

ANNE CHECKS ONLINE TO give me the address of Weber Trucks. I miss the days of the Yellow Pages, Johnny, but she retrieves the information in about half the time. After she assures me she's composed and offers an encouraging word, I drive through the never-ending snowfall to the large dealership overlooking State Highway 28, near the metro's southern bypass. This area has remained popular and prosperous despite the west side's unrestrained growth. Large office buildings, a golf course, and even a supposedly attractive housing development lead into Valley Junction... the eclectic origins of West Des Moines.

A sentinel line of black Kenworth cabs sits on the crest of raised ground that overlooks the highway. I pull into the driveway, my car looking like the slovenly peasant seeking admittance past the castle's stately guards.

In the main office building, I inquire after Jason Weber. A stout man, who'd be more relaxed in farmer's overalls rather than the brown dress shirt and slacks he wears, directs me to the service shop. It's a massive structure separated from the main lot by a peninsula of trees. There's enough space to comfortably enclose eight rigs with room to spare.

Wheeled tool cabinets, each the height of a gas pump and the width of a dumpster, dot the expansive floor. Overhead tracks for hoists line the ceiling. The cold air carries the odors of exhaust, oil, and steel.

I find Jason, clipboard in hand, inventorying parts behind a roughed, scarred, and stained counter. Annabelle's video journal said he'd introduced himself at a Halloween party as James Dean. I note a trace resemblance in the high forehead, gentle round chin, serious mouth, and the actor's distinctive hairstyle. A youthful appearance, though, and I guess he's no more than mid-twenties. He's dressed in a blue work shirt and pants. His left hand curls grotesquely around the top of the clipboard as he scribbles notes.

I once read many southpaws contort their hands in such a manner to better control the pen, whereas the right hand naturally leads the writing implement across the page. He squints at me when I say his name. I introduce myself, my purpose, and ask for a few minutes, preferably in a quieter setting. Grumbling vibrations of engines, while not deafening, are not conducive to conversation.

Jason grabs a jacket, and we step outside. Under the protection of the roof overhang, we watch snow pile up on trailers, storage outbuildings, and a small collection of truck cabs from the seventies rusting away in a back corner. Snow falls and the shop's wall muffles the trucks' engines.

Jason shivers once, but I'm comfortable. There is no wind, and the cold eases around me like a cloak, not yet intrusive. I light up a Lucky, inhale once, and look at the kid. "Tell me about Annabelle."

Hands in his pockets, he shrugs. "I don't know. We went out a few times."

"I understand you two met at a party."

"Yeah, the whole thing was pretty lame. The usual, you know. Music, drinks. I just dropped by to check it out, didn't plan on staying long. She was sitting by herself, so I thought I'd say hello."

Jason and I stand a few inches apart, breaths forming temporary clouds. We're two men in dark clothes in a white world.

"Tell me about her," I repeat.

Another shrug. "She's okay. What's this about? Why are you asking about her?"

"She contact you in the last week?"

"Naw, I ain't seen her since before Christmas. She texted several times, left voicemails."

Texting. Basically, phone email, and a stupid idea. It's a phone, for heaven's sake, not a typewriter.

He shifts his feet a bit. I sense he's hedging. "Talk to me," I urge upon an exhalation of smoke. I toss away the dead soldier to be buried unceremoniously in white. "I'm not here to judge, just wanting information."

He tilts his head to one shoulder. "She's cool, you know? Not like a lot of girls. She didn't act all conceited. Some girls know they're attractive and want everyone to notice."

"Not Annabelle?"

"No. I mean she's pretty. She just didn't show it very often. I thought all girls wanted to look good." He shrugs. "I could talk to her. I don't think she did very well in school, but she is smart. From what little she said, I don't think her family treats her well."

He pauses. This time, I let him come to it by himself. "I thought I could be a good friend. She seemed, well..."

"Lonely?"

He nods. A feeling they both shared. Being lonely together lessened the impact.

"Jason, Annabelle's been missing since New Year's."

"Really? Like I said, I haven't seen her since before Christmas."

"She kept one of those online video journals. I watched some of the entries, trying to find clues to her disappearance." He meets my eye, but waits for me to speak. "Tell me about the photo shoot."

"Well, like I said, she'd been feeling pretty bad about her family. She didn't say anything that first night. You know, you don't bring up problems on a first date."

"Sure." I light another cigarette.

"She didn't seem to like herself, which was stupid. Not her. I mean, she's not stupid, just that she was down on herself. I tried to cheer her up, take her to some fun places. Anyway, I wanted to do something special for her, give her a chance to feel good about herself. Who knows? You hear about some girls who meet the right person and the next thing you know, they're on the cover of fashion magazines."

Or those of prurient quality.

"Uncle Ray pays me pretty well here at the shop, and I'd saved enough, so I thought I'd give Annabelle an early Christmas present. When I told her, she said a friend of hers recommended The Magical Lens."

"What did she think?" I ask.

"She loved it. One of the few times I've seen her enjoying something. The photographer said she'd see if some of the pictures could be featured on the website. Agencies look at photographer sites for potential models. Advertisers for television commercials, too."

As well as other businesses, if the monitor at Prentiss Productions and Leena's story are indicative of anything. I don't want to come across as a custos morum, but I brook the relevant point. "What about the last time you two were together? What happened?"

His chin rises in a sense of honorable defiance. "What do you mean?"

I say nothing, but maintain eye contact as I smoke my Lucky.

When he realizes I'm not going to give any ground, he looks away. "It wasn't like what you think."

"Help me understand," I say.

He hems and haws, but in the end, he gives up and states his case, "I could tell, you know? She'd been thinking about it for a while. I was cool, didn't want to rush or force anything. Like I said, we talked a lot. Along with the photo session, I gave her this small, silver heart pendant I'd seen in some store. Nothing fancy, but I thought she'd like it. Patricia let her wear it during the shoot." His head jerks back to me and fire flashes in his eyes. "That night, she clutched that pendant the entire time. Kept a tight fist around it." His voice lowers. "Afterward, when I helped put it around her neck, she cried. I thought I'd done something wrong, but she seemed so happy." Again, he turns away.

I wait a couple moments before asking, "Were you happy?"

He can't decide on a reaction. "Yeah, I guess. Happy for different reasons."

I smoke some more.

"You know how it is. It felt, well, I cared about her. I wanted to be sure she…" He shakes his head, confused. "She wasn't mean in that it was all for her, but in a way, well, I just can't explain it." He pauses. "Anyway, the next time we talked, she was excited and wanted to see me again. Started talking about getting out of her house, maybe moving in together, what did I think… I mean we'd been seeing each other only a short time and despite the Christmas present and, you know, that one time… well, that was a little much. Too strong."

"You broke off the relationship?" I ask.

"No. I mean, yes." He shakes his head again. "What I said was we should take a break, get through the holidays, and catch up after New Year's."

"You didn't want to celebrate the 'out with the old, in with the new' with her?"

His lips tighten. "Look, I try not to be a jerk around women, okay? But there are limits. Like I said, she was coming on a bit strong, and I'd already made plans with some of my friends. If she hadn't been so… clingy, I might have invited her along."

"How did she react when you told her you didn't want to see her until after the new year?" I ask.

Only a half shrug. "A little disappointed, I guess. Otherwise, she seemed pretty cool about it. Sounded like she was either distracted or was thinking about something else."

I understand. Watching Annabelle's videos, I can explain to him all about it. She, too, cared about Jason, but as a means to an end. I don't believe she went into it with cruel intentions, but she left some scars even if the boy doesn't acknowledge them. She wanted a drastic change from what she'd been living with for years. A chance to start over, do things right with *her* child. She didn't call this week to see if Jason wanted to go out because she had no good news to tell him. By breaking contact after the failure to conceive, she banished Jason to the realm of those who couldn't help, and, in a sense, he didn't matter any longer. Because in her mind, *she* didn't matter.

He looks at me again. "I almost expected her to call sometime this week." He shrugs. "I was going to call her after work tonight. It's a little late and she might have plans, but…" Another shrug. "Do you know why she didn't?"

Yes, but I'm not the one to explain. Why crush his spirit further? He's almost moved on anyway. Better to let him think she ended their relationship just because.

"Do you know where she is?" he asks.

I shake my head, flick away the cigarette, thank the kid for his time, and make my leave of him. I had indicated I was ignorant of the girl's location, but I know differently.

Annabelle may have gone to a place to find herself, but I fear others found her first.

THIRTY-ONE

FRIDAY AFTERNOON. I step out of the car and feel the frenzy of rush hour as a soft, electric vibration on the currents of frigid air. The anticipation and anxieties, the plans, schemes, goals, and dreams for the upcoming weekend.

Freedom. Fewer responsibilities. A time to break out and escape. New Year's is over, but an entire year of Saturdays and Sundays waits to be celebrated.

Except by me.

I open the door to the office.

Anne's head turns toward me. She half-rises. "Sabastian…"

After our *moment* earlier, I told her about the plan to see the last person on my list. Her tight, strained expression now wants to know how I am, where I've been, if a miracle happened and I found Annabelle.

I lean against the door frame, release a long breath, and offer a small head shake. Her pained disappointment lances my heart, but the "I-know-you're-doing-your-best" tilt of her head and soft smiles crushes me.

"I've called a dozen people, Sabastian," she says when I drop onto the couch. "Anyone I thought might help."

I nod. Weariness settles like a thick blanket over me.

My head throbs with a dull ache.

Anne stands and puts an ashtray on the table in front of me.

My limbs feel like anchors, and I don't have the strength to fire up a cigarette.

"Do you want some supper?" she asks.

A nice gesture and any other time I'd accept. "Don't you have some function or event to attend tonight?" I ask. Her calendar is usually booked a couple months in advance.

"Not tonight," she answers. "I thought I'd visit Arlene."

I nod, and my eyes close.

"Why don't you go home, Sabastian? You're exhausted and injured. You're not going to accomplish anything more today."

I nod again. "I will. I'll just rest here for a while. Maybe do some paperwork." I open one eye to see if she bought my line.

Her lips tighten. "You don't have any paperwork, Sabastian."

I shrug.

"When was the last time you filled out a case report?"

I breathe in, think for a second, breathe out, and shrug again. "My girl, Friday," I say. I'm not certain when I last used the sentiment, but she accepts the compliment. I love Anne and need her in my life. I'd fall into a deep pit without her.

A sigh escapes my lips. Jackie's blow to my head must have affected me worse than I thought if I'm waxing romantic. Better jump off the rail before I say something stupid, like asking her to marry me again.

Memories flood in. Happier times when I'd buy her flowers and presents just because. I tried to make the marriage work. She was patient, but I kept rubbing the polish off that patience. Every time she introduced some new technological change, I'd balk. Sometimes she'd return it, other times, she'd keep it to use for herself. Computers and other electronics. Accounting and e-banking, a new car with too many gadgets. Invitations to join her in business ventures even if they were on the side, something for which I could be responsible.

My reaction to all was to shy away, spend more time in the bars. Smoke and drink too much. I don't know what the last straw was, and I doubt it was one particular thing. The accumulation built up, and it was her turn to step back, re-evaluate her life, my life... our lives. The night she laid the situation out, it wasn't an ultimatum—you do this, stop this or else—but rather this-is-the-way-things-are-and-what-they-will-be. I don't recall arguing, begging, or pleading for another chance. I knew the score and accepted it.

Afterward... I'm surprised she's stayed around. I don't remember feeling weird that she became my office manager, financial planner, and arm's length friend. She still supports and encourages me, and she knows I need that. I don't take it for granted, and her presence does help, in some small way, to keep me from chucking it all in and spending every hour in the bar or at home with a case of whiskey.

Anne tidies her already immaculate desk, dons her coat, and, before leaving, lightly kisses my forehead, her palm against my cheek.

See what I mean, Johnny?

"Go home, Sabastian," she whispers, her lips brushing my other cheek.

They're warm and soft, and, if she doesn't leave soon, I'm going to say to hell with my sore head and sluggish muscles, take her in my arms, and consecrate the couch.

"I bought new tires earlier," I say.

The hint of a smile appears, the minutest raising of the corners of her mouth. Her eyes still have a suspicious nature that sees through my half-truth.

"Okay, refurbished."

The smile broadens a quarter inch. "Call me tomorrow," she says. "I want to know how you're feeling. If you get weak or dizzy tonight, call me."

I'm weaker by the second, but not from the injury. Just before she leaves, I say her name, but nothing else. I cannot wrap my mind, let alone my tongue, around words that… well, nothing she doesn't already know.

The room goes silent for three seconds. No breath or rustle of clothing. She gives me a simple nod then walks away.

Anne's gone, but her essence remains. The press of her lips on my skin lingers, but not long enough.

I tilt to one side, slide into a fetal position, and drift off to sleep.

Anne

She rides down in the elevator, walks across the lobby, and outside to her car. At the alley entrance, emotions rise, blur her vision. She shifts back into park. Her hands remain on the steering wheel, her foot on the brake.

Breaths catch in her throat. Her chest hurts with each inhale. She coughs on each exhale.

Sabastian.

He is such a stubborn, stupid man who…

She should march back up there, drag him out of the office, and make him…

He won't change. He can't. All her words and haranguing haven't done a bit of good.

He is what he is, and she understands this. If he were any different, she wouldn't feel the way she does. If he were a different man, she wouldn't have had Arlene visit him in the first place.

Why can't he be different? Just a little bit? Is it too much to ask for just an inch?

Damn, stubborn, stupid man. Doesn't know when to give up. Doesn't know how.

She knows she's confusing his effort in this case with her attempts to make him into a better man in social, professional, and personal relationships. Too often, the two become muzzy, so convoluted she sometimes can't separate which of Sabastian's personalities she is speaking to—the stalwart detective or the obstinate man. Maybe one depends on the other. Or the two are so enmeshed she can't separate them. This could explain her constant frustration at trying to change him. When she plucks at one, she tugs at the other, and the result is only further resistance on his part.

This case, though, has touched a personal note for both of them. He wants to succeed, not only to find her niece but because to fail, in his mind, adds another failure in her eyes.

That notion only brings her closer to him. They shared a tender moment earlier when he showed her Annabelle's video blogs and the troubles in the Lansing household. She'd felt anguish for Annabelle; a touch of anger for her sister, brother in-law, and even her nephew because she understood what Sabastian had mentioned about the apathy toward Annabelle's development over the years with her moving in another direction. What those videos did was spur her to action, making phone calls, including to the police for an update, badgering Pam Hollis and giving her names. Perhaps with the combined efforts of Sabastian and the police, talking to people again, something will slip out, some clue to find Annabelle.

She wipes her eyes, and resolves to, yes, go be a support for Arlene and Roger, but also to talk. The discussion wouldn't be easy, but maybe they would all find something to start the recovery process if they took a cold, hard look at everything.

Easing her way south on Seventh, she understood, she, too, needed a recovery of sorts. Today, she waited for Sabastion and worried when he left. She wanted to—what? Continue the moment from earlier?

Is she crazy thinking this way? That they could ever be a couple, a real couple, a married couple, again? Yes, he still loves her. She knows this, but surely, he has to know it could never work out. Is he thinking it might? Is he wanting to try again? What about her?

Of course not. Okay, she still harbors feelings for him.

Love?

Maybe.

She's smart enough to realize they couldn't live together, be married to each other, but maybe being together, in this current… well, relationship, for lack of a better word, is what works.

Tears flow down her cheeks, drip from her jaw, and she makes no effort to wipe them away.

Her resolution set, she will continue and not rest, as Sabastian won't rest, until Annbelle is found.

No, he won't give up on Annabelle, and she, Anne, won't give up on him.

Later, when Arlene answers the door, Anne shows her a tear-streaked face and a supportive but determined-to-find-answers expression.

"We need to talk," Anne says.

CHAPTER
THIRTY-TWO

HOURS LATER, my neck protests the angle at which it's been forced to endure. The lights in the reception room still shine, and, of course, the heater has decided to also nap. For all of Anne's efficiency and entrepreneurial success, she cannot manage to maintain this one utility to a standard. Well, she's only human.

Since I am conscious, my stomach gurgles for me to give it something more than bourbon.

My head, though throbbing, is relatively clear, the wooziness all but diminished. In a seated position, I allow a few minutes to pass before I stand and step to the phone to dial a nearby pizza joint.

When the food arrives, I fumble in my pocket for some crumpled bills and drop several, trying to hand them to the kid.

He's dressed in a white uniform reminiscent of the Good Humor Man. The name of his employer is stitched onto the left breast of his shirt. His look tells me that he thinks I'm into an early Friday night bender.

I don't care. Money for pizza exchanged, he disappears from my life.

The pizza is lukewarm, under-cooked, and greasy. I ingest every slice. My stomach thanks me, but later will remind me about the lack of real nutrition I've given it.

Before the first flames of heartburn sear my esophagus, I fall sideways on the couch again and drift off to Morpheus's sea.

The jangle of the phone rips into my eardrums, drives me upright. My heart rate jumps ahead of awareness. Just as my brain starts to get up to speed, the clamor repeats, and a migraine stabs my forehead.

Lurching off the couch, I grab for the phone on Anne's desk. For a moment, I entertain a serious notion of flinging the entire unit across the room, maybe through the window. The pleasure of such release vanishes when Leticia's voice says my name.

"Hello, 'Tish," I murmur. My tongue feels as thick and dry as a cotton ball. "Where are you? What's wrong?"

There is no reason she would call me at—I squint at the clock on the desk—just past eleven unless she has information or is involved in a situation beyond her ken to handle. "I'm here at Sammy's diner," she says. "That girl you been lookin' for?"

"Annabelle, yes. Have you seen her?"

"She was walkin' into the back of Zemo's 'bout five minutes ago. Actually, not really walkin'. More like helped along."

I recall what 'Tish said happens beyond the dance floor and the bar.

"She didn't look too good, Sabastian. Better get down here."

"Listen to me," I say, "You don't like them and you don't need to be involved, but you have to phone the police. Right now. I'll be there as soon as I can." I slam the receiver back into the cradle, snatch my coat I'd been using as a pillow, and rush to my car.

The sky spits snow, little *pock-pocks* against my car's hood, windshield, and nearby dumpster. Cars passing on Seventh sound as if they are rolling over crushed, frozen oyster shells instead of asphalt. A far-off siren wails like a cat forced under a shower. A stab of pain in my head reels me. I lean against the car door for a full minute until the icepick subsides to a toothpick.

I scrape the front bumper against the curb as I pull out into the lane and almost run over a figure encased in a heavy coat. He bangs a fist on my hood, then shakes it at me all the way around the front of the car and down the sidewalk.

An accident at Locust blocks traffic. Police and ambulance personnel halt southbound traffic. I'm trapped, heart thumping in desperation. When the ambulance wails off, one officer forces traffic to one lane to trickle through the intersection.

The traffic, weather, and roads delay me at every intersection. A rideshare driver waiting for passengers, flashers on, blocks one lane. I have to wait for an opening before I can pass.

Another car slows the flow when he slides, grill first, into a snow pile created by plows. More waiting. I slam my palms against the steering wheel, frustrated.

The flashing red at Third reduces everything to stop-and-go, one-at-a-time, except for the guy who takes his turn early, misses a car by inches, and veers off to bump up onto the opposite sidewalk.

A snowplow on the Walnut Street bridge takes the center line, slows to avoid clipping the bumpers of the cars parked on the left side, and throws waves of snow on those parked on the right.

Less than a mile and a half from my office, but I reach East

Fourth Street twenty minutes after Leticia spotted Annabelle. I slide to a halt perpendicular behind the row of cars in front of Zemo's, blocking three. Did 'Tish call the police? If so, their record for responding to calls just went down the toilet.

Almost slipping on the pavement, I reach the door. Inside, I'm almost bowled over by the callithump that fills the air. My headache spikes with each drumbeat and piercing guitar riff.

Chaos, confusion, a multitude of voices, a boisterous and drunken mass of moving people reveling for no other reason than because they're capable of doing so. The big holiday bash is almost a week gone, but Friday night is the time to let inhibitions fall by the wayside.

Vision blurs, but I push my way through the crowd of bodies. I'm overwhelmed by the atrocious noise from the stage. Four youths dressed in clothes purposefully shredded and with long hair covering most of their faces bounce and jump like epileptics on speed. Their hands produce tortuous sounds from guitars or beat a frenzy on the drums.

I stagger like a beaten boxer, shove people away, elicit a few curses, but I'm mostly ignored.

Behind the bar, Randall Fisher II and two flunkies hustle nonstop from customer to customer to harried waitress. Their movements are swift but precise, unerring.

To me and my seasick vision, they appear skewed, weirdly angled.

My goal is the door to the right of the bar, the one guarded by a bulky man in jeans and stained, gray sweatshirt. Trying to appear inconspicuous, he eyes the crowd, a frown chiseled upon his lips.

When I reach the door, the sentinel halts me with one upraised palm. I am weak, nearly off balance from the pounding music, the surging crowd, and the mother of all headaches. My head reels from the frenetic energy around me. I don't have a plan, cannot formulate one amid the cacophony. Instead, I rely on the pencil-thin diameter of tunnel vision, the focused motivation. Into this tunnel, I issue a mental command to arms and legs and they respond. I may smoke and drink, but I am not a weak or timid man. I'm not a master in karate, but can put someone down when needed.

When he raises a hand to halt me, I grab his wrist and pull his body forward. A second later, I drive the heel of my palm into his straight elbow. I sweep my left leg into the back of his knee. He's on the floor before the first scream of pain leaves his mouth. I give him a swift kick to his jaw before I'm through the door. No cries of alarm from the crowd, so I don't think anyone noticed.

A poorly illuminated hall with several doors spans north to south. Thin carpet lies beneath my shoes. I open each door. A storage area for liquor. A restroom. A cluttered office. At the end, a set of stairs descend to another hall and more rooms. The air smells musky with old sweat and cheap cologne, along with something lurid and salacious. Muffled grunts and occasional gasps emanate from behind each door.

I kick open the first. Inside, nothing but gray walls, a cheap table, a dingy lamp, and a sheeted mattress on old bed springs upon which lies a scantily clad woman. She's no older than twenty-five, with haunted pupils dilated by drugs.

Not Annabelle.

Farther down the hall, a door opens. Out stumbles an intoxicated man trying to zip up his pants.

I rush toward him, and he collides with me.

"Watch it there, buddy," he slurs. Spittle oozes down his chin. He gestures over his shoulder. "I wouldn't bother with her, man. Bitch barely whimpered. And I gave it to her good."

I sidestep him, and he staggers on.

He left the door open, and I enter the room. Similar in design to the first, except for the girl on the bed.

Naked and sprawled on the mattress is Annabelle Lansing.

I rush to her. Her skin is pallid and dry except for sweat droplets from the recent visitor. A tiny-linked silver chain encircles her neck, and a dull silver, heart-shaped pendant rests in the hollow of her throat.

I kneel, turn her head toward me, and thumb open an eyelid. Her eye rolls like a marble on linoleum. I place two fingers on her carotid and feel a thready and faint thrum of flowing blood.

"Annabelle," I whisper.

She doesn't respond. I repeat her name and, on the last syllable, her pulse ceases.

I stand and, one hand on top of the other, press my palm between her breasts. Up and down, I push on her chest in rapid succession. I lose count, but after I estimate thirty compressions, I proceed to phase two of cardiopulmonary resuscitation. Pinching closed her nostrils, I tilt back her head and force two breaths into her mouth. Then back to step one. Step two. Repeat. No heartbeat. No breathing. In short order, I'm exhausted.

I drop to my knees again, my breaths labored.

My eyes close, as I struggle through the growing dizziness.

My mind settles on two thoughts.

I have succeeded. I found Annabelle.

I have also failed.

She was already too far gone.

New Year gone.

THIRTY-THREE

"WHAT THE HELL?"

I recognize the voice from the doorway. Randall Fisher II. He wants me to believe he doesn't comprehend what is happening or the identity of the girl on the bed.

I know better. He's wondering who waylaid his lackey and invaded his sanctum of sleaze.

With the speed and force of a locomotive, I rise, take three steps, rear back my right arm, and smash my fist into his nose. His system in shock, he wants to fall, but I drive him back until his skull cracks against the opposite wall.

His body collapses to the floor, and I stumble back to Annabelle. More compressions. My motions become monotonous, and I lose count. Two more breaths. Voices and commotion outside the door, but I don't stop. More compressions.

Shouts for help. The room goes dim, but I cannot give up.

Hands ease me away from Annabelle. A voice assures me. I slump against the wall while blurry forms give commands.

The cops and EMTs have arrived, and I'm in for a long, long night.

Until the police organize the chaos, no one leaves Zemo's. Paramedics tend to the other women in the back rooms. Most of them suffer from narcotics injections to ensure compliance.

As a gurney with Annabelle's body moves through the mass of patrons, I'm in a position to observe two familiar faces. Around me, rumors tinged with facts circulate through the crowd faster than fire burning a haystack.

Near the entrance stands Kym Malin dressed in a slinky outfit that clings to her body like Saran Wrap. She's dyed her hair spikes red and plastered on enough makeup to send the Maybelline president on a Caribbean cruise. Nearby, looking the pauper to the princess, Rusty Fisher eyes the scene with awe, fear, and naiveté.

Kym's eyes meet mine from across the room. They widen a fraction, dart to the figure on the gurney, then back to me. Her face freezes in shock. She turns away, either sickened or embarrassed.

Rusty catches up seconds later, also doing the tennis match head swivel. His reaction is to double over and vomit.

I have no sympathy for them.

Hours pass. At police headquarters, I'm questioned once, twice. After further inquiry, I tell my story one more time.

After a long stretch of waiting, Pam opens the door. "Sabastian, how are you?"

I don't reply. A cigarette and a jolt of Ten High would do me a world of good, but I've been denied both.

"It's a hell of mess," she says.

I nod. "Yeah."

"I've read your report. It seems pretty straightforward."

"You think I've lied or held something back?" I say, defensive.

"No, that's not what I mean. I wanted to say that we'll let you go here in a bit." When I stay silent, she says, "Sabastian, you did the best you could. Hell, we'll be sifting through evidence for weeks. We may not even turn over all the stones we want to."

She means Jackie. They'll try, but it'll be a miracle if they make the smallest of charges stick.

"Annabelle," I say. "She… I didn't get a heartbeat. She…"

"From what I understand, you saved her. The latest report is she's in a coma. The bastards fed her a lot of drugs to keep her compliant. Not sure when she'll come out of it or what damage has been done. The brain… you know, it's a tricky thing." She pauses. "Do you blame yourself, Sabastian? For not finding her sooner?"

"No, Pam, I'm fine. Just very tired."

"Okay," she says. "I'll let you know when you can go. Do me a favor, though. Please?"

"What?"

"When you leave, go home to bed, not to a bottle. You need sleep, not booze."

I nod.

"Promise me that you'll not drink."

I sigh. "I promise."

After Pam closes the door to the interview room, I cross my forearms on the table and rest my head. Guilt? No, I don't feel guilt. I did my job. Annabelle was missing for five days, but she'd been lost for months, maybe years. I punched Fisher in the nose, but there are several more individuals I'd like to hit, slap, or shake, then dump a truckload of guilt onto.

At one point during my waiting, an end-of-the-world wail fills the hall and pierces my heart. I close my eyes and hang my head.

Short of a death notification, Arlene Lansing has received news no parent wants to hear.

Near dawn, I'm back in my office. Again, using my coat as a poor substitute for a pillow, I doze fitfully. Images swirl in my dreams. Cries—both my own and Arlene's—deafen me in my subconscious movie house.

Something warm and tender touches my cheek and, from a cosmos far away, someone says my name. Twice more it comes to me before the mental theater darkens, and I open my eyes.

Anne, my beautiful Anne, sits on the edge of the couch. Dried make-up and tears streak her face. During the night that never wanted to end, we saw each other once. She had come with Arlene and Roger. At one point, she managed to get close enough to ask, "How are you?" and I gave her a half-smile and a nod. "I'm okay, but I'd rather be with you in New Orleans, enjoying oyster po'boys."

Which shows you, Johnny, how bad things were. You'd have to truss me up like a hog for me to visit New Orleans, and anything that looks like it came from a giant's nose should not be ingested.

I sit up, and we meld together in each other's arms, two desperate souls yearning and clutching for a quantum of sanity in a world gone black and mad. Fresh tears soak through my shirt, and I hold her even tighter.

I hate this city.

I hate the world with all its cruelty, pain, and chaos.

I hate my life with its nonstop cigarettes and whiskey.

I'm so tired I could lie down, close my eyes, and gladly never awaken.

My one saving grace, my one, ever-present bit of light in the abyss sobs in my arms. I don't know if each of us can be the comfort or the release the other needs.

We can only be.

At this moment, for as long as it lasts, it is enough.

CHAPTER
THIRTY-FOUR
SATURDAY

THE LACK of warmth from the busted, stubborn heater in my half of the duplex doesn't allow me to sleep for more than a couple hours. Just before eleven, I give up and phone the landlord, only to receive the usual animalistic growl-snarl. I finish my morning ablutions, and walk out the door smoking the first cigarette.

Downtown digs out from yet another snowfall that arrived overnight. Piles of white crowd the sidewalks. Gutters flow gray and dirty with runoff. The syrupy sludge rushes toward the nearest sewer, as if it can't wait to escape the surface level, preferring to wander through dark tunnels until it mixes with the greater body of the river. Above the skyline, a wall of solid white hovers, threatening more snow. Short blasts of cold wind whip around the corner, racing each other in never-ending, chilled sprints.

The office hours don't include Saturdays, but even after last night's tragedy and long aftermath of questions and accusations, and crying that lasted until the early hours, I feel compelled to come in. I don't know why. As Anne pointed out the previous day, no paperwork awaits my attention.

Her desk sits empty, clean of files and papers, ready for her return on Monday. I don't know how much sleep she got after last night. I'm sure she'll spend the day with Arlene and Roger.

I nudge up the thermostat and wait until the radiator comes to life before I thunk down in my chair, still wearing my overcoat. My desk is clear of papers and files. Not clean—a thin layer of dust, a stray paperclip, a dog-eared, pocket-sized, spiral notebook, the phone, and other miscellaneous items all waiting for the feng shui guy to arrange them in harmonious order—but clear.

Memories of last night seep into my thoughts. During the previous hour, I had closed the door on them, but didn't bother to fully latch it. Now, they push it open and flow in like an invading line of ants.

Sounds of music and laughter and sirens and crying.

Sights of people and Annabelle and people and Fisher and cops and people.

Wisps of pot smoke and the mustiness of a police interview room.

The memories are a strange combination of both blurred confusion and a clear order of events.

Somewhere while remembering, I doze only to wake up near enough to one-thirty. I lock up the office and ride the elevator down to the first floor and back outside.

The area in front of the small sandwich shop is clear, evidence of Timothy's aunt's dutiful sweeping. The bell sounds hollow and lifeless when I open the door.

Behind the counter, the woman, also moving gingerly, steps to the cooler and removes my usual fare. With a bit of pride, she points to the selection of snacks, my choice of pretzels prominently on display.

I give the food a cursory glance, my satisfaction short-lived as I can't stop staring at the woman's face. Embarrassed, she tries to turn away, but I step into her territory and grasp her shoulders, forcing her to face me. Her head droops, but I cup a hand under her chin and raise her head.

The bruise under her swollen left eye brings my blood to a boil. My heart races, jaw stony. The woman may not be glamour model attractive, but her innocence, her humble nature, and her kindness have been damaged by this caitiff act.

I ask the one-word question. "Who?"

She shakes free. "No, no, he didn't mean it." Turning away, she attempts to place the sandwiches into a paper sack, but the intensity of her trembling hands causes her to rip the paper down one side.

I remember the look in the boy's eyes when he walked into Jackie's office and put together the series of events with little imagination. "He arrived home high," I say. "You confronted him, and he hit you."

Her whole frame quivers. "He didn't know what he was doing."

No excuses, I want to say, but she knows. I sigh, at a loss for words or action.

Part of me pushes back. *Leave it alone. You tried. This isn't your business any longer.*

I silence the voice, because the damaged eye of the woman who wants her nephew to be a good kid won't allow me to leave this alone. My action two days ago resulted in a partial concussion for me, Leon's beating, and, indirectly, this woman's injury. Timothy is to blame, but guilt coats my heart like molasses. I need to put this right. I failed the previous night to reach a girl in desperate straits in time. If I walk away, I'd never again be able to frequent this woman's shop.

Jackie's words, the highlights of his soliloquy about the river and destiny replay in my head. The man, evil as he is, spoke truthfully in one sense. I may not be able to stop him. To put an end to his organization would take forces beyond what I can muster. However, I can stop Timothy. I don't quite know how yet, but a vague outline begins to brighten. I step back around to my side of the counter. "Ma'am, is he still at your house?"

She nods, unable or unwilling to speak or to look at me. "May I have your permission to enter your home and… take appropriate action?"

She raises her head, a frightened expression on her face. She fears the worst.

"No undue violence," I say.

"The police—"

"And no police."

"What will you do?" she asks.

"I will endeavor to make him see the error of his ways. If I cannot do so, my advice to you is to turn him over to the authorities, despite the possible repercussions. At the very least, he would need to leave your house."

"He's only fifteen."

"He's under the influence of powerful narcotics," I say. "He has committed violence, and no matter his state of mind at the time, it cannot be allowed to continue." My voice turns gruff. I do not enjoy pushing her, but she needs it for her own good. I also know when to ease off. "You asked for my help," I say. "Let me try again. I chose the wrong method the first time. I need to communicate directly with Timothy, get him to come up to my level."

I don't tell her I may have to lower myself to his first. She hesitates, but the intensity of her quivers lessens.

I recall what she said two days ago when I showed reluctance and repeat her plea. "Please."

After a moment, she acquiesces and tells me the address. "There's a spare key hanging from a nail on the back of the first post by the door." Before she changes her mind, she plucks a bag of pretzels and two sugar cookies, vacuum-wrapped in clear plastic, and adds them to the meal. Without ringing up the sale, she shoves the sack into my hands. I start to protest, but she turns away and busies herself with a mundane and nonessential project, refusing to look back.

I offer a gentle nod that she doesn't see, turn around, and leave. A child was all but lost last night. I'll do my best—or, as a former coworker at the police department used to say, "my damndest"—not to let another one go down.

———

Timothy lives with his aunt in a small, white, stucco-sided box house on East Diehl, north of Army Post Road. The backyard looks upon one of those large, all-in-one, mega shopping centers featuring tools, home accessories, and lumber. Everything from doors to pliers, clothes, and snacks, all under one roof. The place is too big, too cluttered, and too noisy.

I pull into the snow-packed, gravel driveway. The house's gutter hangs askew from a roof with the most minimal pitch. The stucco has aged, grayed, and saddened, a perfect mimic of the house's owner. A ramp leads to the front door. Snow piles along the edge of the wooden railing. Nature and time have peeled paint and created gaps where balusters have rotted away. One front window displays a thin crack, and the screen door hangs at the same angle as the gutter.

I discard a cigarette to a short, hissing death in the snow and squat to feel behind a post. A sharp nail head scratches my finger, but it holds the key. When I examine the wound, seeping blood coagulates when it meets the cold air.

I insert the key. The front door's hinges squeal like a violin suffering a child's first lesson. I step into a hallway the length of the house. The back door lies in shadow. As I walk along the clean but scratched hardwood floor, I pass a living room, a small and tidy kitchen, an extra room used as storage, and two bedrooms. Timothy's is the last room by the back door.

Where the rest of the house shows regular upkeep, this bedroom is typical teenager pigsty. Clothes strewn willy-nilly, books and folders stacked haphazardly. Dust layers every flat surface. I shudder at the benthic odor in the air.

Timothy, still dressed in the same clothes he wore at Midnight's, lies sprawled across the width of the unmade bed. One arm rests atop a pillow. The black-and-white striped pillowcase is stained yellow by sweat. Before he crashed, he'd removed the windbreaker and flung it on top of a lamp.

Only fifteen and on a downhill slide.

I fortify myself with a sip from my whiskey flask and tell my headache to hold off for a while. Then I grasp the boy by the scruff of his neck and the top of his pants and drag him off the bed out into the hallway. He yowls, but a kick to his butt turns the protest into a yelp.

"Get moving!" My order comes sharp. Sabastian Habeck, drill sergeant. I boot him again.

In his dazed state, he starts to crawl and pull himself along the floor.

"All the way to the front door."

At the door, a rush of chilled air hits us. I clench a wad of sweatshirt, pull him up and outside.

The cold slaps his senses into order. He shakes his head, and his eyes roll but focus on me. "What the hell?"

He tears himself away, steps back, and cocks his arm for an amateurish roundhouse punch. I block the feeble strike and drive my right fist into his stomach. When he folds, I spin him sideways and, again, grab his neck and pants, lift, and throw him over the railing where he lands face-first into the snowdrift.

Around the end of the ramp, I meet him as he attempts to stand, stick my leg out to trip him, and plunge him back into the cold white flakes. He screams, but I hold him down like a bully holds the nerd's face into a flushing toilet bowl. I swivel my head to check for witnesses to my assault on a minor. When his body weakens and shivers in the cold, I release. I wait until he stands before pushing him down. I hate to do it this way, and some people might think I'm getting revenge for Midnight's assault on me. Perhaps a smidgen, but the kid needs a lesson about respecting his elders, especially one of his relatives who provides him a place to live while his father is off making deals in foreign countries. I'm not beating him bloody and bruised, unlike what he might receive should he continue down the narcotics path.

He sits half-buried and glares at me. His expression shows

confusion, but in a moment, there's recognition in his eyes. Jackie Midnight doesn't hold coffee klatches and Timothy's gaze toward me in that back room held only the slightest interest. Now, expletives spill from his mouth like verbal diarrhea, followed by threats of both revenge from Jackie and calling the law on me.

I let him babble for twenty seconds before interrupting. "Shut up!" I raise my fist in another threat.

Sabastian Habeck, motivator for teenage punks.

He gulps and sputters half-formed words. "What? Who?"

"Zip it, son!"

His mouth opens and closes like a fish trying to breathe air.

"My name is Sabastian, and I'd like a chat."

"You broke into my house."

"Actually, I used the key."

Sabastian Habeck, logician.

"Who are you? What do you want?"

"I've already answered those questions," I say.

More confusion.

"Are you ready to stand?" I ask.

He nods. I open my fist and offer my hand. He looks at it as if daggers might sprout from the finger ends. Reluctantly, he reaches up and takes it. He groans when I pull him upward.

I bring him in close, faces inches apart. My wicked grin transforms into a disgusted sneer. "I just visited your aunt," I grate in a low voice. A second passes, and what surely is recollection flashes in his widening eyes. "She thought I should come say hello."

I sock his gut once again and let him drop back into the snow pile. He moans and drools while I reach for my pack of Luckys.

Sabastian Habeck, one hell of a wake-up call.

THE IDEA of driving around the city with a fifteen-year-old dope head wasn't on my itinerary when I rose from bed earlier. However, a throb in my temple reminds me of two nights ago. While I didn't find a solid connection between Jackie Midnight and what happened to Annabelle, Leticia did say he had an interest in the urban renewal project. That makes enough of a connection for me. The man has revved up my ire. While I may not bring down his nefarious enterprise or dam up his flowing river of drugs, I might be able to divert the course of one of his victims. Otherwise, another innocent will be washed away or sucked to the muck-filled bottom.

Timothy offered no resistance when I ordered him into my car. I did threaten further visits to the nearest snowdrift should he vomit in the floor well. There's enough to clean up without adding a noxious odor to the mix.

I drive west on Army Post Road.

"Where are you taking me?" He sounds like a kid half his age being punished for kicking the dog.

While he lay curled up, I retrieved his shoes and jacket. No shower, hair plastered in all directions like the creation of a blind beautician, skin pallid, eyes watery, he looks a step or two past disheveled.

"On a magic ride into the future," I answer.

"What the hell does that mean? Who are you?"

"I'm going to show you what your life is destined to be if you don't get your act together."

"Aw, man," he whines. "You've been talking to my stupid aunt. Screw this, man, and screw you. Let me out."

A red light halts traffic at Southeast Fifth. With one hand, I grab his shirt collar and pull him close. Fear dilates his eyes.

"You should consider yourself fortunate you received only two gut shots. In my day, striking a woman merited blood."

"I'm still calling the cops," he says on a huffy and acidic-smelling breath.

"Where we're going, you'll have ample opportunity to file a report. Meanwhile, sit there and shut up." I push him away as the oval of green allows traffic to move. The mix consists of the lunch crowd and those out to enjoy the weekend. Every car sports streaks of slush and winter grime. Mother Nature holds no favoritism and heaps misery on all.

At Southwest Ninth, I turn left toward the zoo. Half a dozen blocks south, I cut left again on a half-moon-shaped road into Fort Des Moines property.

In 1851, the city became incorporated with the moniker Fort Des Moines. Six years later, people tired of the three-part name and shortened it. Roughly translated as "of the monks" the "Moines" part has also been noted to have come from the Algonquians, meaning either "loons" or the more amusing "excrement faces."

Don't you love history, Johnny?

Not much of the original fort exists. Brick structures look abandoned and lonely. The road winds through the property and offers an obstacle course of potholes, as if enemy aircraft conducted bombing runs during the war.

Some of the buildings—those where the walls weren't stuffed with asbestos—have been transformed into Iowa's Fifth Judicial District. This is the midpoint between county lockup and prison. A sort of second chance offering for sex offenders and drug users. Staff refer to the inmates with the euphemistic name "clients", but everyone knows what they are. Those not confined to the main headquarters are housed for short stints in a single block of former barracks, which I don't think ever receive adequate heat. A fair number are monitored via ankle bracelets. The personnel who track the felons' whereabouts do so from inside an old garage storage building.

I park in front of central command and shut off the engine. "Get out," I say.

Timothy shivers, hands in his jacket pockets. I fire up a Lucky and point out a number of other smokers huddled on steps or iron porches. I explain the living arrangements and the types of felons housed in the long-faded red buildings.

"Sexual deviants and drug users. Your aunt's stucco shack is in better condition and a lot more comfortable."

He's not impressed, but we've only just begun.

A set of lock boxes similar to what one might find in a bank sits inside the first door to headquarters. Employees and felons alike are required to discard any items deemed a threat. This includes weapons, of course, or any item potentially used as a weapon, such as nail files and clippers. Into one of the boxes, I deposit my flask, cigarettes, and wooden matches. I close the door and place the flat-headed key in my coat pocket.

I walk over to the locked glass door and finger the intercom button. Through the window, the reception and monitoring area are a raised, half-circle counter behind which are four computer terminals and various personnel.

A woman with short cropped, auburn hair looks up at the buzz. Her eyes narrow, and a frown forms on her face, as if I've thrown crap against the door. "Sabastian." Her voice sounds tinny through the speaker.

"Joan."

"Heard about Zemo's last night." She eyes me from head to shoes. "You look properly steamrolled this morning."

That's Joan. Never miss an opportunity to kick your shins when you're already hurting. After a day of headaches after Midnight's assault, tussling with Fisher, and snatches of sleep, I'm amazed that I can still function.

"What can I do for you?" she asks.

"Do you have a minute?" I glance at Timothy. "I have a future client with me. I understand you don't normally condone this type of visit, but do you have a little time to chat, possibly show him a few procedures?"

She sighs and gives me a weary stare. Moments pass. If she refuses, I'll go elsewhere. There are plenty of other places to give the boy a perspective of reality.

"Hold on a minute. Let me ask Michael."

"Thanks, Joan."

Joan Nicely. Attractive enough to walk a fashion runway, but too short to be taken seriously as a model. We've known each other for almost a dozen years. Similar to Pam, Nicely and I would frequent the same bars until she jumped on the wagon one day with no explanation given. She's been sober since.

Good for her.

A buzz at the door is followed by a click.

Inside, Joan stands ten feet away, the top of her head just below the bridge of Timothy's nose. "Turn around," she orders. "Put your hands on the wall."

"What the…?" Timothy starts.

I jump in with, "Son, you'd better—"

"Can the 'son' nonsense, Sabastian," Joan interrupts and turns her attention back to Timothy. "No one enters this facility without a pat down."

"Chill out, lady," Timothy whines. "I didn't want to come here in the first place."

"You are here, so you either turn around and submit to a pat down or turn around and walk out the door."

Said door latches closed, though we could be buzzed out. Timothy's eyes dart around for other exits. He shivers, feeling trapped.

The people behind the counter play audience to our little gathering, ready to intervene with appropriate action should circumstances warrant it. Four black men, aged early to middle twenties, halt their progress at the beginning of the hall to watch with both wariness and anticipation. They see a new fish in their pond about to discover the penalty for disobedience and giving back talk to Nicely.

Joan twirls an index finger, indicating to Timothy what he needs to do. He whispers profanity, but turns and presses his palms against the wall. She runs her hands up and down his body, checking for unauthorized materiel. The tension eases as nothing exciting happens. The desk attendants return to their computers, and the youths amble on down the hall.

"Turn around." Joan steps back. When Timothy does, she continues. "Now, stay quiet, listen, and learn."

I've visited the command center before and didn't enjoy the experience. The ambiance doesn't resonate friendliness. High ceiling lights brighten the reception area, the hallways, the meal room, and the recreation room, but this place is still a jail. A gray veil pervades the atmosphere. An odor of painted concrete lingers in the air. This place is sterile, uncomfortable, and despair lingers in every expression and walk of the prisoners. Leniency accompanies confinement, but only so far. This place may offer the aforementioned second chance for those who want to try for a decent existence, but harbors no love for those who turn another way.

Joan leads us up a narrow set of steps behind the reception counter. Each computer terminal is manned by an individual who taps a keyboard to bring up different windows and information. Joan explains about the felons wearing ankle bracelets, and she produces one from a box under the counter and offers it to Timothy for inspection to show how they are tracked. She lists some of the exclusion zones—schools, malls, daycare centers— where these people aren't allowed to travel. In precise terms, she describes the facility's routines, living arrangements, restrictions, as well as punishments for rules broken.

"Yeah, but I ain't one of those pervs," Timothy says. "That's sick, man."

As if on cue, the clip-clop of footsteps echoes off the tile floor. Two men dressed in professional attire escort a gangly individual, hands cuffed behind him. He's white, and the closer he walks, the more his aged face and emaciated features become noticeable. Sunken cheeks, raccoon eyes. The curvature of his ribs protrudes behind his standard-issue prisoner shirt.

"He's only twenty-five," Joan mutters loud enough for only Timothy and I to hear.

Twenty-five, but the man looks twice his age. At the reception counter, one of the officers accepts a clipboard and scribbles on an official-looking document.

The cuffed man raises his head and spots Joan. He offers a weak smile. "Hey, Ms. Nicely."

"Matthew," she states in a flat voice.

Matthew sighs, tired. "I gotta go now," he says in a nebbish tone. "I jus' wanna let you know I had no prob'm with you. You always treated me fair."

"Thank you, Matthew," Joan replies. Clinical. Emotionless.

The guy squints at Timothy, perhaps recognizing a familiar pathos. "You stay on Ms. Nicely's good side, or she'll whoop your ass." He tries for a snicker, but it comes out coated with saliva.

The escort to his right tugs on his arm. "Come on, Matthew."

The door buzzes, and the trio disappears.

Timothy flaps a hand in the direction of the door. "What's his deal?"

"Cocaine and meth," Joan answers. "He can't stop using and violated his probation."

"Where are they taking him?"

"Fort Madison prison to serve out the rest of his sentence." Joan locks eyes with Timothy. The look would intimidate a bulldog into giving up its bone. "Compared to there, this place is a cakewalk."

CHAPTER
THIRTY-SIX

BACK IN THE CAR, Timothy sits, sullen and silent. His expression still shows defiance, but some of the roughness has been chipped away by the operation's center. Modern and bright, but a confinement area, nonetheless. Some inmates receive an opportunity to better themselves, but what is given can be taken away. Does Timothy envision a glimmer of a possible future when he becomes an adult, or imagine himself repeating Matthew's walk of shame? I am certain Joan will remember him if the boy ever becomes a 'client'.

North on Fleur and into Water Works Park. Even in the height of summer, this acreage feels desolate and distant from the surrounding metro. In the depth of winter, it is a foreign landscape, harsh, isolated. The trees stand naked save for a coat of snow, and a desert of white spreads out before me. The park exudes loneliness, barrenness. Skeletal wireframes of Christmas figures line the roadside. During the holiday season, cars jammed the route through the park as visitors enjoyed the lighted display.

Now, those figures resemble emaciated travelers lost on their journey to an unknown destination, never to be reached.

The water treatment plant sits on the northeastern edge of the park. Normally, two eight-foot swing bars block entrance to the plant, but today they point toward the gray sky. I'm thankful, otherwise, Timothy and I would be forced to walk farther than I want.

The perimeter road circles the gawky-looking building and edges the Raccoon River, which snakes through the park. I stop the car, but keep the engine running and motion for Timothy to exit. He exhales another disgusted breath, but obeys.

Outside, I light up a Lucky and tromp through the shin-deep snow to the riverbank. I wait until Timothy trudges to stand shivering beside me. The decline is steep, the shallow, snowy river silent, waiting for the spring when it can threaten the area again with flooding.

I'm grateful because the wind, for the moment, has stilled. A few birds too stupid to fly south twitter in nearby trees, while slushy traffic noises from Fleur barely reach my ears.

I wait.

Timothy's teeth chatter like clicking dice. I smoke.

I almost feel sorry for the kid in his light jacket. Almost. Finally, he says, "What are we doing here?"

I gesture with the cigarette to a cluster of tents on the opposite riverbank, little mounds of white with bits of pale blue or green showing. They're strung along and above a railroad spur. Beyond, and up the hill, a curving line of upper-middle-class residences, and behind those, Terrace Hill. The governor's mansion.

"Stupid time of year for Boy Scout campers," Timothy says, full of sarcasm.

I say nothing. I wait.

Timothy shivers. I smoke.

I glance at him. "Feet cold, yet?"

"Duh!"

Again, I indicate the tents. "The people over there have nothing except what they can pick up at shelters, beg for, or steal. What little money they have goes for food… or drugs."

I smoke for a moment.

"Some found themselves in financial straits through bad investments and too much debt. They couldn't make house payments or the monthly rent." I look at Timothy. "Many lost their homes to drugs, and many turned to drugs when they lost their homes. I couldn't guess at how many are so addicted they'll never recover." I may be exaggerating, but I'm not giving Timothy hard numbers.

I study the dismal and cold-looking tents and contradistin-guish the view. "Look at the scenery, son. People huddled in tents within sight of neighbors in high-priced homes, the state's top government official, and his family. The latter two groups don't care about the first group, other than being annoyed every so often with its presence." I smoke and sigh. "It's hard to care, though, when the homeless themselves, or at least a fair number, don't care enough to straighten up because they can't or won't get off the drugs."

"I'm not like that," Timothy says. "Besides, you said they owned homes, which means they're adults."

I open my mouth to tell him about the children in the tents, but he stops me.

"Listen, man. This is all bull. I told you I'm not like that. I do what I want, but I'm not addicted. I'm not going to be like them or those dumbasses in jail. When I want to stop, I will. Now can we go back to the car? 'Cause it's too damn cold out here." He stomps off.

I finish the last of the Lucky. His attitude doesn't surprise me. His phrases of denial, false bravado, and self-control have been said by thousands over the decades.

Addiction. One doesn't know one is trapped until the jaws bite deep. It can be a miserable and tragic situation. Some people can pry the teeth from their bodies. Others become snared so securely, a miracle is needed. Even then, what have they lost? A job? A marriage?

Before I return to the car, I shake the flask in my pocket to determine the level of whiskey. Then I take a hit and jot a mental note to buy another pack of Luckys.

THIRTY-SEVEN

I NEGOTIATE the streets to the northern suburb of Johnston. Timothy sits in a state of quiescence. Our visits to the Fort and to view the homeless encampment didn't impress him, at least not enough to cause an immediate change in attitude. Of course, I didn't expect them to. In fact, part of me believes this entire endeavor today is a waste of time, that tonight he'll be back at Jackie's, and I can expect another visit from the man in the black Jag or his goons.

The other part of me pushes me to keep trying, to find that one experience that will touch the boy down deep. I could take him out to a women's lockup at one of the local hospitals, but forgo another jail-type facility for a place better suited for his mindset.

Timothy has seen adults living the consequences of their actions, but doesn't have an adult concept of life. He views his teenage years as a "now" circumstance. Adulthood and responsibilities lay in the future, to be dealt with when they arrive. He thinks nothing with which he's currently involved will play any part in determining how he faces them. He expects a clean slate, a fresh start, and probably Daddy's money to help him along.

Terrence Howard—resembling, but with no relation to, the actor—is the director of Iowa Hope House, off Merle Hay Road in Johnston. Away from the busy malls and the chaotic west side, the acreage with its trees and narrow sidewalks promotes serenity. Neighboring businesses exude quiet professionalism. Streets and lawns stay well-tended, and the residents live in abodes that don't scream 'stately' or 'wealthy', even though they could.

Centered among ten acres of sprawling lawn, backed by a copse of trees, at the end of a maple-lined drive, four stories of a cranberry-colored brick and depressing-looking, monolithic structure rises imperious and imposing out of the uniform white.

This is not Disneyland.

Terrence meets us in the lobby. I had stopped at a convenience store for cigarettes and to persuade the cashier to let me use the phone. Claimed my cell was broken. I had called and requested a favor using vague but recognizable phrases.

The man stands seven inches taller than my five-eight, with linebacker shoulders, a face devoid of tension, cheeks slightly marred by patches of acne scars. His size is exaggerated by his casual dress of a black, knit sweater, khaki-colored chinos, and black wingtips.

Terrence knows every inch of his facility because he's a former resident. No one can claim he doesn't know his job or understand what the kids experience because, as he tells it, he was one of the worst cases.

He offers a meaty hand when Timothy and I enter the lobby. "Sabastian," he says, voice deep as rolling thunder.

"Terrence," I return. "Thanks for seeing us on short notice."

"Not a problem." He turns to Timothy, who stands two steps to my right and a step behind.

"Timothy, this is Mr. Howard," I say. "He's the director here."

"How are you doing?" Terrence doesn't offer a handshake, but keeps his hands clasped behind him.

The boy acknowledges him with a typical teenager half nod.

Terrence studies him for a moment, then addresses me, "Sabastian, before we go any further, I have to know if he's in possession of any items—"

I hold up a hand to allay his concern. "Already covered at our first stop. Much to his discomfort, I might add."

"Okay." The big man gestures down one hall. "Let's check out your room, Timothy."

"What?" The kid backs up, and his body tenses. He must have thought Terrence announced the end of his freedom, that his incarceration was imminent. He's ready to bolt.

Terrence steps forward, just enough that Timothy is forced to crane his neck to meet his eyes. "Listen to me," he says, and his voice has as much power behind it as a locomotive. "I'm not here to listen to excuses or denials, because I've heard them all a dozen times over. I'm giving it to you straight, so you listen to me and take what I say as gospel truth. You know nothing about me, and I don't know but one thing about you. What I do know is the road you're on leads to three destinations. Prison, an asylum, or death. This facility is an attempt to divert your course. I'm not going to sugarcoat anything. This is not a fun place. We don't conduct campfire sing-alongs, teach scrapbook classes, and we don't mollycoddle. We're tough and strict. If you end up here, you will be monitored every second of every hour of every day. We'll know when you're lying or hiding something. You earn privileges by obeying the rules and penalties by not."

Terrence halts his soliloquy. With long strides, he walks down the hall. I'm two steps behind. Timothy's options are to follow, remain where he stands, or exit the building, stuck miles from home.

Ahead, Terrence opens a door and waits while we catch up. We observe a similar space in size, appearance, and design to Amos's college dorm room. Double occupancy, small dressers, desks, one closet. This room, though, doesn't have a television or mini fridge, and a steel screen covers the lone window.

"We offer few amenities," Terrence says. "We are not the Radisson."

The director walks to a door at the hall's end. Beyond, we stop in a small waiting area with benches and tables, each of the latter with a surface area twice the size of Annabelle's laptop.

Through a large picture window, the three of us look upon a community recreation room. Couches, chairs, a wall-mounted television, shelves filled with an assortment of board games and a selection of books. Nearly a dozen youths occupy the room. Dressed in drab, institutional-style clothes, their expressions range from passive to jittery anxiety. One boy paces like a caged bear cub, wearing a line around the room's perimeter as if ever seeking an exit. Another sits in a chair, rocking as those afflicted with certain psychological disorders are wont to do.

"These cases run the spectrum of the recovery process," Terrence explains. "Not all started with the privilege of being allowed in this room."

Timothy shifts from foot to foot. "Where were they?"

Terrance gives the inquiry a frown and a pointed stare. "In another part of the facility you are not permitted to visit."

The ex cathedra voice produces dents in the boy's armor. Timothy's jaw tightens, quivers, and his pupils dilate. What must he imagine that part of the facility to be? He studies each occupant of the recreation room, and I wish for the power to divine his thoughts.

Apparently, Terrence possesses a touch of that ability. "The oldest is seventeen." He indicates the pacer. "Later this year, if he has not fully recovered, he will be transferred to another facility. If and when he is released, the law will treat him as an adult come his eighteenth birthday. Should he be caught using, his next stop will be prison." Terrence points to another boy seated at one end of the couch nearest the television. Blond, wearing glasses, the child reads from an open book on his lap. "The youngest is nine."

Timothy's eyes widen and his jaw drops. "Nine?"

Terrence frowns and locks eyes with the teenager. "We've had younger."

We observe the occupants in the room. Most of the area is open space, but off to the far side is a partition that reaches almost to the ceiling. On the other side, at a small desk, sits a boy I judge to be Timothy's age. Fair-haired, he has a lean and wiry body. He could be a running back for a high school football team. Whatever drugs are in his system haven't yet affected him physically. His blue eyes stare at nothing and not one muscle moves. A derisive sneer curls his lips. Behind him stands a man reading a report from a manila folder.

The scene shows the dichotomy of the room. One side activity and the other silence and immobility. Timothy notices and asks why.

"Do you know how hockey has a penalty for infractions?" Terrence says.

"Yeah."

"This is similar. The young man broke a rule in the room. He must sit out for an assigned period of time. He's not allowed to speak or make any unnecessary movement."

"For how long?"

"Depends on the severity of the violation. Could be five minutes to three hours."

"That's ridiculous," Timothy says. "Sounds like one of those stupid 'time outs' I had when I was a kid."

He's still a kid, but I say nothing.

"Essentially, it is," Terrence agrees. "However, should matters… escalate, he will be removed from the room with further privileges revoked."

"Still sounds stupid."

Terrence points to a chair. "Sit."

I'm surprised when the boy obeys. His will is weakening, and Terrence's tone of command brooks no defiance.

Terrence sighs and his stolid, unyielding personality deflates. Sitting on one of the benches, he wipes his brow. "I'm not going to lie to you, son. This isn't a nice place. I wish it didn't exist. I wish circumstances didn't require it, but the world is a big, scary place, and sometimes, people find awful ways to deal with the chaos." He gives me a quick look with a half-smile. "I don't know the details of your situation, son, but I'll bet your story is pretty close to those who are in here. You may not believe me, but it's true." He sighs, exasperated. "I'm not going to lecture you or jump on your back. You don't know me from Adam, and my words may not mean anything to you. At least, not right now. You think you can handle whatever it is you're into, that you can quit at any time." He tilts his head toward the room. "Every single one of those kids had the same thoughts. Take another look in that room and, later today, reflect on the notion that you could be sitting in there very soon."

Timothy takes one more look. For me, the long moment stretches to a distant vanishing point on the horizon. When I return to the moment, I thank Terrence for his time in a quiet voice.

The big man stays seated, but offers one final sentence to Timothy as we leave the waiting area, "When you walk out the front door, I hope you never walk back in."

I met Terrence several years ago, coincidentally on a Midnight-drug-related case. At the time, he invited me out to this facility. Didn't like it then, don't like it now. Nothing much has changed except the faces are different.

In the car, I gaze at the building. A bleak and cold keep. From my angle, darkness resides behind the entrance doors. The darkness of an abyss from which only the fortunate ever escape.

I glance at Timothy and wonder where his thoughts are. He remained defiant throughout our first two stops, but went silent during the visit inside this place. His head angles to look out the passenger window. Hands in his lap, expression blank. No indication of whether any of Terrence's words wormed through his resistance.

I hope so. I share Terrence's regret that his institution and those like it have to exist. Ditto with Joan Nicely and her correctional facility. I don't like to think on these places too often, let alone visit them.

Resistance. Obstacles. They remind me of the soliloquy

Midnight gave me. He expounded on the metaphor of him and his operation to a river. He could have gone farther.

Rivers usually end up in seas or gulfs or oceans. Midnight hopes to continue to feed fresh "fish" to those places, either deceased, or like spawning salmon, wanting to return for more. Rivers also have eddies where one might become trapped in a constant swirl of repetitious destruction.

Of course, I don't think of Timothy as a fish, but he is floating down a river that could turn into rapids. Whether he crashes against the rocks or ends up on the shore is up to him. My hope is that through my words and those of others combined with what he's seen this day, he can veer down a tributary to more placid waters.

THIRTY-EIGHT

I DON'T LIKE HOSPITALS, but not for the obvious reason. Today's hospitals have grown so gargantuan and complex that I could be Theseus in a labyrinth of corridors. I never know if I'm taking the correct route and am always afraid I'll encounter a minotaur in the form of a prune-faced nurse wondering why I've strayed into the maternity ward or a stony-jawed security guard barring my progress into a restricted area.

Despite my fears, I complete the trip across the acreage of parking at Methodist Hospital and, after twice repeating directions given by a receptionist, find Leon Brummell's room.

At first, I think it's a storage closet until a nurse indicates the room number by the door. I don't believe the minimal square footage allotted. The elevator on which I rode to his floor was more spacious.

Timothy trails along behind me, silent until now. "Who we seeing?"

Before we enter, I look down at him. "A decent human being

who didn't deserve what he received for trying to help. I want you to understand what happens to people who get on the wrong side of Jackie."

Crammed into the room are a chair, a boxy machine to monitor patients' vitals, a useless potted plant, a television mounted in the ceiling corner, open shelves for clothes and other personal items, and, of course, the bed upon which Leon lies asleep. Off to my right, another door leads to an even smaller bathroom. Near the window stands a wheeled, C-shaped cart, the top flat surface designed to extend over the bed to hold meals.

A blanket covers Leon to the neck. His arms lay on top by his sides. Tubes and wires trail to the monitor and an intravenous unit drips a clear liquid. A thicker cord snakes down to a narrow head with a push button. It rests in his right palm, and I assume he can administer his own pain medication when needed. I also assume he needs it a lot. His face looks like a train wreck, nose broken, a patch over the left eye. Stitches line swollen lips. Scrapes and scratches flame red and angry. I cannot imagine what the rest of his body suffered.

Timothy stays near the door. I approach the bed, see a finger twitch, and am relieved Jackie and his thugs didn't injure him to the point of paralysis. His right eye quivers, opens, and stares back at me. His pupil contains so much depth, I could lose myself. His stare stabs me in the gut with unspoken statements and accusations. Blame. Sorrow.

What words can I express? What trite phrases can relieve his pains and salve his hurt? None.

"Leon," I whisper, "I'm sorry."

The one eye continues to bore into my soul. Leon may not be the smartest man in town, but he's intelligent enough to put one and one together. He understands what he did for me resulted in his procumbent position in the snow Thursday night and his occupying a hospital bed today.

I, too, suffered from the attempted impeding of Jackie's business, but I wonder if I'll be facing the wrath of the big man once he recovers.

His lips tremble, and he hacks a dry cough as he tries to engage his voice box. A raspy sound issues from his mouth, dry and desperate. "I... know, Mr. Habeck." The end of his tongue attempts to give moisture to his lips.

I search for a water pitcher, but see nothing.

"Not... your fault," he slurs.

His eye moves past me to the door. He stares at Timothy, but doesn't say anything. Timothy stands, not moving, eyes riveted on the large man in the bed. Leon's eye closes, and his breaths even out. He may have fallen asleep, succumbing to administered pain suppressant.

I touch his shoulder before turning away. His inhalation hisses, gurgling and wet. I stop and glance back.

In the quiet of the room, his words are clear, cold, and ominous, "He... should have... killed me."

———

Timothy remains mute all the way back downtown, and I'm content to hear only the purring of the car's engine. I find an open spot in front of Anne's building, half a block from Timothy's aunt's shop, the familiar semicircle of cleared snow in front of the door. We sit in silence. The engine's thrumming vibrates through the leather of the bucket seat.

Neither of us looks at the other. A minute passes. Two.

I say, "You have a number of choices. You may call your daddy and bitch about the way I've treated you. You can report me to the police or Jackie Midnight. Or you march through that door and do what's right by your aunt. At this moment, I'm too tired to care what decision you make." I pause. "Look at me." I wait until he meets my eye. "But if I hear or see that you've mistreated her again, it will take more than Jackie, his goons, the police, or your father's lawyers to stop me from kicking your ass again. Do you understand me?"

His chin dips a millimeter.

"Today, I've shown you ways your life can go once you leave this car. There is also assistance, a little less severe than Terrence's facility, and you don't need to feel ashamed in asking for it. Ultimately, it's up to you, because you have to live with the consequences."

Timothy stares out the window for another minute before he exits the car. He shuffles toward his aunt's store and pauses at the door.

He still might tattle to Jackie and fall back into a life bound for despair, but for one moment, I sense optimism. It breaks through the gray afternoon, riding a shaft of sunlight. The beam blinds Timothy for a second. Then he opens the door and ducks inside the shop.

I spend the rest of the day in the office. I can't help but marvel at Anne's organizational skills. She's arranged the file cabinet drawers for easy access to the files for her projects and clients, financial records, and my case files. With mine, she's arranged them alphabetically and by whether they're old or cold.

I can't win 'em all, Johnny.

I keep most Saturdays open. Few cases force me to work week-ends. Most of the weekend, I wander the capital to see the changes in the city. New restaurants I want to try or avoid. New apartment or townhouse complex locations. I wonder where all the residents originate.

For many of the weekend hours, I sit at home in front of the television. Mindless shows with the occasional old movie. A flip of the coin determines whether I head out to a bar once the sun sets.

Today, I sit at Anne's desk smoking while reviewing cold case folders. I remember each as if I worked on it yesterday. I recall the players and my achievements and failures. Of course, the ultimate failure in each came when I had to give up because I couldn't make an adequate closure. Lack of evidence, death of the person before the confession, stolen items lost forever.

On a handful of cases, I jot a page and a half of notes to recheck old leads or to try a new direction in the investigation. When I find myself lacking new cases and my continued presence in the office exasperates Anne enough, she throws one of these cold files at me and boots my butt out to the street.

The hours pass and two things surprise me. The first is that I sit until the setting sun darkens the room enough for me to notice. The second is that, throughout the time, I don't take a single drink from my flask.

I place the notes on my desk to review on Monday and replace the files in the drawer, double-checking I put them back in the same order. Anne's system should not be altered.

I lock up and trudge to the elevator, scrolling through my mental Rolodex of restaurants. I settle on one in the East Village. D. Mays offers home-cooked meals and sensibly priced drinks. Pie for dessert on a chilled plate. One step up from Sammy's Diner and the sports bars.

A parking ticket flutters from under my windshield. It joins the others in the glove compartment.

Across the river, I spot Timothy and his aunt standing on the corner near D. Mays. I slow because they're not alone.

A wiry man, middle twenties, prevents the pair from crossing the street. He wears all black, a trademark of Midnight's crew.

Timothy's dealer?

I wouldn't have expected Timothy and his aunt to be out so late, despite it being a Saturday night. Taking time to discuss the boy's situation, I hope. Dinner and apologies? Only to meet trouble on the way home?

A quick turn of the wheel and the car jars over the curb. I park with one tire on the sidewalk. Out of the car, I wait for a passing cab before crossing.

I'm halfway to the opposite sidewalk when the guy says, "Come on, man. I tol' you. I make you a good deal."

"Leave us alone," the woman says.

"Shut up, lady. I ain't talkin' to you. What do you say, Tim? Buy one, get one half-price. Jus' don't tell Jackie. What do you say?"

Timothy backs away. "No."

"Man, you just don't know what you're missing. Don't tell me you forgot how good you felt."

"He told you no," I say, fifteen feet away

The man faces me.

I don't stop to argue, but advance, cock back an arm, and slam a fist dead center of his face. When he stumbles back, I take a chance on my balance and stick my right foot behind his.

He tries to lessen the impact, but the angle is off. A sharp snap tells me a bone cracked or a joint dislocated. Either way, the drug dealer is out of action. He lies on the cold sidewalk and moans.

The winter air stings my lungs, but the moment of violence, while satisfying to my avenging nature, has drained me. I haven't fully recovered from the conk on the head from two nights ago. I place one hand against the wall of D. Mays to keep from falling on top of Timothy's dealer.

After a minute, I'm able to raise my head. The minor flurry of action has attracted no attention, but Timothy and his aunt still stand, holding each other. They've switched personalities. Cocky teen shows fear in his quivering jaw and trembling arms. Anxious store owner's posture is erect and defiant.

"Thank you," she says.

I nod, reach for my flask, but stop with my hand in my pocket. Wrong time and place.

"Timothy." He twitches when I say his name. I want to pontificate something memorable, verbalize a slice of wisdom he can keep with him years from now. Instead, I begin to walk away. At the curb, I throw a look over my shoulder. "Remember what I told you before you left my car this afternoon."

His aunt gives him a curious head tilt. Timothy glances once at the fallen dealer, then up at me. His whispered words drift through the air carrying all of the fragility of his reawakened inner child. "Yes, sir."

FOUR WEEKS after the tragedy at Zemo's, I'm back in my office looking at the beginning of another frozen month. The snow won't stop, and the mercury refuses to rise higher than the teens.

I've solved a few cases since that night. Nothing important, more trivial or nonsensical than serious challenges to my skills.

During that time, other events occurred.

Zemo's closed.

Randall Fisher II was treated for a broken nose, arrested, and now awaits trial or, at least, a deal to trade information for a reduced sentence. He admitted to luring Annabelle to the back room with an offer of a movie deal from a previous conversation with Prentiss. A little Valium in some wine followed by other narcotics helped keep her compliant for the pictures at the studio and the subsequent prostitution.

Annabelle, still comatose, was moved to a special clinic where she receives better care than a hospital could offer. Anne told me doctors, when questioned about her recovery, give long explanations full of medicalese but the basic message is they don't know.

Roger Lansing entered a sanitarium after a breakdown. His revitalization plans for Fourth Street fizzled and faded into the ether.

Arlene put the house up for sale and moved into an apartment complex. Anne helps with rent and storage for the family's possessions.

No word on how Amos took his sister's state, but Anne frowns when he brings homework on his rare visits to Annabelle's clinic.

Stephan Marshe and Mel Prentiss hired lawyers to shield them from the splatter of lawsuits and citations. With no honor among thieves, Ms. Kozar cut a deal to keep her sentence reduced by skewing facts to put more blame on Fisher and Prentiss. Her business closed, and Leena found other employment.

Timothy Hawthorne voluntarily entered a rehabilitation center, and I receive positive reports. His aunt, pleased I was the cause of his reformation, promised to discount my sandwiches and pretzels by fifty percent for a month.

One day, I swear I'll learn her name.

Rusty Fisher moved to Council Bluffs to live with his mother.

No word about what became of Kym Malin. No one could establish a criminal connection despite Kozar's insistence she was an accomplice in referring girls for the seedier sessions. She'll survive, but whether she still walks on the carefree wild side is another story.

Jackie Midnight survived the slew of accusations and charges thrown at him. He had enough attorneys on hand to found his own firm. Currently, though, he suffers from multiple injuries, all thanks to Leon Brummell. I'm sure Jackie rues the day he incurred the wrath of the Bull.

———

I learned of Midnight's condition from several sources, but one recent evening, I met Leon, who still fares well for himself, despite his limitations. He accepted my offer of dinner, and, while eating chicken and noodles over mashed potatoes at D. Mays, he told me the story.

He had been ordered to Jackie's headquarters on that Thursday night. He was told his boss wanted a 'chat'. Upon arriving, Jackie was friendly, offered him a chair and a beer.

"How are things?"

"Fine."

"No hassles from police or any of my 'competitors'?"

"No, sir."

Jackie paused a moment, then said. "Leon, I've been good to you, haven't I?"

"Yes, sir."

"Business has been good. You know, I don't expect huge sales from you. Don't expect too many in one night. Every little bit helps, though."

"Yes, sir."

Jackie went into a long explanation about loyalty and solving problems, with something related to the river that Leon didn't understand.

In the middle of the conversation, Jackie decided they should walk. Across University, behind a row of businesses. They stopped near a dumpster.

Jackie placed a hand on his shoulder. "Leon, you've been a good man, but when you actively seek to deny my customers what they want, you cost me money. Employees who do this lose my trust. I can't have untrustworthy people working for me."

The hand on his shoulder clenched into a tight grip, and Leon realized too late it was meant to keep him in place. He heard a rustle of clothing from behind him, and the pain between his legs from one of the bodyguard's kicks doubled him.

He tried to fight back, but five strikes to his head from what he imagined was a sap reeled him enough he went down on his knees, then dropped prone. He suffered the subsequent kicks and punches until he passed out.

When coherency returned, Leon mulled over the situation. Everyone thought he was stupid or, at the very least, slow. He'd overheard the terms "mentally deficient" and "retard" from numerous people. They were all wrong. Sometimes, he needed extra time to comprehend ideas and concepts, but Leon was intelligent. He's a big man, and many people were intimidated by his size, which only added to their thinking him incapable of substantive conversation. Given the right circumstances, they might be impressed by his insight on any number of topics.

He knew drugs were illegal and selling to kids was frowned upon by a lot of dealers. Jackie didn't care who sold what to whom, but Leon didn't want to be involved with the hard stuff and drew the line at minors. A little weed here and there, however, made him enough to keep his belly full. His mistake was telling Jackie during their Thursday night conversation that he'd spoken with me to try to dissuade a teenager from buying more cocaine. When I had visited him in the hospital, Leon could tell, even through the semi-consciousness, that Jackie had punished me, too.

That had been Jackie's mistake... along with the level of violence against Leon. Maybe because of Leon's size, Jackie had allowed his bodyguards a little extra 'fun'. He could have just fired Leon, ordered him to leave, maybe walked him out the door with, at most, a punch to the stomach. That would have been accepted.

Instead, Jackie had crossed the line. He hurt someone he considered a friend. Leon wanted retribution.

Before Christmas, he had visited the downtown library and read a history book about the success of Japan's attack on Pearl Harbor during the Second World War. Many strategists, long before that fateful day, had voiced the opinion the best chance for maximum death and destruction would be on a Sunday morning.

So...

In the early dawn chill the Sunday after he left the hospital, not fully recovered from the worst beating of his life, Leon leaned against the corner of the Walgreens. He stared at Analu's, on the far side of the 'L', the restaurant which fronted Jackie Midnight's operation.

Leon knew an unusual spike in temperature the previous night made for a profitable weekend. Jackie and his men would be sitting around, enjoying the take. They'd be lazy, off-guard.

Leon had been standing at his post for an hour. The warmth of the night had evaporated, and the cold began to stiffen still aching injuries. He ignored any distractions and focused on the storefront.

Actually, on the empty store next to Analu's, a former bakery. The front door was locked, but to the right was another door behind which stairs ascended. Earlier in the week, Leon posed as a potential tenant to the office supply owner, whose business was two away from the Laotian restaurant, thinking there might be an apartment for rent up those stairs.

"No," the man told him. "Years ago, maybe. Now, we use it for storage."

On the other side, above the bakery amidst the exhaust pipes and ventilation?

"Empty insulated space," the man said.

Leon nodded, thanked the guy for his time, and walked out. He'd worked construction a time or two in the past and guessed the space extended to above Analu's… and Jackie's office.

With as much stealth as his bulk could manage, he left his post, eased to the inside 'L' corner, then toward the door and the stairs. All of the store entrances were steel framed, but this door was wooden. Over the years, no one bothered to install anything more secure.

A cheap lock yielded to three hefty shoulder blocks. In minutes, Leon crawled among the insulation, dust, and ductwork. He was cautious and quiet, but frustrated by limited vision from one eye in a dim flashlight's illumination. He kept his mind on the goal.

The gap between Analu's and Midnight's room was narrow and the exposed head of a nail snagged Leon's sweatshirt. He stopped when fabric ripped. Any sound might arouse suspicion from below. With a slow hand, he found the obstruction, tugged the shirt off the nail.

Slower now, he slid on his stomach across the rafters. In the center, he found a hole near where the overhead light fixture was mounted. It was small enough to go unnoticed from below, but large enough that when he pressed his one good eye to the opening, he saw enough of the room below to ascertain only Jackie and two of his bodyguards were present. Jackie's desk was on one side of the room, and on the other, the day bed where some of the hookers napped when they weren't on the streets. He inched over to the trap door above the day bed, a pause to catch his breath, psyche himself, then…

He dropped into the middle of the bed, which collapsed under his weight. For two seconds, his feet tangled in the sheets and mattress. One knee buckled, but he caught himself before he toppled over. Five seconds more to suffer a flash of ache in his ribs and back spasms. During those year-long seconds, he expected a bullet and the end of his plan.

With teeth gritting against the pain, he stepped clear and discovered Jackie and the two bodyguards spent those seconds in complete shock, frozen like the statues in the park next to the library. By the time one of the guards collected enough wits to go for his weapon, Leon was already on the move, plowing into the man. As big as the guard was—same height, less bulk, but more muscle—Leon drove him into the steel office door, a semi against a doe. The man's head smacking the door sounded like a brick dropped onto the sidewalk from a high scaffold. A ham hock uppercut to the chin put the guard out cold.

The second guard's weapon was out and aimed, but Leon had the momentum, and, while Jackie's man was trained to play the tough guy against street punks or to exact revenge on competitor gangbangers, he wasn't ready for an angry and roaring Bull. Leon, with grinding sore joints and recently healed cuts seeping blood, was the irresistible force and the guard fell short of being the immovable object. He faltered for a second, and Leon was on him a second before his trigger finger jerked.

Leon is a big man, but the bullet went wide.

The shot deafened him, but Leon's rage rose above the short-lived echoes. He released long, drawn-out growls as he propelled the guard back, back, over Jackie's desk, right into the drug lord's lap. Jackie's surprise and delay of action cost him. He and his chair couldn't support six hundred and fifty combined pounds of beef.

Leon, the top of the sandwich, brought up his knee and avenged his own suffered groin. Then he half-stood, hauled the guard up with one hand clamped onto the guy's jacket collar and the other in a vice grip on either side of his neck. Leon stomped on Jackie's stomach, took two more steps and another sickening crack of a skull against the wall took care of the drug king's protection.

Similar to a cheetah, Leon expended energy in short bursts. Fewer than twenty seconds had elapsed between his dropping from the ceiling to when he turned and gazed down on Jackie, who wheezed, curled into a fetal ball. Leon's breaths came out hoarse and staggered. Sweat dripped from his face and heat radiated from his body like an aura. Unlike that African cat though, Leon's reserves had yet to be tapped. He waited for his former employer to roll in his direction, saw the unadulterated fear in the widening eyes and a protesting hand in the air, and listened to the start of a choked and stuttering plea for mercy.

I didn't ask for a detailed explanation of what was done to the East Side gang leader, but from later reports, Leon never spoke truer words than on the day I visited him in the hospital. Jackie should have killed him.

Anne still occupies the front desk of Habeck Investigations, tending to her enterprises. She continues to chide me for smoking in the office and frowns when I don't wipe my shoes on the mat.

She smiles at me more often. It's a sympathetic offer, with a little hope peeking at me from the depths. We'll never be husband and wife under the same roof, but we won't be enemies. She'll attend galas and artsy-fartsy society functions without me, but our relationship will be more than mere acquaintanceship. I'm not sure what we are or what we will be, but I can live with it.

And Sabastian Habeck?

He still buys packs of Luckys and bottles of Ten High, resents the modern world, and drives a junky car, albeit one with a repaired headlight and better tires.

Is he content? He doesn't know and doesn't care to contemplate too deeply about it.

I sigh, stub out a cigarette, and lean back in my squeaky chair. My thoughts often turn to Annabelle, and I long for the day when the memories will fade.

Hers was a life so wrong. In another family, she might have succeeded in her own fashion, entered adulthood with dreams to achieve and happiness to enjoy. She never knew true love and laughter, never experienced a genuine family, or started one of her own.

While her brother dropped into a Sisyphean existence, she fell into the well of apathy with the oval of light too far above to reach. With her insouciance cemented, she watched those around her adopt the same attitude of dispassion regarding her. She had no lifeline other than one narrow crack in the cement. Years of suffering the pressure for success, she eased open the door to the corporate world and, with tentative feelers, found temporary respite, maybe even enjoyment in her part-time mall job.

Yet, her one ray of hope faded to black when she discovered her mother's lie. She couldn't find the fortitude to overcome what she considered a betrayal to not only the family but to herself, to her core being. She tried to overcome, albeit in the wrong manner, to prove to herself that she could be better as a mother and as a person. When that desperate venture failed to conceive what she longed for, she accepted what she thought was a way out. Instead of stardom, she found drugs. Maybe she took them not knowing the consequences, maybe as a way to cope. Whether she came to accept the highs, no one can say, but the accompanying hell became too much to endure. Others saw her as a tool for their own depravity. In one sense, she was fortunate she didn't last to suffer future indignities and waste.

She should have had better.

I doze only to awaken long after Anne has departed for the day. She left a ham sandwich on my desk with a note that tells me to eat, then to go home. I touch the sandwich and whisper a thank you.

I sit back, ready to take the first bite, but stop when I wonder why I awoke. At first, I can't fathom the reason for my return to consciousness. Seconds later, my crack deductive powers kick in…

… the heater has shut down again. Damn!

Some things never change, right, Johnny?

END

ACKNOWLEDGMENTS

Writing a book takes time, effort, and dedication. While one may see a writer scribbling or typing away in a coffee shop or park bench, the majority of time is spent alone in his or her cubby hole organizing, researching, editing, and rewriting. However, a writer does not create the book by himself. I wish to give my heartfelt thanks.

To the good Lord for blessing me with the talent and creativity to write.

To my parents and family for their love and support.

To Ozark Hollow Press for accepting the manuscript.

To the Marion County Writers Workshop and the Sisyphean Scribes. These two critique groups have helped me learn the craft and hone my technique.

To Kim McKinney for being a sounding board when I'm stuck on a tricky scene.

To the city of Des Moines. It is rife with material, setting, and characters. The city undergoes constant change. This book was written at a time before many of those changes occurred. For instance, the American Institute of Business no longer exists. Neither does the Texaco station in the East Village. Harding Street has been renamed. The metro has an outlet mall. Even though the story is set in "present day," I have chosen to not update the changes in setting. I hope this decision will not detract from your enjoyment.

Finally, a huge thank you to my fans and readers.

ABOUT THE AUTHOR

Stephen L. Brayton is a sixth degree black belt in the American Taekwondo Association and a marketing associate for a software company.

He began writing as a child; his first short story concerned a true incident about his reactions to discipline. During high school, he wrote for the school newspaper and was a photographer for the yearbook. For a mass media class, he wrote and edited a video project.

In college, he began a personal journal for a writing class; said journal is ongoing. He was also a reporter for the college newspaper.

During his early twenties, while working for a Kewanee, Illinois radio station, he wrote a fantasy-based story and a trilogy for a comic book.

Current publications include *Alpha*, the first of his Mallory Petersen action mystery series, and *Night Shadows*, the first in a supernatural series featuring a homicide detective and an FBI agent.

He is the editor and contributing author of *The Peace Tree Mystery*, a story set in the Knoxville, Iowa/Lake Red Rock area.

He has also been published in numerous anthologies of fiction, poems in *Lyrical Iowa* 2018-2024, and articles in issues of *Plant Engineering*.